Finally heard

ALSO BY KELLY YANG

Finally Seen

New from Here

KELLY YANG

Simon & Schuster Books for Young Readers

NEW YORK · LONDON · TORONTO · SYDNEY · NEW DELHI

SIMON & SCHUSTER BOOKS FOR YOUNG READERS
An imprint of Simon & Schuster Children's Publishing Division
1230 Avenue of the Americas, New York, New York 10020

Text © 2024 by Yang Yang
Jacket illustration © 2024 by Maike Plenzke
Jacket design by Chloë Foglia © 2024 by Simon & Schuster, LLC
Grin stars icon emoji art on page 110 by Tanvir Islam/Essentials/iStock

Simon & Schuster: Celebrating 100 Years of Publishing in 2024
For information about special discounts for bulk purchases, please contact
Simon & Schuster Special Sales at 1-866-506-1949 or business@simonandschuster.com.
The Simon & Schuster Speakers Bureau can bring authors to your live event.
For more information or to book an event, contact the Simon & Schuster Speakers Bureau
at 1-866-248-3049 or visit our website at www.simonspeakers.com.
Interior design by Hilary Zarycky
The text for this book was set in New Baskerville.
Manufactured in the United States of America
0124 BVG
First Edition
2 4 6 8 10 9 7 5 3 1
Library of Congress Cataloging-in-Publication Data
Names: Yang, Kelly, author. | Yang, Kelly. Finally seen
Title: Finally heard / Kelly Yang.
Description: First edition. | New York : Simon & Schuster Books for Young Readers, 2024. |
Audience: Ages 8-12. | Audience: Grades 7-9. | Summary: Ten-year-old Lina wants to create a
viral video to help her mom's business, but as she navigates the world of likes and views with
her two best friends, Lina must find the courage to stay true to her authentic self.
Identifiers: LCCN 2023030790 (print) | LCCN 2023030791 (ebook) | ISBN 9781665947930
(hardcover) | ISBN 9781665947947 (paperback) | ISBN 9781665947954 (ebook)
Subjects: CYAC: Social media—Fiction. | Self-actualization—Fiction. | Friendship—Fiction. |
Chinese Americans—Fiction. | LCGFT: Novels.
Classification: LCC PZ7.1.Y365 Fg 2024 (print) | LCC PZ7.1.Y365 (ebook)
| DDC [Fic]—dc23
LC record available at https://lccn.loc.gov/2023030790
LC ebook record available at https://lccn.loc.gov/2023030791

To the Mrs. Carters of the world

Finally heard

Chapter 1

Mom!" Millie, my sister, protests, banging on the door. "Lina's locked the door again!"

I search through my closet, frantically. *How can T-shirts that fit me perfectly a week ago, now suddenly not fit?*

"I didn't lock anything," I insist, glancing at the doorknob. Definitely locked. "It's probably just stuck again. . . ." I tell my sister to jiggle it harder, to buy myself some time.

I sneak a look back at the mirror. I've gone through growth spurts before, but this one feels different.

I seem to be growing in all kinds of places, *places I'm not ready for!*

"Lina, c'mon! Your sister has to change too," Mom says in Chinese, walking over and knocking on the door. "Can you guys change together?"

Definitely *not.* I grab a blanket and cover myself with it. For a second, I seriously consider cutting a hole in the blanket and wearing *that* to school. At least then I wouldn't feel like microwave popcorn, exploding out of the kernel.

"Seriously, Lina, spring break is over. We're going to be late for school!" Mom says in her *I mean business* tone.

I know I have exactly five seconds before they both come flying in here. I stare at the mirror one more time, closing my eyes, hoping, praying for everything to just go back to the old days.

Days when I could walk into school with a thin white shirt, and not even think twice if anyone stared. When I didn't tower over the boys. When I could play hangman, without freaking out. Last night, when Millie and I were playing, and Millie wrote _ O O _ S, I got so upset, I almost threw a slipper at her. When *actually* her word was *books*.

I felt like a real dope when she added the *K*. Like now, after I opened my eyes. Still the same. Nothing's changed.

I make a final attempt to appeal to Mom.

"Do I *have* to go to school?" I ask through the door.

"Of course you have to go to school today," Mom responds. "Is it the photo? Are you still worried about that?"

I glance at the picture my mom's talking about, taped up on my desk, next to all my doodles. Right before spring break, Catherine Wang, my favorite author in the whole world, came to speak at my school. As her #1 all-time biggest fan, I was the first in her signing line. But as Mrs. Hollins, my librarian, snapped the picture of me and her (I was so worried and self-conscious about my . . . er . . . books), I panicked and put my hands up in front of my chest at the last second.

The result? Catherine looking amazing, and me looking like I'm trying to block a basketball.

"A lot of people have photo anxiety," Mom says through the door. "It's not a big deal."

I *wish* it were photo anxiety. Cringing, I walk over to the photo. I fold it in half. There. Now at least I don't have to look at myself.

But then I think of my immigrant mom, tidying up my room later and seeing the folded picture. She works so hard for me and my sister. Every day she wakes up at 5 a.m. to make bath bombs, which she sells online to support our family, so we can live here and go to a great school. And it really *is* a great school! I'm finally doing well in my classes. I've learned English, thanks to my teachers and my wonderful librarian. And I've made great friends, like Carla and Finn.

I unfold the picture, because I don't want Mom to be sad. I'll just . . . keep looking at my basketball pose.

One day, I tell myself, I won't be an awkward mess. I'll stand tall and proud, with my chest out and my arms down and a smile on my face. It'll happen. Just not . . . today.

"LINA! I'm coming in!" Millie exclaims.

I lunge for the closet and grab a sweatshirt, even though it's ninety degrees in LA and my socks are already sticky. Still, it's better to be baking than to be sorry.

"You look like Lao Lao, with her gazillion layers!" Millie giggles in the car as she moves her arms. My sister is always dancing, even when she's sitting. I frown, envying her cutoff jean shorts and orange tank top. Our grandma loves wearing two puffy vests, even when she's inside her warm and toasty room in her retirement home in Beijing.

"Yeah, are you sure you're not too hot, sweetie?" Mom asks as she drives.

I yank at the neck of my sweatshirt, wishing we had air-conditioning in the car. "Nope, I'm good. Let's call Lao Lao!"

My grandma and I spent five whole years together in China, while my parents and Millie came to America first to get things settled. It makes me sad that she lives all the way on the other side of the world now, but she's recently made some good buddies in her retirement home. And we're able to "see"

3

her all the time, since she finally caved and got a smartphone!

"In a bit. I'm expecting that call from Bella Winters any minute, remember?" Mom asks.

"Explain, again, why we have to pay some influencer to make videos about our bath bombs?" I ask. "And how much are we paying her?"

"Hopefully it's not something outrageous. Her manager said she liked our *vibe*. We absolutely need her. We're getting crushed. All everyone wants to do is buy from the popular brands they follow online. You've seen our sales lately." Mom sighs, holding up her phone to show us.

My sister and I stare at the sad, tiny number. Only three orders yesterday.

It's hard to imagine that just a few months ago, Mom was getting interest from real, physical stores that wanted to carry her bath bombs. Then, overnight, twenty more bath bomb stores opened up on Etsy—all with slick social media accounts. And our numbers fell through the floor.

No wonder Dad had to get a second job, parking cars for the restaurant valet after he's done at the lab. Now he looks like a raccoon when he finally gets home in the middle of the night.

"It's a whole other skill, social media, and I just don't have it. Those videos take *hours* to put together—" Mom's phone rings as she's explaining. Mom screams and shushes me and my sister. "It's her! She's FaceTiming us! Everyone be quiet!"

Mom clicks accept. Bella comes on the screen, smiling and fluttering her extremely long lashes, like a burst of sunshine.

"Hi! Bella!" Mom says, switching to English, pulling over

the car. "We're sooo excited you're interested in working together—"

"About that," Bella says, holding up her Pomeranian, whose rainbow coat matches her eyelashes. "So I talked it over with my manager, and he says I can't go lower than five thousand dollars a video."

Millie and I lunge forward, our heads almost falling off. *No, Mom!* We gesture wildly in the rearview mirror. Forget the video. For that price, we can buy an entire bath bomb *car*.

"Five . . . Wow, that's a lot," Mom takes a second to find the words. "We don't have that kind of money. We just a small business, just me and my daughters. Only five sales a day—"

"And without social media, that's where you'll stay," Bella says. "Five sales a day, dead in six months."

Dead? I frown. She doesn't know that! I poke Mom not to listen to her; I don't care how colorful her eyelashes are.

"Look, I'm offering you a pretty good deal, considering . . ."

"Considering?" I chime in, crossing my arms.

"Considering you don't have *any* social media presence. I'd literally be making a video about a company NO ONE'S ever heard of—"

"I've heard of it!" I remind her.

Bella repeats, to my great annoyance, "NO ONE'S ever heard of, and asking my followers to believe me that it's legit—not some gross, moldy ball of baking soda that's going to crumble in your hands like vacuum dust."

My sister's and my jaws drop.

"Well, it's definitely not *that*," Mom responds sharply.

"'Course. I believe you. But the internet? It's a harsh place. And who knows what they'll believe, unless you have someone like me vouching for you. But it'll cost some dough," Bella says sweetly. Before we can say another word, she waves her long manicured fingers and says, "Text me your answer. Ciao!"

The call ends.

"So much for liking our vibe," Mom mutters, switching back to Chinese.

"Mom, you *cannot* pay five thousand dollars for a video!" I blurt out. "You could buy a whole bath bomb factory with that!"

"We could buy a new air conditioner!" Millie says, fiddling with the vents in our car.

"We could buy eighty thousand new shirts for me!" I add. *That actually fit.*

"First of all, no one's getting any new shirts in these circumstances," Mom says, starting the car again. My hopes sag along with my thick sweatshirt. "And there is no way I'm giving her five thousand dollars. If I *had* that kind of money, then I wouldn't need her help. Business would actually be good!"

I shake my head. It's so unfair. How can Bella charge so much for *one* video, when my parents grind away for just pennies?

"What if we did it ourselves?" Millie asks. "I could dance to your bath bombs!"

"That's actually not a bad idea!" I add. We can totally do this ourselves. "Millie, remember when you used to make dance videos? How many followers did you have?"

"Fifteen . . ." Millie says.

"Fifteen!" I beam at Mom.

"And I can juggle the bombs to show they don't crumble!" Millie says.

"And I could . . ." I pause, trying to think of something I can do that wouldn't involve showing my awkward . . . er . . . books. "Stack them on my head?"

Mom gives me a funny look as the phone rings. It's Lao Lao calling.

"Lao Lao!" Millie exclaims. "Tell Mom to let us make videos for her for social media! C'mon, it'll be so good!"

"The girls, on social media?" Lao Lao asks, putting her comb down. She stares into the camera at Mom. "Oh no, they're way too young. All my friends here who have grandkids, they never let their grandkids on WeChat," Lao Lao says, referring to China's largest social media platform. "I thought you were hiring someone."

"We were, but she wanted to charge five thousand dollars," Mom tells her.

"Oh, that's ridiculous! For five thousand, you guys can fly over and see me. I'm so lonesome in my room, all by myself. . . ."

I lean in, concerned. I thought things were going better for Lao Lao there. My grandmother had been telling me her arthritis was improving.

"Is everything okay?" I say in a soft voice. "Is it your friends? Are they not being nice?"

"Oh no, it's not that. They're fine," Lao Lao says. "I just get a little sad, that's all. The ambulance comes at least once a day. Put it this way, we're all painfully aware that this is the end of the road."

"It's not the end of the road. Hang in there," Mom says to Lao Lao emphatically. "We'll be back to see you soon, I promise. I'll . . . figure something out."

"I hope so," Lao Lao says as Mom pulls up to our school.

My sister waves to Lao Lao and jumps out of the car, shooting off across the yard. I wave at Lao Lao too, but linger for a second, staring out at all my classmates. How come *their* buttons don't look like they're about to pop off? *Their* pants don't look like they were chopped at the ankles by a woodpecker?

The questions multiply in my head, until five whole minutes have gone by.

Mom turns to me and pulls her sunglasses down. "Don't worry . . . we'll find a solution, sweetie."

I know she's not talking about my shirt situation at all, but I imagine she is, and it helps.

I put on my bravest smile, as I get out, so Mom knows I'll be all right.

And I will be. I think.

Chapter 2

Across the schoolyard, Carla's unicorn backpack stands out in a sea of black Lululemon backpacks. It's a bigger version of a backpack Millie has, but Carla's is ten times shinier. I love how it glitters in the sun every time she moves, and it is so much more interesting to look at than the boring designer ones all the other girls are carrying.

I don't know exactly when the black backpack trend started.

I think it started with Jessica. Then it spread to Tonya. Then Nora and Eleanor. Before long, nearly every fifth-grade girl swapped out their colorful backpacks for funeral ones. Even the boys got in on it.

I gaze down at my own maroon one, the same one I've been carrying since third grade. Sure, it's a little tattered around the edges, but who has the money to switch backpacks *midyear*?

That's another thing about all this growing. It's so *expensive*. Thankfully, I've only had to ask Mom for new shoes once.

I bounce in my secondhand Vans, skipping over to Carla. I pass by Principal Bennett, with his bright Lego tie. It's thick and colorful and looks like the whole tie's made out of little plastic squares. I wave to him as I skip.

"Welcome back, Lina!" he says, smiling.

For some reason, the sidewalks in America are so much

wider, making it ten times more fun to skip on. I'm soaring through the courtyard, when Jessica—my classmate and the drama queen of fifth grade—looks up from her phone, flips her silky straight hair, and makes a face, like she's just seen a snail blow his nose.

I stop midskip.

Is there gum in my hair?

Is there a bee on my sweatshirt?

Is it *me?*

The last thought makes me want to grab one of my classmates' phones and record myself skipping in slo-mo, just so I can analyze myself.

On second thought, maybe not.

I tell myself to not let Jessica get inside my head. After all, she was the one who tried to get my favorite book by Catherine Wang banned last year. And guess who got it unbanned. *This girl.*

That's right! Boy, did I show her!

I smile at the memory as I speed-walk the rest of the way to Carla. My best friend listens with rapt attention as I tell her word for word what Bella said.

"Boo! Ditch her! She sounds so rude!" Carla says, unzipping her backpack and pulling out an old Popsicle-shaped Pop-It. She hands it to me. I channel all my frustrations into popping the Pop-It in record time as we walk over to the library.

"She was totally rude. She wouldn't even let my mom talk. And she called our bath bombs vacuum dust," I add, popping.

"Why would anyone in their right mind pay her anything?" Carla asks. "Especially since it's so easy to make good videos by yourself. I've been studying more movies—listen to this!"

Carla stops walking and, with all her enthusiasm, pitches

me a new movie she's cooked up over the break. Ever since Carla and her mom moved out of Old Man Pete's—a terribly grumpy and exploitative employer that Carla's mom and my dad used to work for—Carla's been obsessed with watching Netflix movies. Especially romantic comedies.

"It's called *You've Got a Package.* It's like *You've Got Mail* but about two people who fall in love when an Amazon package gets delivered to the wrong house."

I giggle. I love how unselfconscious my friend is when it comes to romance. Me? I still wriggle when I get to the scene when Elastigirl tells Mr. Incredible that he's flexible.

"What do you think?" Carla asks.

"I'd watch it," I say.

"I've already started writing the script!"

"Really?"

"All day Sunday, when my mom wouldn't let me finish watching *Runaway Bride!*"

"Why wouldn't she let you finish watching *Runaway Bride?*" I ask. I've never seen it, but judging from the title, it sounds like a movie you want to stick around to the end for.

"She says it's too mature, even though it's rated PG. *And* she's let me watch *Red Notice* before, and that's rated PG-13!"

"I love *Red Notice,*" I say.

"I think she just doesn't like rom-coms for some reason . . . ," Carla says, sad for a second.

"Because . . . of your dad?" I ask softly. Carla lost her dad about three years ago. I could see Mrs. Munoz not wanting to be reminded that the love of her life is gone.

"Maybe. Or maybe she thinks I'm not ready . . . ," Carla says, glancing down at her petite body.

At five feet one, Carla's body is not popping out of any kernels yet.

I used to envy her, until I learned how she felt about it.

"I just wish my body would hurry up," she whispers. She glances up at the sky, throwing her hands together. "Just give me one boob. Doesn't even have to be two."

I laugh so hard. Carla can be ridiculous sometimes, and I love her for it. Finn comes running over to us. Carla and I both press our lips together, trying to be all serious.

"There you guys are!" Finn says. "You going to the library?"

We nod.

"Good, because I have to return this to Mrs. Hollins," Finn says. He holds up a copy of *Middle School: The Worst Years of My Life.*

"Is it really the worst years of your life?" I ask.

"No, but I want to be prepared. This kid! You wouldn't believe how much trouble he gets into!" Finn says.

"Like what?" Carla asks.

"Well, the book *starts* with him sitting in the backseat of a police car," Finn says.

Our jaws drop.

"Yeah. He breaks so many school rules." Finn starts listing them. "He pulls a fire alarm and vandalizes school property—"

"Vandalizes school property?! Pulling a fire alarm? That's not going to happen to us," I tell Finn.

"We're student librarians!" Carla adds. "The only thing we're pulling are library cards."

I bump Finn's shoulder. "Stick with me and Carla, and everything will be fine."

Finn gives me a faint smile.

"I know. I'm not *really* worried. But it was like he was possessed. He just kept making bad decisions, one after another. And I couldn't stop reading about them. I was so intrigued and horrified at the same time. It was like watching my mom fake laugh for endorphins."

"Wait, what?" Carla and I both blurt out.

"She just starts laughing sometimes."

"For no reason?" I ask.

"She says it's good for when you're feeling down. Something about our brain and serotonin."

Finn demonstrates, bursting into laughter. He laughs so loud, two of his friends—Preston and Nate—walk over.

"Finny, my man!" Nate says, jumping off his skateboard and giving him an elaborate handshake. "Haven't seen you all break! Wanna see a cool trick? Dude, I can jump off the benches now!"

Preston barely looks up from his phone while his friends talk. Another trend that has suddenly swept through our grade—everyone getting their own phones. It started with Preston, who convinced his mom that he needed it in case she was running late to pick him up and he couldn't find her after school. *And* he definitely needed it for soccer practice once he was in middle school. Even though none of us actually go to middle school yet, T-Mobile was running a big family promotion. One by one, all the parents caved, even Finn's . . . making me and Carla the only two holdouts.

"What kind of trick?" Finn asks.

"I'm calling it the dragon flip! C'mon, I'll show you!" Nate says.

"Here?" Finn asks. I can see him fretting—there's a strict

no-skateboarding-on-school-grounds rule, which Principal Bennett is always reminding us of. Nate nods.

"C'mon, it'll only take a sec . . . ," Nate says. "There are no teachers around!"

Finn nervously glances down at his *Worst Years* book and says, "Actually, I have to go and return this. . . ."

"You and the library, man," Nate mutters, shaking his head.

Finn's face turns red. "What?" he asks.

"Never mind." Nate smiles, exchanging a look with Preston. "The library's cool."

I study Nate. Something about the goofy grin on his face makes me wonder what he really thinks. I hate that even though I know English now . . . there's still so much I don't *know*. Like when people say, "Yeah no"—do they actually mean "No" or "Yeah"?

Preston slaps Finn's shoulder as Nate turns toward the benches. "See you online later?"

"For sure . . ." Finn nods, fist-bumping Preston.

Finn waits until both of them have skated away, before turning to me. "C'mon, race ya!"

As we hurry to the library, I glance over at Nate and Preston, envying that they have this whole other life with Finn online. I wonder what they all do on there. Maybe online, Preston and Nate are completely different. Maybe they're kind and sensitive and don't just say "the library's cool" with a sarcastic grin. Either that, or Finn is a dragon-flipping rebel who breaks all the rules.

I'd love to find out. Hopefully soon.

Chapter 3

ina, Finn, Carla, welcome back!" Mrs. Hollins, our librarian, says when we walk in. "I've been dying to show you what I've been working on!"

Finn pops his book back into the check-in slot. Then we join Mrs. Hollins behind her desk. She points at her computer. It's a neon green website with the words *Winfield Reads* flashing in giant Comic Sans.

"What do you think?" she asks. "I made it myself!"

"It's . . . nice!" Finn volunteers.

Bless Mrs. Hollins. She tried so hard to make it look fun and lively. But in the process, she might have gone . . . a little overboard. Every neon font color on the planet is splashed across the page. If highlighters could make a website, that's what it would look like. Still, it couldn't have been easy to set up, and I give Mrs. Hollins an enthusiastic thumbs-up.

"Great job!" I say.

"I worked all spring break on it. Look, there's even a section for student book recommendations! I was thinking maybe you guys could each give a book talk, and I could record it for the site—"

"Like a video?" Carla asks excitedly.

Mrs. Hollins nods. "It'll just be for our school. What do you think, Lina? You've been loving that new graphic novel *Frizzy*!"

I do love *Frizzy*. But a video? I wriggle in my sweatshirt. I can already feel it getting too small, my neck too sweaty, and my hand freaking out at the last second and doing that basketball thing again. "I don't think so."

"I'll do it!" Carla throws her arm up. "Can I do *Love Double Dutch*? There's a dreamy middle school dance scene!"

"Sure!" Mrs. Hollins says. "And, Finn? What about you?"

Finn looks eagerly over to his book, lying in the check-in box. But then his eyes drift to the window . . . to Nate and Preston skateboarding, and he shakes his head shyly.

"I don't know, Mrs. H. But I can definitely help film with my phone!" He holds up his shiny phone.

I eye it enviously.

"Great!" Mrs. Hollins says. She goes to grab *Love Double Dutch*.

As Carla sits down to write her speech, I see Eleanor and Nora walking by. Eleanor is my fellow graphic-novel-loving classmate. I dash out to say hi. Right before the break, I'd set the latest Babysitter's Club book aside for her, before I even had a chance to read it.

"Hey!" I say to Eleanor.

"Oh, hey, Lina!" Eleanor says. She and Nora stop walking. Nora, who holds the longest record for gum chewing in our class, smiles at me, then goes back to chewing. "How was your spring break?"

"Good! Did you read the book? What happens?" I ask. "No, wait, don't tell me!"

Before Eleanor has a chance to respond, Nora cuts in. "Can I just say, your English is so good now. It's almost kind of terrifying."

My tongue turns scorching hot. I wish I could answer: *Well* . . . when you go to a nearly all-white school like me, you have no choice.

Instead, I mutter, "Thanks. I guess it's from reading a lot."

"The book was amazing," Eleanor says, pulling her copy out of her black backpack. "It saved me from a completely boring break."

"You stayed home too?" I ask, maybe a little too hurriedly. Because Nora and Eleanor both stare at me, like I'm some sort of bedridden lizard.

"No, we went to Palm Springs . . . but the resort was really packed," Eleanor says. "And my parents were working the whole time."

Finally, something I can relate to. "Mine too!" I say. "My mom's *always* working."

"I mean we're supposed to be on vacation! Can't she take a break?" Eleanor asks.

"Exactly!"

Jessica walks over and joins us.

"You should have FaceTimed me," Eleanor says to me with a smile.

"She can't," Jessica butts in. "She doesn't have a phone."

I glare at her. *Thanks a lot!*

"Anyway, here's the book back," Eleanor says, handing it to me, gazing distractedly at Nate doing his skateboard tricks. I flip through the moist pages. "Sorry I got a little water on it!"

"It's okay. I'll just . . . dry it with a fan."

"You're the best, Lina!" Eleanor says, flashing me a smile.

Jessica gives me a little wave as they head over in Nate's direction.

"Maybe we can talk about it later, when I'm done reading . . . ?" I ask, but Eleanor is already halfway across the yard.

I head back to the library, where for the next fifteen minutes—while Carla makes her funny and captivating book talk video—I sit in the corner fanning Eleanor's book for her. I try to cheer my friend on, but all I can think about is the way Jessica said it—*she doesn't have a phone.* Like I'm a character in *The Wizard of Oz*, and she's explaining to Dorothy that I don't have a brain.

I wish I could do something to show them, in my terrifying English and lumpy sweatshirt, that I'm just as good as them. As Carla wraps up and Mrs. Hollins casts a hopeful glance at me, my heart thumps in my chest. Slowly, I stand.

Do it! Do it! Just get up there and speak from your heart!

But my shaky knees give way and I sit back down. I'll get there. I know I will.

Chapter 4

Jon Butterkatz, my neighbor, secretly watches videos on his phone while Mrs. Carter teaches.

We're learning about the life cycle of a plant. I'm doodling a beanstalk in my notebook, wondering where I'd be in the plant life cycle.

Leaf development?

Stem elongation?

I gaze down at my arms. Somehow plants look so much more elegant when they grow.

I pick up a green color pencil and start drawing a long rose stem. Mrs. Carter made us switch seats right before break, saying our interpersonal skills would improve if we sat next to a new person, which is how I got stuck with Jon. So far, the only skill that's improved is my arm-watching skills.

I have to say, his shirtsleeve is a pretty good hiding location for a phone. His phone is tucked just enough in that Mrs. Carter can't see but far enough down that Jon can still sneak a peek by moving his arm an inch.

I watch as Jon scrolls through videos about everything from banana smoothies to race cars to bathroom pranks to tree houses, a seemingly nonsensical string of videos that makes me wonder if it was curated by a pet monkey.

All of a sudden, my mom's face pops up.

"AHHHHHHH!" I scream.

"What is it?" Mrs. Carter asks, tearing her reading glasses off.

I point to Jon's phone. Jon immediately yanks his sleeve down and hisses "Don't you dare!" at me. Not wanting to be a bad neighbor, I immediately move my finger to the floor.

"Nothing, I, uh . . . I saw a . . . uh . . ."

"Ant!" Jon whispers.

"An ant!"

"Oh." Mrs. Carter puts her reading glasses back on. "Well, it is getting warmer. So we might see a couple of them inside the classroom. But getting back to the process of photosynthesis. . . ."

I sit back down and nudge Jon. "Can I see that again? Please? I think that was my mom."

"No way! I'm not giving you my phone!"

"Just for a second!" I try reaching for it, but he flinches away. "Please, it's important. . . ."

Reluctantly, Jon pulls his phone out of his sleeve ever so slowly and hands it to me under the table.

I sneak a glance at Mrs. Carter. My heart's pounding. Did Mom finally decide to take the plunge? And what did she SAY?

"How do I hear . . . ?" I ask, pointing to my ears.

"You can't," Jon says. "Just read the captions."

I scroll up in the app until I find Mom's video again, then tap on it with trembling fingers. Crystal-blue water laps calmly behind her. *She filmed this at the pool? How'd Mom get it so clean?* Though our apartment complex has a pool, the filter's broken and there's usually a layer of leaves thicker than my sweatshirt.

As the auto captions appear, I cross my fingers and toes.

"Hi, everyone," Mom says. "My name is Jane Gao. I am the owner of JML Bath Bombs, a small family-owned business. This my first video. I want to talk about reality of running small business that's not so famous. Every morning, I wake up at five to make these beautiful bombs."

Mom holds up our Luxury Lavender bomb.

"I make all from scratch. Then I package and I ship. I do inventory. I track my sales. All this while I try to raise my two daughters. I used to believe that if I just work hard enough, eventually I succeed. I want to show my daughters: 'Hey, girls, just think BIG IDEA, and work hard. You can make it.'"

Mom looks earnestly into the camera and shakes her head.

"But now . . . I don't know. Because the last few months, my business really suffering. And I know the reason. I don't do social media. Why not? Because I don't think I 'have it.' I can't sing. I can't dance like it's 1999. I just want to do my job, work hard, be a good mom, and give people great products. So I guess I'm just hoping . . . that if there's anyone out there who wants to hear from just a mama. Not an influencer. Or a celebrity. Or a big famous person. Let me know."

My heart explodes with pride when Mom finishes her video. It was perfect! God, I hope Bella Winters is watching this. I hope the whole world is watching this, because it took guts for my mom to put it out there!

I feel the power of her inspiring words as I hand Jon back the phone. She's right. I just need to get over this fear of my new body and be my true best self!

· · ·

As soon as school is over, I bolt out of the classroom, racing all the way to Mom's car.

"MOM!" I exclaim. "I saw your video!"

"You did?" She grins. As Millie and I climb into the car, she fills us in. "I was sick of not doing anything! Being scared! Not trying. So I took my phone and went to the pool! And, girls, it's been bananas! You wouldn't believe the orders coming in!"

"Like how many?" I ask, taking Mom's phone and showing Millie the video.

"Fifty in the last *hour*," Mom says as she pulls out of the school parking lot.

"You're kidding!" I exclaim.

"Mom's video has 5,239 views!" my sister reports, holding up Mom's phone. She grins from ear to ear, bouncing in her seat.

"OH MY GOD!" I shriek. "Mom's going VIRAL!"

We're screaming and laughing. Mom pulls over, instructing me and my sister to read the latest comments to her.

Love your energy! Automatic buy!

You're not just a mama—you're a modern mama!

You can absolutely make it without dancing like it's 1999! I'll support you!

We love an honest queen!

I used to be scared of social media too! But don't be scared—we're with you, Modern Mama, and I can't wait to try your bath bombs— I've just ordered!

You have two daughters? Can I ask you for some parenting advice??

Your skin is beautiful!

Congrats on taking the plunge!

This was the content I needed today.

Brb . . . purchasing ALLLLLL your bath bombs.

Love that it's a family business! So sweet and authentic!

Admire your courage and how open you are! You are the American dream!

Tears stream down Mom's eyes as I read her the comments. I can't even heart them fast enough; that's how many of them are coming in as the views continue to jump.

"Look, now it's at 6,828 views!" my sister says.

A second later, I call out, "7,293!"

It feels almost like a video game! But I know it's real—I can feel the love pouring in, filling the car with hope. Mom's crying. Millie's practically bounced a hole in our backseat, but no one cares because this is the greatest day of our lives!

"You girls were right! I should have taken the plunge a long time ago. I don't know why I was so afraid—the internet is a true equalizer!" Mom says, wiping her tears, as she restarts the car.

"Hear that, Bella Winters?" I yell, rolling down the window. "An equalizer!"

"Our whole lives can change! With just a phone! Can you imagine?" Mom cries. "We don't *have* to get left behind!"

I yank off my sweatshirt and throw it in the trunk. I'm so hyped by Mom's words, I don't even care how I look!

"We gotta go to the store! Stock up on baking soda! We gotta fill all those orders!" Mom says, stepping on the gas.

"Can we stop at the ice cream shop?" Millie asks. "For two seconds?"

We both give Mom our biggest *pretty please* eyes. Mom relents.

"Fine, but only for two seconds!" she says. "I still have to clean the rest of the pool if that's where I'm going to film!"

"Wait, why the pool?" I ask.

"Well, it's the only half-decent place we've got. Our apartment is so . . ." I wait for Mom to find a good adjective. Messy? Cozy? She finally settles on "Sad-looking."

Ouch. I feel the sting of her word, even though I know why she'd say that. Our sofa has a giant hole in one of the cushions. My parents sleep in the living room on a yoga mat, which they use for a mattress. But surely all that stuff can be moved around. There must be *one* corner that doesn't look . . . sad.

But Mom shakes her head firmly. She doesn't want to take any chances.

"I'll help you with the leaves," I offer.

"Actually, you really want to help me? I need ideas for what to post! I saw this video—this lady said, to really grow on social media, you gotta post *all the time*. So if I'm going to do this, it can't just be one video!"

"I'm on it!" I yell, grabbing a notebook from my backpack and a pen. "You can count on me!"

"Can I be in one of the videos with you?" Millie asks, putting a hand under her chin and smiling at the rearview mirror.

Mom laughs.

"We'll see . . . ," she says.

"To JML Bath Bombs!" I cheer, thrusting my pen up.

Mom looks back at me with misty eyes. "To us, taking control of our lives!"

Chapter 5

----

walk into school the next day with "Unstoppable" playing in my head. Last night was too amazing for words. The only way I can describe it is with sounds:

The opening of the door when Dad came home early from work. He surprised us with mapo tofu from the restaurant!

The swish of my hair as I danced with my sister while Mom responded to comments from her fans. She stayed up till one in the morning—there were that many!

The buzz of the fan blowing in our faces as we frantically mixed the baking soda with the Epsom salts to fill the orders.

The thump in my heart as Mom held up her phone and snapped a selfie of her and me and my sister, and posted it on her Instagram Stories with a message: *Overwhelmed with gratitude. Thank you for all your support.*♥

The most amazing thing? I didn't do basketball hands or reach for a Trader Joe's bag and try to wear it over my chest. I just smiled!

I skip toward Finn and Carla in the library at school with my good news. Maybe I can do this. Maybe deep down inside, underneath fifty pounds of sweatshirt, I have the same confidence flowing inside me. All I have to do is post it like Mom. But I need help from my friends coming up with ideas!

"I'm so in! Finally, my chance to be a writer-director!" Carla says.

"This is great!" Finn says. "I know all about social media from Brooke!"

"Who's Brooke?" I ask.

"This lady my dad hired to help him with his social, for his construction company. She charges an arm and a leg, according to my dad, but he says she's the best there is!"

I grab my notebook and start taking notes. "So what did she say?"

"So far, I think she said, post consistently. Let's see, don't take too long to get to your point. Oh, and come up with a good hook!"

"A hook?" I ask, picturing a pirate hand.

"It's the thing that gets people's attention. Tells them immediately what the video's about! Like, you know, those descriptions on the front of a book?" Finn asks.

I smile. Leave it to Finn to talk to me in a language I can understand.

"You mean *How can you be yourself if no one sees the real you?*" I ask, pulling *Invisible*, one of my favorite graphic novels, off the shelf.

"Yeah! Or *Standing up for who you are is no joke*," Carla says, reading from the cover of *Stand Up, Yumi Chung!* I grin. Another one of my faves.

Finn grabs another book and reads the title. "*My Life As a Potato*. Now, if someone made a video with that hook? C'mon, that's gold."

Carla's head jolts up. "What if we made a video—'My Life as a Bath Bomb'?" she asks. "We could *be* the bath bombs!"

"Ohhh! That's good! I like that!" Finn says.

"We could be *two* bath bombs meeting in the bathtub!" Carla continues. "It could be a meet-cute!"

"What's a meet-cute?" Finn asks.

"In every rom-com, there's a moment when two people meet and fall in love. . . ."

I like the idea. But I'm not sure about being a bath bomb for my first video. "I don't know. . . ."

"Well, I can't meet-cute myself!" Carla says. "Finn?"

"Oh noooooo! Preston and Nate would never let me hear the end of it!" Finn says firmly.

Finn's answer is so loud, Carla and I both fall quiet.

I put my book down. "Why do you hang out with those two anyway?" I ask gently.

Finn stares at his shoes.

"They're not that bad . . . ," he finally mutters. "Preston's all right."

"Preston gave Mrs. Carter a tattoo for teacher appreciation week," Carla reminds him.

"It was a temporary tattoo," Finn says. "He was trying to be funny."

"It was a tattoo of toilet paper."

"So she'd never run out!"

We give him a look.

"Okay, it wasn't that funny," he finally admits. "Look, it's not been easy, okay, with my parents' divorce. And Preston . . . he's the only one who understands."

My face softens. So that's why. Poor Finn. Here I thought things were getting better for him now that the divorce was final. He seemed excited that he had two houses and two of

27

everything, including two computers to play video games on. I put a hand on his shoulder, feeling bad for giving him a hard time over Preston.

"Is there anything we can do?" I ask.

"Yeah, let me be the cameraman!" Finn says. "I'll get the best shot and edit it to perfection!"

"Fine," Carla says, turning to me. "Lina, what do you say? Ready for your close-up?"

I'm glad she said close-up and not zoom out. Maybe if we keep the camera focused on my face, I won't ever need to do basketball hands.

"Yeah, but do we have to *be* the bath bombs?" I ask. "What if we made one about the people who use bath bombs?"

"Like interview your customers? That could be fun!" Carla says.

"Or maybe we could do a super-in-depth process one," Finn says. "Behind the scenes of how bath bombs are made!"

"All of this sounds so good!" I say. "Let me write down these ideas, and I'll ask my mom which one she likes!"

I'm scribbling as fast as I can, when Jessica walks in. It takes every ounce of willpower not to blurt out what we're doing. I imagine her shock when she scrolls through her phone and sees my smiling face!

I hope it'll prove to her once and for all—I may not have a phone, but I definitely have a brain!

Chapter 6

Mom is *wild* about the "My Life as a Bath Bomb" idea.

"I love it!" Mom says.

"Oh, can we be mother-daughter bath bombs?" Millie asks. "Please, please?"

Before my mom can answer, my sister grabs a towel from the dirty laundry pile—there's a *large* pile from all of us being too busy staring at Mom's phone yesterday—and drapes it around her face, acting it out.

"I'm so confused, Mommy. Why are we going in this water?" Millie says, getting into character. "Oh, that feels nice. . . . Oooohhh, yeah, that's the spot." Suddenly Millie screams. "Is it just me, or am I disappearing? Help!"

Mom chuckles.

"That's cute!" Mom says. "Why don't we try it?"

"Really?" Millie asks, her eyes sparkling.

I open my mouth to say *what about me*, then close it. Mom's clearly excited to film with Millie. And someone has to hold up the phone. Maybe next time.

"Just give me a few minutes to change into a new outfit, and I'll meet you by the pool!" Mom says.

"Wait, why a new outfit?" I ask. I like the red flower dress Mom has on, with the poofy sleeves.

"I've already filmed something in this today," Mom says, gazing down at her dress.

"But it's so nice," I tell her. I remember when Dad got it for her. It was on Valentine's Day, back when business was still good. And even though my mom made a big deal about how it's just a silly American holiday invented by chocolate companies, she smiled when Dad surprised her with the dress.

"Yeah, but I can't wear it twice. What will people think?"

"That you have a nice red dress?" I ask.

Mom shakes her head. "I can't have just one nice red dress. I'm Modern Mama, remember? I need to have a variety of outfits!"

I twist my eyebrows at Mom's logic. I guess it makes sense?

Twenty minutes later, Mom's in a denim shirt and beige pants, and we're setting up the chairs at the pool for Millie and Mom to sit on. The water's sparkling blue, thanks to the hours Mom spent raking the leaves yesterday. Millie's brought Rabbity, her favorite stuffed animal, to watch. She's putting Rabbity on a chair when Lao Lao calls.

"Hey, Ma, can we call you back? I'm about to film a video with Millie!" Mom says, waving to the camera.

"Thought we agreed the girls weren't going to be on social media," Lao Lao says, looking worriedly at us.

Mom hesitates. She looks at Millie, who holds up the bath bomb in her hand, all ready to go.

Mom sits down on a pool chair next to Rabbity.

"I know, but Millie's excited. And the fans, they're so kind and supportive. I think she's going to do so great . . . ," Mom says.

"Oh, I'm sure she'd be fabulous! She's a firecracker, Millie. But are you sure it's good *for* her?" Lao Lao asks.

"Look, the kids are going to be on this stuff anyway. I see them, with their YouTube and whatnot. They're watching it. They're consuming it. This way, at least they'll learn to be creators, not just consumers, right?" Mom asks.

"I'm just worried. Millie's *so* young. And Lina—"

"Lina's the brains behind all this! This video we're doing is actually her idea!" Mom says.

I raise a finger. "Actually, it's my friend Carla's, but I have other ideas!"

Lao Lao looks at Mom. "I just hope you know what you're doing . . . ," she says with a sigh.

Mom looks out at rays of light reflected in the rippling pool water. A nostalgic look falls over her face.

"You remember when my cousin Xiao Lan got his first computer?" Mom asks.

"How could I not? Your aunt wouldn't stop bragging about it. She practically glued the receipt to her forehead."

I snort, missing Lao Lao and her humor.

"But remember how scared you were of letting us go to their house? You thought we were going to get addicted!"

"No, I didn't," Lao Lao denies.

"Yes, you did. You thought we were going to become gaming zombies and you'd find us starved to death in an internet café somewhere," Mom says.

"Well, it could still happen!" Lao Lao says in her defense.

"No, it can't. And it didn't. All that happened was Xiao Lan was so much better at typing than I was, and I had to learn it anyway, years later," Mom says.

Lao Lao falls quiet.

Mom holds her arm out to my sister and me. We all

squeeze into the frame, so Lao Lao can see the three of us. "I'm done being scared. I'm going to teach the girls that technology's nothing to be terrified of. We have everything we need to change our lives . . . in our palm. And we're going to use it."

A small smile appears on Lao Lao's worried face. "Well, when you put it that way . . . ," she says.

I blow Lao Lao a kiss. My grandmother catches it and tucks it into her pocket.

As Mom taps the end call button, she hands me the phone. As my sister and mom get into position, I stare at the sleek, silver edges and feel the power pulsating from the screen. *Is it really true? Everything we need to change our life is in my palm?*

"Ready?" I ask.

Mom and Millie nod, holding up their bath bombs.

"Action!" I yell, tapping record.

As Millie smiles her missing-tooth smile, the screen explodes with her cuteness. I can almost hear Mom's fans screaming for more Millie. A thousand red heart emojis! All the flowers and dancing icons! The entire world is going to fall in love with her!

It only hits me what I've done after I've pressed upload.

Chapter 7

The comments pour in like a flash flood. My sister's smile is as wide as the pool. Mom snaps a selfie of me, my sister, and her in front of the water as I read the comments:

CUTENESS Overload!

I'm dying!

OMG who is this bath bomb princess?? She's the BEST!!!

Y'all are adorable! I need this TV show!

Love your daughter! Baby girl has PERSONALITY!

She's giving Lily from Modern Family vibes!

The missing tooth! The dimples! She's PERFECT!

Those baby cheeks! SOOOO CUTE!

As I read the last one, my own fingers travel up to my face. Do *I* still have baby cheeks?

I push down on my cheeks with one finger. *Boing. Boing.* They *feel* soft. But I know they're not baby soft like Millie's anymore.

A worry creeps up. What if, with all the growing I'm doing, I'll never be cute again.

I suck in a breath as Mom gathers all our stuff and starts walking back to the apartment. I think of the movies and TV shows I love. In every single one of them, people love the little kid more than the big kid. Whether it's Jack-Jack in *The Incredibles* or Maggie in *The Simpsons*. Even little Simba was so much cuter than big Simba.

What if I'm doomed to non-cuteness forever?

Millie jumps up and down next to me, trying to reach for my phone with her tiny hands. Dang it, even her fingers are cute.

"How many views did I get?" Millie asks, hopping from foot to foot.

"I don't know," I mutter.

"Tell me! Did I get a hundred? A thousand? Did I get five thousand?" Millie's pupils flash as she gasps. "What if I got a million???"

"You didn't get a million," I tell her flatly.

"You don't know that! It *could* be a million!" Millie says, hugging Rabbity. "Let me *see*!"

"Let's just look at it later," I urge.

"Good idea," Mom says, taking the phone from my hand and putting it in her pocket. "You can see the view count *after* you've both done all your homework, set the table, and eaten dinner."

"And read," I add. "And take a shower."

Millie rolls her eyes. I'm aware that I'm sounding like a party-pooper scrooge, instead of a proud big sis, but I can't help it. She broke the internet with her cuteness on her very first try. She didn't even need a script! All she has to do is *show up*.

"Fine, then after that, can I look at the views?" Millie asks.

Mom nods distractedly as she opens the apartment door.

"And if it's super super high, can we do something fun to celebrate?" Millie asks.

I look over at Mom.

"Like what?" Mom asks.

I fully expect my sister to say *let's go for some ice cream* again. But instead, she asks, "Can we make another one?"

"Careful now, or I might have to fetch you from an internet café in Beijing," Mom says. Millie giggles as Mom makes zombie hands at her, and we walk inside.

Later that night, I'm standing in front of the closet mirror, squishing my cheeks, when Millie walks in with Rabbity.

I immediately put my hands down.

"What are you doing?" she asks.

"Nothing," I say.

"Guess what my views are?" she asks, plopping down on my bed.

"Fifty trillion million?" I ask.

"Nine thousand four hundred and seventy-one!" Millie gushes, tossing Rabbity up in the air.

I try not to let any emotion show, even though I'm stewing with envy. That is a LOT for thirty seconds of standing in front of the pool. She didn't even dance! Wait till the internet sees her dance!

I'm in deep deep trouble.

"What do you think I should do for my next one?" Millie asks. "Maybe a dance duet with Mom?"

"No!" I shake my head firmly. "Mom, dance? That won't turn out well."

"Then I'll dance by myself!" Millie says.

"Nope. Finn says we have to be consistent," I tell her. Actually, what he said was *consistently* post, but Millie doesn't need to know that it was an adverb.

"So what do you suggest?" Millie asks.

Think quick!

"I think you should try being behind the camera. Part of the creative team!" I suggest. "Learn how to make these things. It's the only way you're going to grow as an artist!"

I blink at her, hoping she buys it.

"I am really good at choosing music," she says after a long pause.

"There you go!" I smile.

"I'll get Mom's phone and start going through Spotify," Millie says, jumping up. She gets to the door and stops. "Oh, and, Lina?"

"Yeah?" I ask.

"Next time . . . I think you should be in it too," she says.

I fight back tears. She doesn't know how much I needed to hear that. I hide my face in the shadow, feeling like an ogre of a sister for trying to stop her stardom when all she wants is to include me.

"Thanks, Millie," I choke.

Chapter 8

My friends run over to me on the stone bench the next morning in the courtyard. Carla's unicorn backpack bounces against her. Finn's waving his arms wildly, like he has something urgent to tell me.

"Guess what? I talked to Mr. Packett! He said we could borrow a music stand from him when we film! To keep the phone steady! Like a tripod!" Finn says.

"What'd your mom say about the idea?" Carla asks. "Did she like it?"

"She liked it so much, they already *did* it," I tell her.

"You're kidding! Who's they?" Carla asks.

"She and Millie. It was a huge hit, too!"

"That's great!" Carla says. Finn pulls it up on his phone. Carla dashes over to watch the video with Finn. "Dang, Millie's good."

"Tell me about it," I mumble.

Finn giggles as he watches, liking the video so much that he plays it over again. As he taps on his phone, Carla walks over to me.

"What's wrong?" she asks, taking a seat next to me on the stone bench.

I shrug.

"I don't know . . . ," I say to my hands, then peek over

at Finn. Thankfully, he's too deeply engrossed in whatever video is after Mom and Millie's. I confess to Carla, "Everyone was going on about how cute she is in the comments. And it just made me wonder about all this." I gesture at my growing, lumpy body.

"What about it?" Carla whispers back.

"Do you think I'll ever be cute again?"

"'Course you'll be cute!" Carla insists. "You'll always be cute!"

I glance at her, not entirely convinced.

"Cute's not just baby kittens in tiny baskets, you know. Cute's a lot of different things. It can be a really great movie. Or a cool hat."

A hat? That's what she's going with?

"Or have you seen those tiny drawings in those bitty glass bottles, that people wear as necklaces?" she asks.

"No, but go on," I encourage. I imagine my doodles going into one of those bottles one day. That would be really cute.

"And strawberries dipped in chocolate!"

"Maybe we could put them in those little cake trays?" I ask. "You know, like, for afternoon tea?" I smile, thinking of Lao Lao. She *loves* those petite silver trays. We never had a chance to go for afternoon tea in Beijing when I lived there, but we always talked about it.

"Absolutely! They have that in hotels, in New York City!" Carla says.

"Maybe my grandma can go with me!" I add.

"And just think, afterward, you can put on your cute suede fringe boots and take a walk through Central Park. . . ."

I close my eyes, imagining my future self exploring New

York City with Lao Lao. Going shopping. Catching a musical. It does sound pretty fabulous. There's only one thing that would make this day even better.

"Can I meet up with Catherine Wang for lunch?" I add shyly, chewing my lips. I want so badly to meet her again but under better conditions. Like, when I'm an adult and no longer blocking basketballs.

"Of course! You guys will have so much to discuss!" Carla smiles. "Such as the new super-cute cover that you just drew for her newest book!"

I grin, bumping my shoulder lightly with Carla. Way to make me feel like a million dollars.

"Thanks, Carla."

Finn finally gets off his phone and claps his hands. "So should I go get the music stand? We still have fifteen minutes before class! We could try making a video!"

"C'mon, Lina, what do you say?" Carla asks. "You ready to show the world what you got?"

My heart thumps with adrenaline. Future me would not hesitate for a second.

Still, it's scary.

Time stills. I breathe in deeply, reminding myself I can do this. I've done scarier things. Like coming to America. Telling my grandmother I couldn't stay in Beijing with her forever. Standing up to Jessica and her mom when they tried to get my favorite book banned.

With all my courage, I nod back to my friends. "I'm ready!"

At that moment, I know there's no turning back.

Chapter 9

Carla stares into the camera with the intensity of a cheetah about to outrun Usain Bolt.

"Showers are for followers," Carla says to the camera, while Finn zooms in. "You're a *leader*. You need to be covered in luxury foam, your boss fingers and toes bathed in possibility. And if you want to use five bath bombs, you'll use five bath bombs, unapologetically, because you *deserve* it. And you're not getting out for *anyone*. Not for the pizza guy, not for your gardener, not for *anybody*. You'll get out when you *want* to get out. On your terms. A handmade bath bomb fit for a queen!"

Wow, I mouth, shocked at how Carla took my idea and just *ran* with it!

"Ummmm, you need an agent, like, right now," Finn adds.

Carla puts a hand to her chest, flattered. "Thank you, thank you." She smiles, pretending to sign autographs for us in the air.

"All right, Lina, you're next!" Finn says, pointing to the spot where Carla was sitting under the tall oak tree.

I gulp.

As I take a seat, I start thinking about all the things that can go wrong. What if I fumble my lines? What if an acorn falls and smacks me in the nose? What if a bird poops on my head?

"Are you okay?" Carla asks.

I throw her a panicked look. I know we're filming my idea and Carla already slayed, but I don't know if I can do this. Carla must have read me like a book because she tells Finn to move over.

Carla steps behind the camera. "It's just me. You're just talking to your best friend, no one else. . . ."

I nod, waiting for my lungs to unfreeze, for my vocal cords to warm. When at last the butterflies in my stomach have stopped fluttering, I smile at Carla.

"You work hard every day," I say. "You're always taking care of everyone else. You deserve a threat."

I smack my forehead. *Treat!* I was supposed to say *treat!* Why do I always get my English words mixed up when I'm nervous?

"It's okay! We all make mistakes. The great thing about the phone is I can just edit it out! Keep going!" Finn assures me.

I nod and start over. This time I close my eyes and picture Mom. She's at home making me and my sister xiao long baos. I picture the look on her face, seeing this video. Seeing me put myself out there, like her. Not being afraid. Taking charge of my future.

"You deserve a treat," I continue. "I know it wasn't easy for you to leave everyone you love behind in China, like my grandma and aunt. To come here and try something new— making bath bombs, so everyone in the world can relax. But, Mom, when was the last time *you* relaxed?"

I gaze tenderly at her, on the other side of the camera.

"I know it's hard. You're always so busy making sure that my sister and I have everything. But *I* want you to have this. . . . I need you to have it. Time for yourself. Because you deserve it. You are the most amazing mom in the world. And you deserve all the bath bombs!"

"And CUT!" Finn exclaims. Carla squeals as she runs over to me.

"That was amazing!" Carla says.

"Really?" I ask.

"It was *gold*!" Finn shrieks as the bell rings. His fingers work fast, putting the video together in the time we still have left before class. I watch over my friend's shoulder as he edits. It's thrilling and strange to see my face zoomed in and pinched out, our performances spliced, captioned, cropped, and cut a million different ways!

Finn holds up his phone. "What do you think?" Finn asks.

Carla and I huddle our heads together, watching the playback. *It's magnificent! Ten times better than I ever ever imagined.*

"Every mom is going to literally cry when they see that," Carla says.

"And *buy*!" Finn grins. "Cry and buy!"

My friends' words fill me up, even more than having baby cheeks or dimples, or everything else I can't control. But *this* I can control. *This* I can edit. *This* I can film over and over again until it's perfect. Until I'm perfect.

"Should we send it to your mom?" Finn asks.

"Send it to her! Right now!"

As Finn shoots the video off to my mom, I whisper a prayer to the internet gods.

I know I hunch my shoulders in real life, and my sweat-

42

shirt's not been washed in days, and I still get my English words mixed up sometimes, and I've got three tiny hairs under my armpits, which no one knows about, not even Carla.

But please, just let me taste the spellbinding magic Mom and Millie felt . . . just this once . . . *and let me go viral!*

Chapter 10

Finn lets out a high, piercing cry, like there's a pigeon stuck in his throat.

"Are you all right?" Mrs. Carter asks.

He nods, but he still can't speak. Instead, he thrusts his phone up in the air, like there's something *really really* important on there. Mrs. Carter notices too.

"For the eighty-fifth time today, class, I need *everyone* to please put away their phones—"

"But, Mrs. Carter, what if Finn's having a medical emergency?" Preston calls out. He jumps out of his seat, with his own phone, pulling up WebMD. "What's wrong, buddy? Is it your kidneys? Your spleen??"

Finn shakes his head and finally manages to speak. "Lina, your pencil! I remembered I still have it!"

Mrs. Carter frowns at Finn, like, *That's your big emergency?*

I give him an odd look too. I don't remember loaning Finn a pencil.

But Finn stares at me, like, *Will you just get over here?*

I rush over to Finn's side. As he's fumbling for his pencil, Finn points to his phone in his hand. It's Mom's Instagram— with our video posted! She put it up! My pulse pounds as I lean closer to read the views. But Preston's big head is blocking me.

"Does it take three people to get a pencil?" Mrs. Carter asks. She tells Preston to go back to his seat. But Preston stays right where he is, and both our heads are practically stuffed into Finn's hand.

Finally, I see it—10,294 views!

"HOLY TALKING COW ON A SURFBOARD!" Preston announces to the entire class. "Lina and Carla just went VIRAL!"

"What??!" Jessica asks, jumping up.

"We did?" Carla asks, scrambling over. She throws her arms around me, and we both hug.

"Ten thousand people saw their video on bath bombs!" Preston continues.

"That's *impossible*," Jessica says.

"No, it's true!" Finn exclaims. "I helped them film it! It's going bonkers on Instagram!"

Mrs. Carter frowns at Finn. "You're not supposed to be on Instagram, you know. . . ."

"I'm not!" Finn insists. "She sent me a link!"

"Uh-huh. Just like Lina lent you a pencil?" Mrs. Carter deadpans.

As Mrs. Carter orders all of us to go back to our seats, I'm still trying to process that gigantic number. That's more than the number of people in all of Winfield! If Carla and I had gone around to every single person in the entire city and told them about my mom, we still wouldn't have reached as many people!

Best of all, the look on Jessica's face as I walk back to my desk makes me burst with pride. *That's* a doodle worth putting on a necklace!

As soon as the bell rings, I fly out of my seat and race to the parking lot.

Mom's the first car waiting in the pickup lane.

"Did you love it??!" I ask her, jumping in the car.

"I loved it with all my heart!" she says, reaching over and giving me a hug. "I cried when I saw it."

"I meant every word," I tell mom. I reach for her phone. "Can I see the comments?"

She hands me her phone. I punch in her code and log into the app, as we wait for my sister.

Wouldn't it be amazing if it was at twenty thousand views? Then all our problems would be solved—business would be good again. Dad wouldn't have to park cars after work. We'd be able to see him every night for dinner! We could finally get a bigger apartment! I could get more clothes, maybe even a bra!

My face flushes at the thought. *Is that the next step?* I glance over at Mom. I know she's always wearing one, but she also hangs them to dry on the towel bar in the bathroom. Like a giant jellyfish. All those straps. Overwashed to a gray pulp. I felt it once. There was a wire on the bottom—hidden in the stretchy band, the width of a power cord. I shudder.

I don't want to wear a power cord!

On the other hand, it was really hot filming in a sweatshirt today.

My sister gets into the car. I load the video, crossing my fingers. And the view count is . . . 12,304.

I can't help but feel a tiny tinge of disappointment. Just two thousand more since this morning? It's been *hours.*

46

"What's going on?" Millie asks.

"Your sister made a video for my channel, and it went BANANAS viral!" Mom says.

I flush at Mom's exaggeration. I mean, it's true. But not true. I tell myself that's still a lot. If you'd asked me this morning, I would have been happy just to receive two thousand total!

And I still have so many ideas! Now that I know what it takes, I bet I'll beat 12,304 next time.

Still, the tinge lingers, like a tiny worm wiggling across my skin. Inching along. Asking, *why can't I have just a few more views?*

I try to cover up my disappointment as Millie high-fives me.

"Three for three!" Millie says, grinning her toothless grin.

Mom talks as I read the comments. My face blooms from all the kind words pouring in.

"Thank you for what you said—you're absolutely right, I do need to prioritize myself, but it's just so hard," Mom continues. "Especially now with this *consistently post* thing. Do you think that applies to the weekend, too?"

I nod, half listening to Mom as I reply *Thank you!* 😊 to all the people who commented.

And then I see it.

Can't believe this "Modern Mama" is using her YOUNG daughters on social media to sell her products! What is she thinking??!

Whoa.

My cheeks boil, reading the comment. It's so MEAN. How can they say that? They don't know anything about me! Mom's not using me. It was *my* idea. I want to help her! It's a family business!

47

"What's wrong?" Mom asks, glancing at me in the rearview mirror as she drives.

I swallow hard.

"Someone . . . just left a mean comment on the video," I tell her reluctantly.

"Let me see!" Millie says.

Mom immediately pulls over. She reaches for the phone. I tense, expecting Mom to burst into tears. My hands curl into fists. I want to reach into the screen and let this *User294055* know they can't talk to my mom this way! To my surprise, she chuckles.

"Haters will be haters," she says. "We'll just go ahead and delete that. . . . There!"

"Wait, you just deleted that? How?" I ask.

"It's easy." Mom shows me. "All you have to do is swipe and tap. Done!"

She hands the phone back to me.

I stare at the spot where the comment used to be. Sure enough, it's gone. Poof. Evaporated into the ethers of the internet. I put the phone down and close my eyes. The comment still lingers in my head, though. *Do they really think Mom's using me? And how come Mom's not more bothered by this person?*

"Look, there's going to be a lot of haters in the world," Mom says. "And part of growing up is learning to have a thick skin. Not letting anyone get underneath it, because the truth is, some people are just going to hate, no matter what."

I nod, pinching my own skin to see how thick it is. Millie sees me and reaches over and starts pinching me, too. It *really* hurts. But I don't say "ow."

Instead, I lean over and ask Mom, "When did you . . . uh . . . grow a thick skin?"

I still haven't talked to Mom about all my changes yet. There was one time, I came close. We were watching *The Princess Diaries* with Dad, and Mom was saying that Mia has a case of the "teenage awkwards." I held in a breath, hoping she'd say more. But then the whole discussion turned. It became a talk about kissing. Then *that* turned into a discussion about the birds and the bees, which I'll never forget. Dad got so choked up at the thought of me growing up, he burst into tears. Mom had to do all the talking.

To be honest, I'm kind of glad we haven't talked about what's going on with my body. Because if I tell her, and she confirms it, then it's real.

Then I can't deny it anymore.

At night, though, the questions bubble up like foamy suds. Did Mom start early, too, like me? And *is* this early? I lean forward, waiting for Mom to respond. Except it's not exactly the answer that I was hoping for.

"Ever since I was a kid," Mom says. "I remember my cousin making fun of me for trying to sing like Whitney Houston."

Oh.

I sit back, disappointed, but Mom starts belting out "The Greatest Love of All." Mom's pitch is . . . er . . . interesting. But she doesn't hold back. She sings big, with all her heart—after a minute or two, you forget that it's off-key.

"If I fail, if I succeed, at least I'll live as I believe . . . ," Mom sings.

Mom holds each word in her mouth like it's alive, and I realize this song is more than a song for Mom. It's her battle cry. Her life motto that she's been trying to follow ever since she was a little girl, fighting for her right to sing it out of tune in front of her fast-typing cousin.

By the end of the second chorus, Millie and I are both singing along.

Mom glances at me in the rearview mirror when the song ends and whispers, "Don't ever let anyone take away what's yours, you hear?"

I won't, I mouth back, misty-eyed.

I smile the whole rest of the way home, vowing to grow a thick thick skin, just like my mama, along with all the other things I'm growing.

Chapter 11

That night, I FaceTime Lao Lao. My video's reached 15,489, and I don't even know what to do with myself! Carla and I screamed for hours on the phone, refreshing the views, until finally her Mom made her go to bed.

"Lao Lao, the most amazing, incredible thing is happening! The internet thinks I'm funny! And cool! And this lady said I inspired her to call her mom!" I inhale and exhale into the phone.

"You are very inspiring!" Lao Lao laughs. "And funny! I've always told you that."

"Yeah, but 15,489 people also think so!" I say to her. "Can you believe it?"

Lao Lao chuckles.

"I can believe it," she says. "But, seashell, I hope you know, even if 15,489 people didn't watch it, you're *still* special. . . ."

I smile. "Thanks, Lao Lao. It just helps to hear it from, I don't know, a bunch of people, I guess."

"Because they're snazzier than your old grandma?"

My face reddens. "What? No! That's not what I meant."

"I'm just teasing you," Lao Lao says, laughing. Her face softens. "Actually, you inspired *me* with your video."

"How did I inspire you?" I ask.

"Well, you inspired me to put on this . . . ," she says, pointing to a silk scarf around her neck.

I lean in to get a closer look. I've never seen that scarf before.

"Is that a new scarf?" I ask.

My grandmother smiles, taking it off to show me. I admire the deep-indigo-blue silk.

"It sure is. I got it at the gift shop. You know, I used to think, what's the point of wearing something nice when I'm just going to be in here all day. Not like I'm going anywhere."

Again, I feel a lump in my throat. I think about how I would trade all 15,489 views for Lao Lao to be able to come here, right now.

"But lately, I've been thinking. Why do I have to wear something nice for someone else? Why can't I wear something nice *for me?*" she asks.

"Yes!"

"Everyone here, they think this is the end of the road," Lao Lao continues. "And I used to think so too. But then I started thinking. . . . For the first time in my life, I don't have to worry about cooking or cleaning. I finally have time *for me!* It's just like you said in the video!"

I'm smiling tears of happiness that my little video is making Lao Lao feel better about her circumstances.

"Maybe this is the beginning of my life, not the end!" Lao Lao says.

"YESSS!" I cry. "It totally is!"

I do a little twirl, and Lao Lao does too, in her deep blue scarf.

"Thanks for reminding an old bird that she's seventy years

young," Lao Lao says. "I can't wait to see what your next video's going to be on. And remember—it's not how many people look at it; it's what you say that matters!"

I dream of Lao Lao coming to America that night. The two of us are in New York, eating tiny cakes on petite silver trays. I'm in town for *Good Morning America* with Carla.

"And this morning, on *Good Morning America*, we're speaking with America's favorite new internet sensations, Carla Munoz and Lina Gao, whose video about bath bombs has taken the nation by storm!"

I walk out, waving confidently at the camera. In my dream, I'm not slouching in a sweatshirt. I'm standing tall and proud in a stunning dress. One that hugs me in all the places I'm too scared to look at in the mirror.

In my dream, I carry myself with grace. As I take a seat next to Carla on the interview sofa, I look out to the audience at my lao lao, clapping for me. Catherine Wang is sitting next to her, cheering me on. And Mom and Millie and Dad are there too.

A huge, hot, beaming spotlight descends from the ceiling, blasting me with the light of fifteen suns. But I don't do my basketball hands; nor do my armpits become swimming pools. I sit there, cool as a cucumber. Comfortable. Like I've had this body my whole life. And I'm *proud* of my curves.

When I wake up, I lie in bed for an extra five minutes.

I want so badly to go back to the dream.

The next day at school, I try to channel that confidence as Jessica walks up to me.

"I saw your video," she informs me.

I tense, bracing myself. *Thick skin, thick skin, thick skin!* At the same time, my legs turn to jelly as I look up at her hopefully. Maybe she thought it was cool?

"Your boss fingers and toes bathed in possibility?" Jessica starts giggling. "Who came up with that? Was it Carla?"

I refuse to let my best friend be the subject of her mockery.

"I did," I say, crossing my arms.

Carla runs over. A crowd gathers. I remember Mom's words, not to let anybody take what's mine. I stand tall, refusing to let Jessica rob me of my pride.

"It went viral, for your information," I tell Jessica.

"15K? Please, that's not viral," Jessica says. "That's what my mom gets for just sneezing."

I fume.

"You want to go viral? Look at this lighting. It's horrible. And do you even have a Lavalier Lapel mic?" Jessica says. "Or a tripod?!"

"We used a music stand," Carla informs her.

Jessica laughs hysterically.

"I hope your mom's not relying on these to sell bath bombs. She'll get two customers."

"She's already getting *tons*," I tell her.

"You didn't even put a trending sound on it!" Jessica says. Then she asks me, point-blank, "You *do* know what trending sounds are, right?"

No, I don't. Panic sets in. I glance around at my classmates, whose amused grins tell me this is something I *should* know. I feel my thin cheeks flaming. Jessica's shoulders are rattling with laughter. Boldly, I step up to Jessica. "I don't need to," I inform her. "I *am* the trend."

"Ohhhhhh!" my classmates gasp.

Jessica stews as I turn and walk away. Carla walks next to me, reaching out her hand. I low-five her as we hurry out of sight.

"Did I just say 'I am the trend' to Jessica?!" I whisper to her, shaking.

"Yup!" Carla whispers back when we turn the corner. "And it was *amazing.*"

Chapter 12

All right, everybody." Mrs. Carter blows her whistle. We're standing outside with our protractors and our clipboards. "We're going to put our math *and* science knowledge to the test today. I want you to pick something in nature—it could be a leaf or a branch—and measure the angle you see with your protractor."

I skip over to Finn as Jessica glares at me from across the crowd. She holds up her protractor, like she's measuring *me*.

"You wanna start with the pine cones?" Finn asks, pointing at the cones blanketing the feet of the tall juniper.

"Sure!" I say. I lean close to Finn, who bends down, sneaking a peek at his phone. "Hey, what's a trending sound?"

Finn doesn't hear me at first. He's too distracted by something on his phone.

"What's wrong?" I ask.

"Nothing," Finn says, typing back. "Just something Nate said on Discord."

"What's Discord?"

"This chatting thing," Finn says, quickly putting his phone in his pocket. I gaze over at Nate, juggling pine cones in his hands. He gives Finn a goofy smile.

Mrs. Carter claps twice. "No more phones! Jessica! That goes for you too!"

"But I have a protractor app on my phone!" Jessica says.

"That's nice, but I'm not asking you to show me what your phone knows," Mrs. Carter says. "I'm asking you to show me what *you* know."

Jessica sulks. As she takes her sweet time putting her phone away, I look around and see at least five other kids secretly pulling theirs out—from hats, pockets, and even socks—and checking. *What are they always checking?*

I glance over at Carla. She's crouching by the daisy bush, examining the flowers with her protractor.

"Look at this daisy, Mrs. Carter! It's got pointy petals!" Carla says.

In the split second that Mrs. Carter walks over to Carla, Jessica goes right back to looking at her phone. Mrs. Carter whips her head around and sees. "Jessica! What did I just say? And you too, Nora and Preston! And Tonya!"

"But I just need to reply to this one thing!" Preston says. "My friend posted a video of milk coming out of his nose!"

"You can do that later!" Mrs. Carter says.

"No, I can't! I've already liked it!" Preston waves his hands wildly. "Do you know what it means if he sees just a like and no comment? He'll think I hated it!"

I scratch my head. There's so much about being online that I still have to learn. It's like a whole other language, social media. So far I've just been responding to comments with a splash of emojis and some words of thanks. But now I'm thinking, should I write more?

"He will not think you hated it," Mrs. Carter assures him. "He'll think you're in school."

"My friend who goes to Torrey Prep Academy says they

let her use her phone even during class," Jessica informs Mrs. Carter.

Finn whispers to me, "That's cap. Torrey Prep is *so* strict. My neighbor goes there."

"Well, may I remind you that you're at Winfield Elementary. Where we have a firm no-phone-in-class rule and *definitely* no social media," Mrs. Carter reminds everyone. "Which all of you are too young to be on, anyway."

"We're not!" Preston promises, trying to look all innocent.

Mrs. Carter looks at him, like, *I was born at night, but not last night.*

"My mom says social media is the future. If you don't have a big platform like her later, forget it. You might as well be fossilized earwax," Jessica tells Mrs. Carter. "None of this stuff we're learning now is going to matter—math, science, reading, and writing."

"Oh, it absolutely will matter," Mrs. Carter argues. "Let's say you come up with a great scientific discovery! How's anyone going to believe you? You have to persuade them with your research and your words!"

Jessica shakes her head. "Nah. You just need a killer video. That's how my mom launched her broccoli water over spring break—"

"Broccoli water???" Finn asks, looking like he's about to hurl. "That's the most disgusting thing I've ever heard!"

All around me, my classmates pretend to gag. Jessica's face stiffens. "For your information, it *tastes* just like regular water."

"What'd you do? Boil the broccoli?" Preston asks.

Carla jumps up from the daisies. "It probably has pesticides!"

"No! There's no pesticides!" Jessica assures us.

But everyone's already on their phones, searching it up for themselves. One glance at Finn's phone, and I gasp at the price of the tiny bottle of broccoli water.

"Eighteen dollars for a tiny bottle of water?" I blurt out. That's like two T-shirts that actually fit, maybe even three!

"It's *infused* with broccoli essence," Jessica says. "We collect the moisture from when you steam broccoli—it makes your inner light glow!"

"You're charging eighteen dollars . . . for steam?" Finn asks.

I'm infused with outrage.

But that's not even the biggest shocker.

"Guess how many people bought it?" She looks at me. "Thirty thousand in one week! From *seven hundred and fifty thousand* views, which is what it takes to *actually* go viral."

I quickly look away before Jessica can see the envy in my eyes.

Jessica turns to Mrs. Carter. "Which is why I need to have my phone out. I have to be on the lookout for *my* big opportunity. I don't know what my brand will be yet, but once I decide, I'll go viral, before anyone else in this class."

"We'll see about that," I mutter under my breath.

As Mrs. Carter reminds Jessica that the only brand she'll be working on is a brand-new math worksheet at recess if she sees her phone out one more time. I look to Finn. That can't be right, can it? Thirty thousand orders in one week, of broccoli steam?!

And more importantly, Jessica can't go more viral than us, can she?

Chapter 13

I t's possible, I guess," Finn says later, in the library. He's shelving *The Marvellers* by Dhonielle Clayton. "Brooke says anything can happen online. If people share and like something enough, it can spread beyond anyone's control! Like those face rollers my mom's always buying!"

"Oh, my mom likes those too!" Carla says.

"All that rolling—it's like she's making pizza dough with her face!" Finn complains.

I stifle a giggle, putting away *The Book of Beetles,* a nonfiction title that's surprisingly fascinating. "Did you know that some beetles can escape a toad's stomach after two hours of being eaten?" But my friends are too distracted by face rollers to hear beetle facts.

"They're so expensive! Thirty dollars for a new one. There goes my college money. Instead of a degree, I'll get fifteen face pizzas." Finn shakes his head.

"Can't she just use one?" Carla asks.

"She always thinks whatever the latest one people are talking about online is better," he tells us, somewhat sheepishly. "Guess she's a little worried. She's . . . trying to meet a bagel."

I glance over at Carla, who looks just as confused as me. "Huh?"

"It's this app. Coffee Meets Bagel," Finn says. "It's for dating."

"So, she's trying to *date* a bagel?" I ask slowly.

"No. She's the coffee. She's looking for a bagel. It's a metaphor!"

"Ohhhhhhhh," I say.

We learned all about metaphors right before spring break. I came up with the most in my small group, but I never thought about people as caffeinated drinks before. I glance over at Finn, who looks like he wants to jump into the *Marvellers* book, so he doesn't have to deal with any of this.

"When did she start . . . bagel-ing?" I ask.

"She's not," Finn insists. "She's just on it, just to see. It might not even happen!"

"Do you want it to happen?"

"No way," Finn says. "But then I feel bad for her, especially when I see—"

Finn suddenly stops, his eyes clouding with worry.

"What'd you see?" I ask.

"The other day, I came home and I saw Brooke sitting super close to my dad. They were brainstorming at the dining table."

"How close?" we ask.

"Like if we were eating popcorn at the movies, and you accidentally dropped a kernel in between our seats. That close."

I try to imagine this, even though I haven't yet been to the movies with my parents since coming here. We usually just check out what's available at the library. I wonder what it's like to go to a real movie. Dad's always saying he's going to take us, but every week there's a new bill that needs paying.

Finn quickly adds, "They could have been actually eating popcorn!"

"Yeah! Or looking over bills?" I ask. My parents always sit super close when *that* happens.

"Or strategizing over a remodel?" Carla says.

"Right, exactly!" Finn's face brightens. Then the worry returns a second later. "I guess it's just . . . hard."

Finn looks like he could sure use a hug. But as I start moving my arms out, I suddenly freeze.

Can I still hug boys?

I gaze down at my bumpy sweatshirt. The question flies around my brain like an untied balloon, until I yank both hands down. "It's going to be okay," I tell Finn, putting a hand on his shoulder instead. Except I'm so tall, my hand accidentally lands on his ear.

Luckily, Mrs. Hollins walks over. She beams at me, holding up the graphic novel *Frizzy*.

"Lina, I saw your bath bomb video! It was magnificent! What do you say about sprinkling some of that online charm on a book talk for the library website?" Mrs. Hollins asks.

I blush at Mrs. Hollins's kind words. I think about Jessica and how rude she was earlier, dismissing my video like the mist from a sneeze. With a determined look, I take the book from Mrs. Hollins.

"Sure, I'll do it!"

Chapter 14

R eady?" Finn asks, positioning his phone. I nod and hold up *Frizzy.* "Action!"

"Hi! I'm Lina, and I want to talk to you today about a book that I read and loved," I start. "It's called *Frizzy,* and it's about a girl named Marlene. She has beautiful curly hair, which she's unsure about in the beginning. And I can definitely relate. My hair's really wavy, compared to my sister's. My grandma used to say my hair's not messy—it's big with emotion, just like me."

Carla's holding up two thumbs: *You're doing great! Keep going!*

As I'm talking, I catch Jessica walking into the library. She watches me from the back, and it's so unnerving, I almost want to stop. But I tell myself to keep going. I have to show her I'm not intimidated by her words. I don't need broccoli steam or some fancy mic. I have just as much of a shot at going "actually" viral as her.

"Brava!" Mrs. Hollins claps when I'm done. "That was *beautiful!* I'm going to put this up on the library website right now! I'll be sure to send a copy of the link to your mom!"

I glow with pride. I wait for Jessica's firecracker laugh to fill my eardrums. But strangely enough, when I turn around, Jessica's not there. She ran off.

It's not until later that day that I find out why.

. . .

After lunch, I'm back to arm-watching. Jon has discovered a new hiding spot. And it's a pretty good one.

This time he's placed his phone on the floor, right between two chair legs. Every two minutes, he conveniently drops a piece of paper and bends down to get it and looks at his phone.

As I sneak a peek over my arm at his chair leg, I see the unmistakable pink of the *Frizzy* cover. I gaze at Jon, baffled. Could Mrs. Hollins's website be catching on?

"Are you watching my book talk?" I whisper to him, pointing at his phone.

"What book talk?" he whispers back. "And quit spying on me!"

"On Mrs. Hollins's website!"

"What website?" he asks.

Now I'm really confused. I drop to the floor and pretend to tie my shoes. That's when I see it—it's not my face holding up *Frizzy*. It's Jessica's! I jolt up, bumping my head hard against my desk.

"Ow!" I cry.

"Lina, are you all right?!" Mrs. Carter exclaims.

"Yeah," I mutter, my eyes flying over to Jessica. *When did she make this??*

Jessica continues staring into her pencil case like there's a fascinating diamond inside. That's when I realize her phone's in there. Suddenly, she yelps out, "The author of *Frizzy* just liked my video and reposted it!"

"What?!" my entire class screams.

"Calm down, everyone!" Mrs. Carter says, but it's too

late. The thrill of a famous author liking and reposting sends our classroom into chaos. Everyone's out of their seats and rushing over to Jessica. The walls are vibrating. The floors are trembling with rushing feet. Eleanor and Nora scream to confirm that the author of Frizzy definitely reposted it, as Jon plays Jessica's video on full volume.

"I love that *Frizzy* reminds me that my wavy hair's not messy—it's big with personality!" Jessica says in the video.

Wait a minute! That's almost word for word the same as what I said! Reading my mind, Finn's hand shoots up.

"Mrs. Carter, Lina made a very similar video on Mrs. Hollins's website this morning—"

"What, two people can't both like *Frizzy*?!" Jessica immediately cuts in. She turns to Mrs. Carter with a hand to her chest, insisting, "I love this book. I was *very* inspired by Maureen."

"It's Marlene, not Maureen," I cry. "Did you even read *Frizzy*?"

"'Course I did!" Jessica's face reddens. "I'm going to become a major book influencer!"

"Since when?" I ask.

She holds up her phone, flashing all the fire emojis that she got in her comments. "Since now!"

"Eight fire emojis, *dang*," Eleanor says, high-fiving Jessica.

I shrink in my seat. The most I've ever gotten was three.

"You know what's literal fire? When the air gets too dry and moisture evaporates from a plant's leaves—" Mrs. Carter says, trying to bring us all back to science. But it's hard to think about plants when Jessica's laying out her master plan to take over the universe.

"I'm going to make book talks on all my favorite books and

tag the authors, so they'll repost. Then *their fans* will repost! Just think! Within a week, I'll be the biggest influencer in the whole wide world!"

I put my arm around my tummy, feeling ill. I pretend to tie my shoes, so I can hide my face. Of all the things Jessica could have picked to talk about online, why did she have to go with book influencer? That's my thing—*I'm* the student librarian!

"Raina Telgemeier, for sure! Oh, and Katherine Applegate! I've *got* to do a book talk on *The One and Only Ruby*! And *Invisible*, my new favorite graphic novel," Jessica continues breathlessly.

"Not *Invisible*, too," I squeak from under the table.

"Don't forget *Stacey's Mistake*—it was so good!" Eleanor calls out.

I cover my ears. Now Eleanor's giving Jessica recommendations that I gave her! I curl into a ball, next to Jon's stinky shoes. Thankfully, the bell rings. As everyone grabs their backpacks, Jessica says to Eleanor, "Tell me more about it on Discord later!"

"Another perfectly good lesson plan ruined," Mrs. Carter laments. "Haven't had this many kids jumping out of their seats since the year there was the lice outbreak!"

Jessica gives me a little wave as I crawl out from under the table. I grab my backpack and bolt for the door as Mrs. Carter calls out, "That's it, we're learning about the human brain tomorrow. If y'all are going to be this addicted to social media, you might as well learn why!"

The only thing on my brain is: *It's on.*

Chapter 15

Mom! I gotta make more videos! A lot more videos!" I say as soon as I get into the car. Before I can say more, I notice Mom's new bob. "Did you cut your hair?"

"Yeah, it's a long story. Oh, Mrs. Hollins emailed me your book talk—great job!" Mom says, beaming. She hands me and Millie a bowl with some cut-up apples in it. I look down. We usually get a bowl of wontons when we get home, or some scallion pancakes. What's with the apples? And why are we eating them on the road?

"So are you going to do more book talks?" Mom asks.

I shake my head: definitely not. Mom's too busy tapping on her phone to ask why. "Hold on. I just posted a video about trusting your kids! And now my comments section is going bonkers!"

"Really?" I ask. "What are people saying?"

"They're asking me a million questions, like how young is too young to trust your kids? Can you let a six-year-old go to a sleepover at a new friend's house?" Mom drinks from her ginormous forty-ounce travel coffee mug. When did she get that? It's bigger than my head! "I don't know! It's a lot of pressure! All these people think I have the answers because I'm Modern Mama."

"So what'd you say?" I ask.

"I said yeah!" Mom says. "Sure! Have the sleepover! You gotta trust your kids, right? Because if you don't trust your kids, then how are they supposed to become full, independent, well-adjusted young adults and—"

Mom pauses from talking a mile a minute to take another huge sip from her coffee mug.

"Mom, how much coffee have you had?" I ask.

"Oh, just ten cups since four a.m.," she says.

"Ten cups?" I lunge forward and ask.

"You were up at four?" Millie adds.

"Well, there were lots of bills that we've been ignoring. And now we can finally start paying them, thanks to all these new orders. Let me just see if they've gone through," Mom says, starting to pat all her pockets. "Have you seen my phone?"

We point beside the cupholder. "It's right there!"

Mom exhales in relief, like it's been hours, not mere seconds, since she last held it.

"So did you get *any* sleep last night?" I ask, peering at the dark circles under her eyes.

"About three hours," Mom says. Millie's and my jaws drop. No wonder Mom's chugging that coffee like there's no tomorrow. "It's not easy making all this content! It looks easy, but for every video, I have to do twenty takes. And I'm running out of clothes to wear and getting sunburned filming at the pool!"

"You're still at the pool? Just move inside!"

"And have them see all my piles of laundry, and my dirty dishes stacked to the ceiling?" she says, frowning. "I'm supposed to be the source of inspiration for these parents! If they see I'm just a mama . . . and an exhausted one at that, they'll leave."

"Can you take a little break?" I suggest.

Mom holds a shaky, extremely caffeinated finger up. "For the first time since coming to America, I have a voice! I thought when I left China, that wasn't ever going to happen to me again. But now, by some random click of luck, all these people have stumbled onto my page—I'm not going to give that up. I don't care how late I have to stay up or how sunburned I get."

Mom takes a sharp right, stepping on the gas.

"Where're we going?" we ask. Our apartment's in the opposite direction.

"IKEA!"

Millie and I look at each other, confused. "Why?"

I expect Mom to say she's running low on hand towels or buckets for the bath bombs, but she tells us she wants to *film* there.

"It's perfect! They have all those cute little living rooms, all set up! And it's so big, no one will even notice."

She's kidding, right?

But Mom points to the ring light and the tripod on the passenger side seat—she's dead serious!

"We can't film at IKEA!" I protest, thinking of what Jessica's gonna say when she sees our next video!

My sister claps excitedly. "I-KEA! I-KEA!" she chants.

"What about all those price tags? The signs everywhere? Everyone will see!" I ask.

"Don't worry, I have a plan!" Mom says.

Chapter 16

Twenty minutes later, Mom's sitting on an IKEA bathtub, in a pink IKEA bathrobe, with her hair up in an IKEA towel. I glance worriedly at all the tags in the little fake bathroom, which my mom stuck to the side of the bathtub and the sink with putty. It works okay. Still, I'm terrified someone's going to catch on.

"You recording?" Mom asks.

I'm leaning forward with her iPhone, and I nod. "Action," I whisper.

Several people walk by, giving us funny looks. But Mom keeps her focus on the camera.

"You ever feel like you just want time-out, as an adult?" Mom says in English. "That's how I feel today. I went to UPS to send all my bath bombs. Well, he couldn't accept my credit card, because machine broken. I had to go to bank. Well, they not believe me, because my hair's different from my ID. So then I go to the hairdressers'. It took *all* day. You know what kept me going?" Mom points to the empty bathtub. "This. Knowing the minute I get in this water, everything going to be better. All my problems and stress going to melt away like jelly."

As Mom tosses a bath bomb into the fake bathtub, she smiles into the camera. "Here's to us giving ourselves a time-out."

"CUT!" I yell, as Mom dips her toes into the "water."

"How's it look?" Mom asks.

"That was perfect!" I tell her as my fingers edit the video. "Did all that really happen today?"

Mom nods, her face falling. She looks longingly at the tub. "At least we got a great video out of it! Can you tell it's IKEA?"

I shake my head. "Nope! The putty really worked. Here, you want to see?"

"In a sec," Mom says. Millie and I stare as she lowers herself into the empty bathtub. "I'm just going to lie down here for a bit." Before we can say anything else, her eyes are closed.

"Is she . . . ?" Millie asks, walking closer.

I peer at her tired, spent face, sleeping soundly in the empty tub. She's worked herself right to the bone. "Let's let her sleep," I urge.

As our exhausted, famous mother catches some Zs in the middle of IKEA, I turn my attention to editing the video. My sister skips over to a fake toilet just across the aisle and sits down on it.

"Lina, look at this toilet! It has a lit-up bowl!" she says.

I ignore her pretending to flush it. I want to get this video done and posted before Mom wakes up.

"Lina, get in; the water's warm!" my sister cries. I look up. Has she fallen *into* the toilet?

No, she's just found another bathtub. I shake my head, turning back to the phone.

"We're in IKEA!" Millie protests. "C'mon, let's play!"

"Can't. I'm working," I tell Millie.

"How about a pillow fight over by bedding?" Millie asks

hopefully. "Or a scavenger hunt in the kitchen section?" When I don't say anything, she grabs a loofah from the bathtub and throws it at me.

"Ow," I exclaim, pretending it hurts more than it does. "This isn't fun and games, Millie. It's serious! We're here to make content. So if you want to help me, think of some more ideas on what to film while we're here!"

Millie sinks her head all the way to the bottom of the tub. "You're no fun anymore . . . ," she mutters.

I put the phone down, feeling bad. "I thought you wanted to be a big viral star . . . ," I say softly.

"Yeah, but I want to hang out with you more . . . ," a voice squeaks from the tub.

I get up and walk over to her. I realize I'm taking out my frustration over Jessica on my sister. And it isn't fair. I sit down on the glowing toilet. "I'm sorry . . . ," I mutter. "I'm just mad about something at school today."

Millie wiggles back up. "What happened?"

"It's . . . complicated. You wouldn't understand."

"Why?" she asks.

"Because . . ." My face grows hot, trying to find the words. I don't know how to explain why it bothers me so much that Jessica copied my book talk. Because it took *so much* courage for me to give it, in my new body and my awkward clothes. I shake the pain away. "I don't know how to explain it. You're . . . too little."

I glance at Millie, worried I hurt her feelings. I hadn't meant it like that. It just . . . came out.

Luckily, my sister pats the spot next to her in the bathtub. "You heard Mom. . . . It'll melt all your problems away!"

I hesitate. Slowly, I put the phone down and hop into the tub. I guess I could use a time-out. As I lean back in the bathtub with my sister and close my eyes, I imagine a day in which nothing I make can be copyable, because everyone in America will know my words. Know my story. Know *me*.

Mom's right. It feels nice.

Chapter 17

At school the next day, everyone's whispering about Jessica's newest video.

According to Eleanor, it's on the latest Katie the Cat-sitter book, which I have to admit, I haven't read yet. Eleanor says it was a great video. I'm tempted to watch it.

Instead, I'm sitting at my desk, furiously brainstorming possible new video ideas in my notebook, so Mom can take a *real* nap, when I catch my neighbor Jon twitching his nose.

Is he okay? Did he accidentally hide his phone up his nose?

I turn my attention to Mrs. Carter, who's explaining the different parts of the brain to us. There's the cerebrum, the brain stem, the cerebellum, and—*did Jon just lean over and sniff me?*

I give him a sharp look. His nostrils flare. He definitely sniffed.

And now he's moving his seat an inch away from me!

Do I smell? I lift my armpits slightly, taking a whiff.

Jon reaches with his hand to cover his nose. I feel almost light-headed. Armpit hair's one thing—I can hide *that* under a pile of sweatshirts—but what do I do about body odor?

Suddenly, I have a whole other emergency to brainstorm. One that's not going to go well. I can just picture the arguments with my parents.

"No way! Deodorant? That's too expensive! I need the money for gas, so I can go to IKEA every day!" Mom would say.

"Eight dollars for a little stick? You don't need that stuff. That's so American, spending eight dollars so you can smell like laundry. I'm telling you, deodorant's a made-up concept, like conditioner," Dad would argue.

"Conditioner's not made-up!" I'd argue back.

"I never had it growing up in China! All you need is shampoo!"

I slide down in my chair, thinking about my impending stinky doom.

After school, I run through campus with my arms up, hoping the breeze will fan out my armpits. I keep my arms up, even in the car. Mom says we need to stop at Albertsons.

"I'm making dan dan noodles for dinner!" Mom says.

At the mention of my favorite dish, my face brightens.

"We're celebrating me getting to five thousand followers! And we're going to be taking some over to your dad, too, at the restaurant!" Mom says.

"Yay!" we cheer.

A family dinner! Millie and I clap wildly, until I remember my odor problem. Does clapping my arms make it worse? I plunge my hands down and keep them glued to my sides before Millie's sharp nose detects any scent. I wish there were some sort of manual for what I'm going through.

Inside Albertsons, while Mom looks for garlic and mushrooms, I make my way over to the Personal Care aisle. I gasp at the rows and rows of deodorants. There are so many. Enough to fumigate a T. rex! My eyes boggle at the bazillion solids, sprays, and roll-on ones that line *both* sides of the aisle.

How can there be so many different items for the same thing? Unless they're not the same.

Maybe every armpit is different.

Maybe every *day* every armpit is different, like at the cafeteria, when you don't know what you're going to get; it could be pizza, it could be burgers, or, if you're lucky, Tater Tots.

Or you could get soggy fish sticks. What if my armpits are soggy fish sticks?

I shudder at the thought.

I pick up the Salty Sierra, then the Hard Spice, then the Ice Pick, and finally the Bear Glove, smelling them all. They all smell horrible.

Then I look at the price tag and I nearly gag—$14.99.

That *really* stinks.

How in the world is it so expensive? I take the cap off one and am holding it up to my nose when, suddenly, Millie appears out of nowhere.

"Lina?" she asks. "What are you doing?"

I jump, knocking the deodorant straight into my nose. *Owww.*

"Great, now there's a nose-shaped hole in the stick!" I cry out.

"Why were you eating that?" she asks.

"I wasn't eating it!"

"I saw you! You were eating it!" she says.

I shake my head, putting the deodorant back. I start walking down the aisle, toward the much safer territory of toothpaste. "I was just smelling it. Forget it. You wouldn't understand."

"Because I'm too little?" she asks.

I stop walking. I consider pretending I didn't hear her. Or distracting her by pointing to a watermelon-flavored toothpaste. But what if she brings it up in the car, in front of Mom. Then I'd die.

"Just tell me!" Millie cries out.

"Fine! Because my body's changing!"

There, I said it.

I turn around slowly. Our eyes meet.

"Is that why you were all sad in IKEA?" Millie asks.

I look down at my hands. I instantly regret not doing the scavenger hunt in IKEA yesterday. I should have just done it with her, rather than get dragged down this long, awkward road of questioning.

"No . . ."

"You didn't want to play, remember?" she asks. "I suggested that we have a pillow fight, but you said no. Even though, who turns down a pillow fight. *Then* I suggested—"

"Fine. You want to play? Let's play!" I grab her hand, and we take off running.

"Where we going?" Millie asks.

Somewhere far far away from the deodorant aisle!

We race to the front of the store, squeezing by all the empty carts, until I get to the one place that I know will crush any doubt in my sister.

The toy claw machine!

We've walked by it a million times, always marveling at the beautiful stuffed teddy bears lying inside, just waiting to be grabbed by the almighty claw, but Mom never lets us play. She says it's impossible to win on those things. And maybe it is.

But today I have to make the impossible possible—prove that I'm still a kid and that despite how salty and ice picky I smell, I can still play.

I dig in my pocket for quarters. My sister's eyes light up as the claw machine roars to life.

I move the claw, razor focused on my prize: a soft white teddy bear. Millie rubs her hands together, giddy with excitement. Unfortunately, the metal claw graces the bear's nose, *so* close, but it slips away. I dig for more quarters. I am *not* losing today. Not when my childhood's on the line.

This time I wait for the claw to come all the way down, until it's snug around my bear's shoulders. Then I go in for the win.

"YESSSSSS!" I scream.

As the machine deposits my new bear, my sister squeals so hard, the entire store looks over.

"Awwww, look at those little girls," a lady says.

I grin, the words warming me to my toes. Take that, scary deodorants! I snuggle my new bear—Snowy, according to his tag—tight to my chest, nuzzling his soft fuzz and kissing his pink nose.

I look into Millie's eyes. "I still want to play, okay?" I tell her.

She nods, throwing her arms around me. I smile into her hair, grateful I can convince my sister. And myself. For one more day.

Chapter 18

Millie describes my dramatic victory to Mom one more time on the way to Dad's restaurant, while I hold the steaming-hot dan dan noodles carefully in my lap. She's been talking about it nonstop since Albertsons.

"The claw was like baw-ha-ha, no chance. But then Lina was like, we'll see about that! And she jammed on the joystick! And the bear was like, game on!" Millie grins, reaching over to rub Snowy's head.

She brought Snowy along for the ride. I pick him up and pretend he's gobbling up the noodles.

Millie laughs. She looks at me eagerly. "Hey, can we play the stuffed animal game tonight?"

I hesitate. Millie's stuffed animal game is basically group therapy for inanimate objects. First she puts all her stuffies in a circle, then goes around asking them about their day. It takes *hours*.

"You said you'd play with me . . . ," Millie reminds me gently.

"Okay okay," I quickly agree, not wanting to risk her going into *that* in front of Mom. Millie bounces victoriously in the backseat.

Mom turns down the radio, 104.7 FM, her favorite station. *Southern California's Home for All Your Old-School Jams.*

"I remember the first time I ever won a stuffed animal. It was at the town carnival," Mom says. "I was twelve. I had to shoot a foam heart through this basketball hoop! And even though I was the shortest of all the girls, I won!"

"Wait, you were the shortest of all the girls?" I ask. Mom nods. That means she hadn't gone through puberty early, like me. I slide back in my seat, disappointed.

I have my answer.

"Well, I'm the tallest in my school . . . ," I mumble.

Mom glances in the rearview mirror. "Don't worry. The boys will catch up. You just have what my Aunt Feng calls—"

But before she can get the rest of her sentence out, a song comes on that makes Mom squeal.

"It's 'My Girl'! The Temptations!" she exclaims, waving her arms as she turns on the radio.

Millie grabs Snowy and holds him up like he's a mic. "Here we go!" she says.

"Wait, what did Aunt Feng say I have?" I ask.

But Mom's already singing. "I guess you'll say . . . ," Mom starts.

Millie elbows me to get ready. As we belt out "My Girl" at the top of our lungs to Snowy, I fill in the rest of Mom's sentence in my head.

You just have what Aunt Feng calls the earlies. Early to bloom. Early to shine. Early to be everything you can be!

I sing the words in my head as loud as I can.

Later, we're eating dan dan noodles with Dad in our car. Mom hands Dad the chili oil.

"This is so wonderful," Dad says, sprinkling the chili oil all over his noodles. "Oh, I almost forgot!"

He digs out a fortune cookie from his pocket that he tells us he got from one of his customers who didn't want to tip him. He hands it to me to open. Carefully, I break the seal. Mom sucks in a breath as I reveal the fortune.

All things will be difficult before they are easy.

"It's so true," she says, breaking off a piece for me and Millie. Mom probably thinks it's referring to her social media struggles, but I think it's for me.

"Can I keep it?" I ask Dad.

"Sure," he says, with a smile.

I stuff it deep in my pocket . . . and in my heart.

Chapter 19

That night, my sister introduces all her animals to Snowy.

"Everyone, say hi to Snowy," Millie instructs. "He joins us from the faraway, mystic land of Albertsons. . . ."

I muffle a chuckle as Millie grabs her stuffed bunny.

"Hi, Snowy!" she says on behalf of Rabbity and the others. "How did it feel getting picked up by Lina?"

I pick up Snowy. "It felt awesome!"

"Did you think you were going to get picked?" Millie asks.

"Nope! I remember seeing that claw machine coming down and thinking there's no way it's gonna be me. But the brave, confident little girl at the joystick was like . . . don't worry, I've got you!"

"The not-so-little girl . . . ," Millie corrects.

I flush at the reminder.

"What's it like? Turning into a woman?" she asks.

I can't believe we're talking about this here. In front of all these plastic eyes. I feel like burying my face in the stuffies. But I remind myself, I'm the one who brought it up first, in the grocery store. Can't blame Millie for being curious.

"It's like your body has a train to catch. And all your mind wants to do is slow down and read a book."

"What kind of train is it?" she asks. "Is it comfy?"

I think about today, Jon sniffing me. "No . . . ," I answer honestly.

"Well, is there good food at least?" she asks.

"Oh yeah, sure. You can eat whatever you want."

"Is that why you've been inhaling two bowls of rice at dinner?" Millie says.

I chuckle.

"Hey, it's hard work, growing all the time. I'm constantly hungry," I tell her.

"And you're always clogging up the shower drain with your hair!"

"Am not!"

"You're like a koala!"

A koala? I twist my face, glancing worriedly at my armpits. I don't think I'm *that* hairy.

"How fast is the train going?" Millie asks.

"For me? Really fast," I tell her. "But maybe it'll be different for you. . . ."

"And *where's* it going?"

"That's the thing. I don't really know," I confess. "Somewhere cool, hopefully?"

Millie hugs Rabbity tight. "Hope it's not somewhere where all you do is drink coffee, work, sing badly, and never sleep!"

I laugh at her description of Mom. "Oh, that's not gonna happen to me. I love sleep way too much."

Millie gives me a lopsided smile. "So, was it weird when you first noticed?"

"Super weird."

She falls quiet.

Then she asks, "Is that why you're always cranky in the morning and locking me out of our room?"

My cheeks blush. It hits me that I haven't been the nicest to my sister. Especially in the mornings. As hard as my metamorphosis has been on me, it probably hasn't been easy on her, either.

"It's okay," Millie says, reaching in her dresser drawer for a bag of Flamin' Hot Cheetos and offering me one. "Mom said that you might get moody. . . ."

Wait, Mom talked to her about this?

"What else did Mom say?" I ask.

"Just that you're growing up and you need privacy," Millie says, licking the Cheetos dust off her fingers, then wiping them on her carpet, which is totally disgusting. But I don't have time to reprimand my sister about her Cheetos-eating habits right now—I need to know more.

"Did she say why it's happening to me so early? And what else is going to happen?" I ask her, grabbing a fistful of Cheetos and stress-eating them.

"Nope!" Millie says. "Why don't you ask her yourself?"

I cringe at the memory of the mortifying *Princess Diaries* birds-and-bees sob session. "Too embarrassing."

"Well, you can always talk to me and Rabbity about it," Millie offers. She holds Rabbity up high, then looks down for a second. "I know you think I'm just a little kid. . . ."

"No, I didn't mean that," I say to Millie. It would be easy to blame my blunt words on my body changes. But I decide that the *grown-up* thing to do is to take responsibility. I take a deep breath.

"You want to know why I said that? You know Jessica in

my class? She copied one of my videos. Just went ahead and ripped it off, word for word. Like I was a lost sock in the bottom of the laundry that no one would even notice if she stole. But what she didn't know is . . . how hard it was for me to make that video in the first place."

Millie sits up, her nostrils flaring. "You're so much better than Jessica is! We'll show her! I'll help you. We'll all help. Right, guys?" As she grabs each stuffed animal and gathers them up, I wipe my eyes, moved by her solidarity.

"Thanks, Millie," I say. "I'm sorry I said you were just a kid."

Millie reaches out her arms, and I hug my sister. Afterward, she hands out a stack of Albertsons sandwich order forms. I didn't even know she took them.

I glance down at her scribbled handwriting as she gives one to each animal. "Now, if everyone can fill out a brief survey to let us know how this session went, that would be greatly appreciated."

Rank the following with 1–5 stars:
I enjoy participating in the Stuffed Animal Game:
_____stars
I feel a lot better: _____stars
Here's a problem I want to discuss next time:

_____

"Really, now? We're doing Yelp reviews for the stuffed animal game?" I tease Millie with a smile.

"Five stars for feedback!" Millie grins.

I roll my eyes, chuckling. Grabbing a pen, I give my sister a well-deserved five stars!

Chapter 20

When the last of the stuffed animals is put away in our closet and both Snowy and Rabbity are deep asleep on our beds, I crawl out.

I tiptoe through the maze in our living room—bath bomb ingredients, packaging material, and my parents' mattress—careful not to wake them. I reach for Mom's phone, in her fingers.

I made it through almost the whole day without checking Jessica's latest video, but now my curiosity has finally gotten the better of me. I can't sleep without checking.

As I'm pulling it out of her hands, Mom's phone starts to vibrate. It's Lao Lao! I swipe to answer, taking the phone into the kitchen. "Hi, Lao Lao!"

"Why are you whispering?" she asks.

"Because it's midnight here," I tell her.

"Oh dear. I always mess up the time difference," she says. "I was just calling to say I *loved* your book talk! Your Mom sent it to me! It was so real and authentic . . . and I loved that you even included me in there."

I smile into the phone, trying not to let Jessica's copycat video sour my pride. "Thanks, Lao Lao."

"Your librarian must have been so thrilled!" Lao Lao says,

eyes widening. "You know what you guys should have at the library? A dance party!"

"Oh no." I shiver, thinking about my sweaty armpits. A dance party's the last thing I need.

"Why not? I'm thinking of hosting one at the retirement home! Every week!" Lao Lao says. "Help us all get on our feet and get moving again!"

"Err . . . yeah, that's not going to work."

"What's wrong?" Lao Lao holds the camera closer to her eye, studying my face. "Come on, out with it."

I pause, trying to dodge the question. But even under the pale moonlight of the velvet night, there is no hiding from my grandmother.

"Because I probably smell," I finally say. "Some kid at school wrinkled his nose at me in class. And now I think I need deodorant!"

Lao Lao puts the phone down on her coffee table. "He *wrinkled* his nose at you? Who is this elitist donkey? Probably got a pencil stuck in his nose. You do *not* need deodorant, sweetheart! You smell like a spring peach."

"How do you know? You haven't smelled me in months!"

"'Course I have. I have a special feature on my phone," Lao Lao says. "Comes right through the speakers!"

"Very funny." I smile, rolling my eyes.

"The reason I *know* is because all the women in our family smell like a spring peach, starting from your Tai Lao Lao all the way down. Your Da Lao Lao, a glowing queen of a peach. Your Mom and your Aunt Jing, lovely honey peaches!"

"But what if I'm different? I'm already going through *puberty* so early," I tell her, cupping my hand around my mouth. I think I'm saying the word right. My lao lao and I never talked about it in China. We didn't have to. I was still a wee sprout then.

Who knew I would shoot up like a palm tree as soon as I landed and started chomping on string cheese?

I hold my breath for Lao Lao's answer.

"First of all, there's no early or late. Everybody's different," my grandmother says. "Take me. I still have all my lush hair. They have to arrange to get a special hairdresser to come in here to cut it for me. Look at that hair!"

My grandmother fluffs her long, flowing, silvery hair with her hand. It sure is beautiful.

"You do have great hair," I agree.

"The best! They call me Silver Belle here! While everyone else's hair is thinning, mine's coming back thicker than it ever did. I'm going the opposite of bald!"

I giggle.

"The point is, everyone's timeline is different. Forget about this kid. You don't need deodorant. You are a divine peach."

I wrap my arms around my chest and squeeze tight. I wish Lao Lao could be here to hug me in person, but this will have to do. "Thank you, Lao Lao."

"Gotta go. I have a meeting with the management to discuss my dance party!"

"Good luck, Lao Lao!" I say.

"Hopefully, I can convince him that we old birds deserve

a dance party to let loose and feel young again!" Lao Lao says, blowing me a kiss.

"I'm sure you will!"

I bid Lao Lao good night, tiptoeing back to my room. Crawling under the covers, I dream of glowing, radiant peaches.

Chapter 21

L INA!" my sister shrieks, banging on the bathroom door the next morning. Millie screams so loud, I almost squirt the peach that's in my hand into my eye. "Rosa and Alfie need our help!"

I instantly put my peach down. I'd asked Mom for it at breakfast, then spent about an hour in the bathroom, rolling it around under my armpit. Like a fruit deodorant. I *hope* it'll work?

The next thing I know, I hear Alfie's bark. I open the bathroom door to see Rosa, our neighbor, standing there with her dog in her arms. His left leg is all bandaged up.

"What happened?" I ask, going over to little Alfie.

"He fell jumping out of my taco truck," Rosa says.

"Oh nooooo," I cry. Alfie whimpers as I pet him.

"Vet says it's gonna cost three thousand dollars for surgery. I don't know what to do." Rosa sniffles.

"Come sit," Mom says, moving all the boxes off our hole-in-the-cushion sofa.

Alfie curls up on the couch as Rosa explains that since Red Russo came in with their giant taco trucks, her taco business has taken a hit.

"They don't even make their own hot sauce!" Rosa says. "They just buy from the store! Meanwhile, I getting up at five thirty in the morning to cut up my habanero. But the people, all they see are their ads. They're killing me with their social media!"

"How can we help?" Mom asks.

"The videos you're making," Rosa says. "You say they're helping your business, sí?"

"Yes!" Mom points to all the boxes of bath bombs she's finished packing that are ready to ship. "Business is getting better!"

"Can you make one for me?" Rosa asks. "If I can just convince the mayor to let me be the official taco truck at the Winfield Concert at the Park next Sunday, I think with my savings, I might just be able to scrape together three thousand dollars."

"Of course!" I offer. "My friends and my sister and I could totally make a video for you!"

"Let's go!" Millie adds.

Mom nods enthusiastically. "Absolutely! You'd be doing me a favor—I *need* the content for my channel! I think they're onto me at IKEA!"

"Really?" I ask Mom.

"While you two were at school, I tried to film an entire bathtub filled with bath bombs yesterday . . . and let's just say, it didn't go well."

"What happened?" I ask.

"Everything was fine until the manager walked over," Mom says. "He asked if I intended to purchase the bathtub."

"And?" we ask.

"I stuffed as many bath bombs inside my shirt and ran out of there!" Mom says. "I was like a hen, dropping eggs all over IKEA!"

Millie giggles.

"Well, hopefully this will help make it up. And I will pay! Fifty dollars for our young artists for your trouble," Rosa offers.

"Oh no, that's not what I was getting at," Mom says, shaking her head.

"Please, Jane, I insist. No one should have to work for free. Take it from me—I learned the hard way, when I was a young child, working in my mother's taqueria. Fifty dollars, that's my lowest, and highest, and final offer."

"I'll take it!" I smile.

Rosa holds out her hand. "It's a deal!"

Alfie barks. I reach over to give Alfie a kiss. "Hang in there, little buddy. We're going to get you all better!"

After Rosa leaves, Mom pulls me in for a tight hug.

"Your first customer! I'm so proud," Mom says.

I smile back, my eyes misting slightly. I don't understand why I'm getting so emotional, but I am. To know that someone believes in me and is putting their hopes and trust and money in me and my ideas! And my creativity! It's one step closer to not ever being a lost sock again.

"I'm not going to let Rosa down," I promise.

"I know you won't," Mom says.

Then she does something truly unexpected. She takes her phone and hands it to me.

"Here, take my phone," she says.

"What?" I ask.

"I want you to have it."

"Like, *have* it, have it?"

My heart pounds. I can't even move, I'm so shocked. How long have I been dreaming about this moment, pining for the day I get to join the phone group?

Mom nods. "You can use it to film! Don't worry about me. Now that we have more sales, I can get another phone, something on Facebook Marketplace."

I wrap my fingers around the phone's silvery edges. I've felt it a hundred times before, but it feels entirely different now that it's mine.

Magical almost.

I breathe in the air of possibility.

"I want you to take this and use this. Now that we've seen the power of social media, use this to lift our community and give hardworking folks like Rosa a fighting chance again. Let's change everyone's lives for the better, not just ours!"

I wipe the tears from my eyes and nod with all my heart.

"Yes, Mama!" I cry.

I stare at the enormous power sitting on my palm, my insides doing somersaults, until it hits me. If I have a phone, that'll make Carla the very last holdout.

She'll be all by herself.

Chapter 22

'm so racked with guilt that I don't touch the phone all day Sunday. I think of fifteen reasons to give it back to Mom. But my brain also pumps out fifteen reasons to keep it.

Monday morning rolls around, and I hide it deep in my backpack.

Maybe Carla doesn't have to know. Maybe I'll just keep it in my backpack the whole time at school.

In the car, I ask Mom, "Are you sure you don't need a phone?"

"I just talked to a guy," Mom says. "He's going to sell me his old phone! It's all arranged! I'm going over there right now, after I drop you two off, to pick it up!"

"But how much is it going to cost?" I ask.

"It wasn't too bad. Besides, it's a business expense. An investment. So we can pay off the credit card bills, faster!" she says, pointing to the stack of bills in her purse.

I nod. With trembling fingers, I unzip my backpack and take the phone out. Maybe that's what I can say to Carla too. Now that we have a new business, which is paying us fifty dollars a video, this is just equipment. Like if you're a director and you're shooting a movie, you gotta have a camera.

Except *she's* the one who wants to be a director. She's going to definitely want a camera.

I go back to my original plan, never to take it out at school. But as Mom pulls up to school, I spot Jessica—strutting across the yard, the wind blowing in her perfect hair, her sparkly nails holding up her phone to snap a selfie—and I know.

I am *definitely* pulling it out.

I stroll across the school with my new phone, Beyoncé's "ALIEN SUPERSTAR" playing in my head. If this were a movie, Carla would run over and high-five me. We'd hold my phone up like a shield as we walked by the cool kids. Nate would hop off his skateboard and return a book he'd borrowed to Finn. Preston would be juggling Cheetos. I'd catch one in my mouth as I'd walk by Eleanor, who would text me, Welcome to the club! ❤

I'm all smiles, watching my movie play out in my head, when I hear Jessica sneer, "Nice phone *for a mom!*"

Uh-oh. That's not supposed to be part of the movie.

I spin around to face her. "There are no mom phones and kid phones."

"Uhhh, yes, there are. That thing has a *coral*-colored cover," Jessica remarks. "That's like holding a salmon."

She's a salmon. I shoot daggers from my eyes. "Well, maybe you should get one too, since you copy everything I do."

Jessica jerks her head back. "What'd you say?" she asks.

I don't feel like repeating it for her, so I turn and start skipping toward Carla. But before I can break into a trot, Jessica calls out, "If I were you, I wouldn't be jumping."

"Why not?" I ask.

"Everyone knows, Lina. You have *b* double-*o b*s."

I feel my whole world black out.

- -

Chapter 23

My brain's completely singed by the time I get to class. I can't hear a thing. My eyes are foggy. All I can think about is the spelling of a certain word.

She couldn't even say it.

It was *that* embarrassing.

And here I thought I was doing such a good job hiding them under my sweatshirt! I stew in a pool of sweat at my desk. Who else knows? I glance over at Tonya. She must know. She's friends with Jessica. Oh God, if she knows, that means Nora and Eleanor must know too.

Do they all talk about it on that Discord thing? I hope not!

Mrs. Carter sees me squirming.

"Lina! Would you mind coming up to the board and drawing the human brain for us and labeling the prefrontal cortex?" she asks.

I shake my head, eyes pleading with Mrs. Carter. No offense to the prefrontal cortex, but I've got other prefrontal issues!

Mrs. Carter wriggles her whiteboard marker at me. "What's wrong?" she asks, studying me. "You love drawing!"

How do I explain to Mrs. Carter that I do love drawing but not enough to risk going up in front of everyone and having the whole class look at me? Even if they can't tell, I'll think they can tell, and I'll squirm like I have a hundred ants in my sweatshirt and then they'll *really* be able to tell.

Call on someone else, PLEASE. Anyone!

Jessica jumps out of her seat and volunteers. "I'll do it!"

Great.

"Thank you, Jessica!"

I watch as Jessica grabs the whiteboard marker and gleefully draws a human brain. Except it's way too big and looks like a giant hamster. She even adds stars and sparkles to it! I frown at her obnoxious glittery hamster. I picture him folding his arms and staring at me, asking:

Are you just going to sit there? And let your b *double-*o b*s stop you forever?*

No! I glare back at him.

For the rest of the class, I avoid eye contact with the sparkly hamster . . . even though he has a point.

At recess, I sit underneath the tall oak tree, watching Jessica's latest video. As if this day could not get any worse, she's just made one on *Flea Shop*!

Catherine Wang's *Flea Shop*.

My favorite book and the very book she tried to ban from our classroom last semester!

As Jessica hugs the book, expressing her enthusiasm to all the people on the internet who don't know any of this, I curl up into a ball on the grass.

Carla and Finn skip over toward me. I quickly hide my phone in my pocket.

"You want to hear my new awesome idea for a bath bomb video?" Carla asks. "So, we open with the two of us shaking out a humongous towel—"

I quickly stop her. "No shaking," I tell her. "At least I can't be the one doing the shaking."

"No, the *bombs* are going to be shaking, on the towel—"

"I can't." I look down. Ever so quietly, I mutter, "I think I'm going to be behind the scenes from now on."

"WHAT?!" Carla asks.

"Why? You're so great in front of the camera!" Finn says.

I don't say anything.

Carla turns to Finn and asks, "Will you give us a minute?"

Finn nods and runs off to find Preston and Nate.

Carla sits down next to me on the grass. "What's going on?" she asks. "I thought we were great together!"

"We are! I'm sorry. I just can't," I tell her, tears pooling in my eyes. Slowly, I whisper to Carla what Jessica said.

"She said *boobs*?" Carla asks.

I nod, immediately putting a hand to my chest to cover them. My head spins to make sure Finn can't hear, but thankfully, he's all the way on the other side with Preston. Still, I feel so naked and exposed.

"Yeah, *boobs*," I whisper back. "She didn't even say *books*."

"Why would she say *books*?" Carla asks, confused.

"Never mind," I say. "It's a hangman mistake."

"Well, don't let her get to you," Carla says. "She's probably just jealous."

"Jealous of what? That I have to wear sweatshirts and worry about people seeing me change in PE? Or obsess about how I'm gonna need to buy deodorant and . . . I don't even know what comes after that. Crushes?! I'm not ready for that!"

"You're not?" Carla asks.

I stare at her. Now I'm worried for a whole other reason. "Are . . . you?"

"I mean . . ." She leans back on the grass and whispers to the leaves, "If the perfect boy came along . . . someone who's funny and sweet, maybe?"

WHAT? How long has she felt this way?

"I'm not talking about the banana heads in our class," she quickly adds.

Oh, good. At least it's not a real, active crush.

"It'd have to be someone super mature and kind," she adds.

I nod, playing along.

"Someone with nice-smelling hair," Carla says.

I try to think of qualities to contribute to her list, if I were crush-ready. Which I'm definitely *not*.

"Someone who doesn't copy my ideas?" I ask. "Then takes credit for them?"

"Oh, absolutely. And it'd have to be someone who believes in protecting the environment," Carla agrees.

"Someone who takes care of his library card?"

"Who has clean fingernails!" Carla adds.

"Definitely. And a clean pencil case. With colored pencils!" I smile, relieved my must-haves are in line with Carla's.

"Which he'll use to write a really great Valentine's Day card! An actual poem!"

Carla looks up at the canopy of leaves, like, *Wouldn't that be nice?* And I pretend to long for that too. Even though what I *really* want in a Valentine's Day card is a Michaels five-dollars-off coupon, so I can maybe paint Mom's coral-colored phone cover purple.

I frown, disappointed at myself for thinking it. There's nothing wrong with Mom's phone.

"How'd this conversation with Jessica even come up?" Carla asks.

I shake my head, sneaking a glance down at my phone, still snug in my pocket.

"She just came up to you and said, 'Hey, you've got boobs'?" Carla asks.

"Not exactly . . . ," I hesitate.

"So what happened?"

"Nothing, she was just giving me a hard time about something."

"About what?"

Because I hate lying to Carla, I pull out my new phone.

"Whoa!" Carla's eyes go wide. "This is yours now?" She sits up, reaching for my phone. "How long have you had this?"

"Since Saturday. My mom just sorta gave it to me. . . ."

"Oh," Carla says.

Her *oh* is so light and small, but it sucks up all the air under the tree.

"It's just for making videos, because our neighbor, she needs our help! It's not even that cool. It's salmon colored!"

The more I ramble, the quieter Carla gets. She twirls a blade of grass around her fingers, around and around, and doesn't say anything, not even when I tell her about the fifty-dollar offer from Rosa to make a video! That's when I know she's *really* sad.

"You know what, I shouldn't have brought it to school," I

finally say, quickly taking my phone back and putting it back in my pocket.

"No," Carla says, stopping me. "It's your phone. You should bring it everywhere."

Her words sound sincere, but her eyes look like a puppy died.

"Are you sure?" I ask.

"I'm happy for you." She manages a small smile. "Don't worry, I'll catch up. Especially if we're getting fifty dollars a video."

I let out a huge sigh of relief. "Yes!" I cry.

"Imagine if we slayed at the video!" Carla says, her eyes suddenly dancing.

"We will."

"*We,*" Carla repeats.

She looks into my eyes, and I nod, wriggling in my sweatshirt.

"Don't let Jessica get you down. They're just a body part. If I had them, I'd walk around like this." All of a sudden, Carla jumps up and starts strutting around the grass with her chest out. It makes me laugh so hard.

I pull her down, my face mortified, but I'm grinning.

"Seriously though," Carla says. "Wear them proudly."

I smile. That afternoon, as Carla and I huddle our heads together and plan the most epic taco video for Rosa, I'm filled with determination. Carla's right. I can't let a body part stop me from going after my dreams. Just like Carla and I can't let a little phone get in the way of our friendship.

Chapter 24

Mom, listen to this idea!" I blurt out when I get into the car.

I tell Mom the *genius* idea that Carla and I came up with for Rosa.

"You know how Rosa said that Red Russo just buys their hot sauce, but she gets up every morning to cut fresh peppers and make hers from scratch?" I ask. "What if we did a taste test with . . . ? Drumroll, please!"

I point to my sister. Millie drums her hands along the car window.

"Flamin' Hot Cheetos!" I announce.

But Mom's too busy tapping on her new phone. It's blue and metallic, with a silver chrome cover.

"That your new phone?" I ask. I reach for it, but Mom holds it out of the way.

She can't seem to tear her eyes from it or move the car, despite Millie and I already getting in. "Hello?" I ask.

I hold up the text from Dad: LOVE IT! It's gonna FIRE! Or slay. How do you kids say it these days? Anyway, can't wait to see it!

"Dad liked my idea!" I add.

I love that I can now send Dad texts anytime I want. Mom finally looks up.

"What were you saying about Cheetos?"

"Did you hear any of it?" I ask.

"Sorry I was just dealing with some ridiculous comments," Mom says, finally putting the phone down and turning her attention to us. She reaches into her bag and hands me a cut-up pear in a sandwich baggie.

"What kind of comments?" I ask, popping a piece of pear in my mouth and offering some to Millie.

"Oh, you know, the usual trolls, saying I'm a lazy parent. A selfish mom. All I want to do is take baths, while my kids play video games," Mom says.

"What?" Millie and I both cry out. The piece of pear nearly drops out of my mouth. I never play video games! We don't even have a real bathtub!

"Don't worry, I've blocked them all!"

I'm glad Mom isn't that bothered by all of this as she pulls out of the pickup lane. I'd be *super* bothered. Though I'm proud of myself for not reacting to Jessica's *b* double-*o bs* comment. I pull at my skin, wondering if it's getting thicker.

"So tell me about your Cheetos idea!"

I fill Mom in as I swipe open my phone, curious to read the comments Mom's talking about. The other great thing about having her phone is now I can go into her account whenever I want! But she must have deleted them all, because there are no mean ones. As I'm talking, I get a text from Finn.

Hi Lina, can u read this? Or is this still Mrs. Gao? Hi Mrs. Gao!

I smile.

It's me, Lina! Hiiiiiiiiii!

I still can't believe you have a phone now!

Me neither!

Does your mom like the Cheetos idea?? he asks.

I look up at Mom. "Finn's asking if you like the idea."

"I think it's great!" Mom says. "Bring on the hot sauce!"

Millie gasps. "Oooh! I have the perfect song!" She reaches for my phone and starts playing "Hot in Herre" at full blast. As the beat of the music takes over the car, Millie starts doing a dance in the backseat.

I text Finn: She loves it, and my sister wants us to play "Hot In Herre" for the video.

That song is the GOAT!

I furrow my eyebrows. Goat? What goat? I scratch my head, looking around for a furry creature with a goatee. But he can't mean *that*.

"What's a goat?" I ask my sister.

"A goat? You don't know what a goat is?!" Millie asks, cracking up. "It's the thing that goes *baaa*!"

"No, I know that!" I say. Millie slaps the seat of the car, still cracking up. "You know what, you're not helpful."

I turn back to my texts.

So you think we should use it?

Bet!

Bet? Now he's betting me?

So when r we going to shoot it?

Finally, a sentence I actually understand.

"Hey, Mom, do you think you can drive us to Rosa's tomorrow, so we can shoot it at her taco truck?" I ask.

"Sure!" she says.

Let's do it tomorrow!

👍 👍

A second later, Finn types, So now that u have ur own phone, what r u gonna join?? Snap?? TikTok? Pinterest? BeReal? 👹🐣🐒

I recognize some of them. TikTok obviously. And I know from looking over Jon's shoulders that Snap means Snapchat. I constantly see my classmates on it. I haven't decided whether I'm going to join all of them. I'm already part of a club Carla's not. It seems extra cruel to be a part of other clubs within the phone club.

But I am curious. . . .

What do u do on these apps? I ask Finn.

Everything? Finn types back. Swap pics, text, talk . . .

Can't we do that thru FaceTime?

Yeah but . . . it's just funner!

I move my finger over to the App Store icon.

"Hey, Mom, you think I can download some apps?" I ask.

"What kind of apps?"

Finn continues typing. There's one for sharing doodles! And Pinterest is good for sharing mood boards—that could be useful for us brainstorming a video. Oh and there's even one for sharing books! It's called Goodreads.

My eyes pop. An app for sharing books?! That's it, I'm so joining. I repeat all this to my mom.

"Sure!" Mom says. "Sounds good."

That was easy!

"Just wait till we get back to the house. Save mobile data! And don't spend all your time on it," she says to me with a smile.

"Yes, Mom!" I promise, counting the seconds until I have Wi-Fi again.

That afternoon, while Mom responds to fans and my sister twirls around the apartment dancing to "Hot in Herre," I join every single social media app—even the ones you have to be thirteen for.

Chapter 25

Oh my God.

How can my classmates have closets that are bigger than my entire bedroom? And chairs that hang from the ceiling? And bookshelves organized by color in their living rooms? Not tiny living room sets either, like at IKEA. Real ones, bigger than anything I've ever seen!

My legs are noodles in the bathroom. I've been in there for hours, staring at my phone. But I can't move. I'm too upset by all the glistening pools.

Who lives this way???

My classmates, apparently. There's Nora with her mini fridge just for her skin care. And Preston with his Ping-Pong table in his *air-conditioned* four-car garage! And Tonya with her *two* puppies. And Eleanor with her own private library! And Jon Butterkatz with a life-size replica of R2-D2 that he got from Disney World!

Meanwhile, my own body's going *BEEP BEEP BEEP. Stop! Look away!* But I can't. I'm hypnotized. My fingers can only keep scrolling.

I tap through spring break photos, of boats, and hotels, and expensive restaurants. I guess I knew my classmates all went places, but I didn't *really* know. Until now.

I tap and swipe until I land on a video.

It's from Eleanor's birthday party. Eleanor had a birthday party this past weekend? And she didn't invite me?

My throat goes dry.

I watch as all my classmates sing "Happy Birthday" to my friend at an indoor trampoline park. Jessica, Nora, Tonya, Preston, Nate . . . and Finn? Finn's there too!? I stare at the screen, at everyone eating the triple-layered chocolate cake. The pizza. The endless chips and guac! Every minute of the celebration captured in mind-blowing detail.

It's like watching people inside a snow globe.

I thought Eleanor and I were friends. Why didn't I make the cut?

Finn texts me as I'm watching the videos.

Hey! I saw you're on Goodreads now! Add me back! 📚😎

No, I reply. I'm mad at him.

Why??

Because you got to eat cake and I didn't, I want to type. I shake my head. Way too embarrassing. But I don't understand! What did I do wrong? I'm always so nice to her. I set books aside for her. She even told me to FaceTime her!

Is it because I gave 4 stars to The Cricket in Times Square? he texts.

No, it's because you gave 5 stars to a party I wasn't invited to!

Fine, I'll change it to 5, Finn writes. Two seconds later. There!

I tap on the emojis bank, trying to find the right one to describe my emotions. Am I a 😔? Or a 😣? If I wait a few minutes, will I forget about the party and become a 🙂? Or will I always be a 😵?

Lina?? Everything ok?

I sigh. Yeah. It's not about The Cricket in Times Square

Then . . . what is it?

I take a leap of courage. Just kinda weird seeing inside every-one's life, on all the apps.

Yeah I know. . . . Sometimes when I see pics of people with their mom and dad, I feel a little funny. But I just swipe away.

My anger melts as I read my friend's words. I go over to Finn's Snapchat account, looking through the pics of him with his dad in his dad's backyard. You wouldn't be able to tell from the photos that he feels sad at all.

How are things going with your parents?

Not good.

What's wrong?

My dad and Brooke went shopping yesterday and LOOK AT THIS.

Finn sends me a pic of his dad wearing ripped jeans. I giggle. They look really ridiculous on him. I imagine my own dad wearing ripped jeans, and a smile sneaks out of my mouth.

😫😫😫, Finn types.

Lots of people wear ripped jeans, I remind him.

Not 45-year-olds!, who eat fiber gummies and hold their phones up to their eyeballs to read the screen! 😬

I chuckle at Finn's spot-on description of dads.

Maybe he thinks he needs to look cool to be on social media . . . , I say, thinking of my mom and her many outfit changes by the pool.

Maybe, or he thinks he needs to impress Brooke.

I sit up. Has Finn's dad met his bagel in Brooke? You don't think . . . ?

No. I'm scared to ask him, I don't want to confirm it.

I nod, understanding fully. I know exactly what he means. Maybe it's nothing!

Yeah, maybe he just suddenly needs holes for his hot knees! 🧖 ♂

I smile.

Hey, those fiber gummies can be 🔥🔥🔥

Lol! Thanks, Lina. Speaking of 🔥, I didn't know you have a pool!

I look at his text, confused for a second. Then I remember the selfie I posted on my Snapchat an hour ago, the one Mom took after we finished filming Millie's video with Mom. I start typing, It's not really mine. But I delete the words. Thanks! ☺

I feel bad for misleading Finn.

Though I can't help but wonder if I'd posted the pool pic earlier, would I have been invited to Eleanor's party?

Chapter 26

'm drawing a snow globe at my desk because I can't sleep. I'm half tempted to unfollow my classmates, so I don't have to see all the super-cool stuff I don't have shoved in my face. But the other half of me *needs* to know. My phone rings. It's Lao Lao calling.

"Whatcha doing?" Lao Lao asks.

"Just drawing," I whisper to her. It's late. Millie's already snoring happily. "How's your dance party planning going?"

"Tomorrow night!" she tells me. "I've put flyers up all over the retirement home. Everyone's ready to boogie!"

I smile.

"Do you think I should go with understated chic?" she asks, holding up a tanned blazer and khaki pants. Then she reaches for a red dress. "Or something fun?"

"Something fun, definitely," I tell her.

"All righty!" Lao Lao does a little swirl, holding the dress up to her neck. She points to my paper. "Show me your drawing!"

Reluctantly, I hold up my doodle.

"That's an interesting snow globe," she says, squinting. "Why are there tiny fridges and chocolate cakes?"

I sigh. I tell her about the posts.

"Oh, seashell," she says, sitting down at her vanity table. She props me up in front of her mirror. "You know this was what I was afraid of when your mom said she was letting you on social media."

I cling to my phone, shaking my head.

"No, I'm fine!" I insist.

"Well, *I* wasn't when I got social media."

"You had social media?" I ask. "When!?"

I definitely don't remember a smartphone phase when I lived with her.

"For about two days," Lao Lao says. "Your aunt Jing got it for me a couple years ago. You know, she works in tech, so she thought I would like it. And she downloaded all the apps for me and showed me how to work everything. So I went on it."

"And?"

She reaches for a cup of chrysanthemum lemon tea and tells me all about seeing her classmates on WeChat.

"It's like I had this front-row seat to everyone's highlights. Every family vacation. Every new car and house. And I just . . . I couldn't handle it! I hadn't seen your mom in so long, or Millie, and yet here were all my old classmates, all united with their families. Going to Shanghai Disneyland, eating, drinking, laughing up a storm, and I just couldn't bear it."

"Oh, Lao Lao," I say. I wrap my arms around the phone, wanting to hug her. Wanting to reach inside and grab her and take her to Disneyland.

"It just seemed . . . so unfair! We all went to the same school, ate the same bowls of rice. Why did these people get to have these perfect full lives now?"

"That's exactly how I feel!" I say to her. "They have *so much*. This girl Nora? She has a walk-in closet just for her shoes. And Preston? He has an entire garage of games!"

"I believe it! One of *my* classmates still skis at seventy years old! He's been all around the world!" Lao Lao shakes her head. "Another woman in my class opened a hotel in Japan and has rubbed shoulders with Hollywood movie stars! I remember gawking at her post. I was fascinated, and nauseated, and disturbed. Yet I couldn't put it down!"

"Me too! I still can't feel my legs. They're numb from standing in the bathroom!" I tell Lao Lao.

"And I felt so gross, lurking like a salamander," Lao Lao adds.

"So what'd you do?"

"I turned the thing off, stuck it in a drawer, and never touched it again," she tells me.

Oh.

"I'm just kidding!" I laugh nervously. "My legs aren't really noodles. They're more like . . . super-crunchy egg rolls! I'm totally fine."

Lao Lao sets down her tea and looks seriously at me.

"Are you sure?" she asks. "Because it's perfectly okay to admit that you can't handle—"

"I can handle it!" I insist. "All I have to do is swipe away."

"Because *I* couldn't handle it."

"Well, I have Mom's thick skin," I assure her.

Lao Lao's face softens. "All right," she says, holding up her arms. "Then show me."

I furrow my eyebrows. "How?"

She gets up and, to my surprise, starts swinging her whole body, moving her hands through the air. "Let's do some tai chi. Show me you've worked the jealousy out of your system."

"Tai chi?" I ask.

Errr . . . they don't exactly teach us that in PE here. But my grandmother insists we try. Reluctantly, I get up and mimic her moving her hands through the air. I can't believe I'm doing this.

"Just copy me. Make your mind and your arms move as one. I want you to push away the negative energy."

I try to move my arms, but I just look like I'm doing some weird dance.

"Catch your greatest fear and release it like a tiger," Lao Lao urges, closing her eyes.

"*When You Trap a Tiger*!" I smile. "That's the name of a book at the library!"

Lao Lao opens one eye and reminds me, "Pay attention."

I close my eyes and imagine myself chasing a giant Siberian tiger. A voracious beast filled with all my doubts and worries. What are my biggest worries? That I'll never be able to confidently put my shoulders back. Or wear a bathing suit and go swimming with my classmates, even if I had a glistening pool like theirs. That actually worked. Or go jumping at a trampoline park. That I'd never get invited to anything. Soon, I'm breaking out into a sweat, chasing the tiger closer and closer. I can feel its fur with my fingertips. I lunge forward, but at the very last second, it slips away.

"Did you catch it?" Lao Lao asks, opening her eyes.

I quickly nod, not wanting to lose my phone.

"Mm-hmm!" I assure Lao Lao. "Don't worry about me, Lao Lao. I'm fine! Really!"

My grandmother smiles.

"Good," she says. "Remember, it's all about balancing our minds."

I thank Lao Lao for her tips and wave good night to her. I fall asleep, dreaming of the tiger. Except in my dreams, the tiger is smirking at me. *You'll never catch me,* he says with his eyes. *Not in a million years! You don't have thick skin like Mom!*

Yes, I do! I cry back. I yank on my cheeks to prove it.

Then go up to Eleanor tomorrow and ask her why she didn't invite you!

Fine, I will! I charge toward the annoying tiger, trying to shut him up.

I wake up in a pool of sweat in the morning, right before I find out whether I caught the tiger or not. As relief fills me that I'm safe in my bed, I remember my promise. Am I really going to ask Eleanor?

sneak peeks at Eleanor while Mrs. Carter teaches us about the hippocampus.

It was just a dream. I don't have to ask Eleanor anything.

"The hippocampus is located in the inner region of the temporal lobe of the brain," Mrs. Carter says. There's a row of giggles from the back row. "What now?"

"Just this meme of broccoli water on Discord—" Nate grins, glancing at his phone.

"Hey!" Jessica protests.

I glance over at Jon's phone. Discord is one of the only apps I couldn't join, because Mom's phone was running out of space. But Jon doesn't have it either. "Private chat," he mutters to me.

Nate continues cracking up.

"That's it, you're so getting it later!" Jessica warns Nate.

"Okay, that's enough." Mrs. Carter walks over, taking Nate's phone.

Nate cries out, "Unfair!"

Jessica smiles at him. Mrs. Carter asks, "Finn, can you remind everyone what we were just talking about? Where the hippocampus is located?"

Everyone turns to Finn.

"Errrr . . ." Finn hesitates, scratching his head. "In your inner ear canal?"

"In the inner temporal lobe of our brain," Mrs. Carter corrects.

"Oh yeah!" Finn quickly says.

"Oh yeah." Mrs. Carter turns to the class. "Every time we say *oh yeah*, that's a memory that didn't make it into our hippocampus. You might be surprised to hear this, but all this endless phone checking and scrolling, it's doing a number on our memory."

Jon looks up from his phone.

"What do you mean?" Jon asks.

"We're focusing less," Mrs. Carter says. She walks by Preston's desk and sneaks her hand under his book, to withdraw his phone. "The second we're even a tiny bit bored, we turn to our phones."

"So that's great! We're never bored," Preston says.

"But did you know? Boredom is important!" Mrs. Carter says. "It forces you to think, to slow down, to contemplate and reflect. When you're bored, your brain actually activates, trying to solve your boredom by making connections, finding a new way for you to understand, so you're *not* bored. Then voilà! A breakthrough happens!"

Mrs. Carter walks around the room, snapping her fingers all around us. "Your brain's firing away! Thinking! Coming up with something new!"

We smile. *This is fun!* We all start snapping our fingers.

Suddenly, Mrs. Carter freezes. "But *now* that we're never bored, and all those long, awkward moments are filled with never-ending interesting things to look at on your phone, your brain's just snoring. . . ."

Jessica raises her hand. "But, Mrs. Carter, we're also learning about *more* stuff on our phones!"

"True!" Mrs. Carter says. "But how much of it will we remember? It turns out, when people know they can watch something on YouTube or they can Google something, they don't bother to remember the details as much."

"That's cap!" Preston complains. "How can I remember something less if I can watch a video of it? I love watching videos!"

"Me too!" Nate adds.

"It's a great way to learn, for sure," Mrs. Carter agrees. "But we're talking about memory. And if your brain knows there's a video of an experience versus no video of that experience? It knows you can simply watch the video again to remember the experience. So it's working less hard to remember it."

I glance over at Eleanor. I'll bet I remember more details about her party than she does, having watched her video eighty-five times.

"You've heard the term *use it or lose it?*" Mrs. Carter asks.

All around me, my classmates nod.

"That applies to our brains as well. They did a study at Princeton—they divided people into two groups. Both groups watched an engaging talk. Turns out, the group that took a photo or a video of the talk remembered fewer details than the people who did not. It's called transactive memory. By taking that video, you're taking yourself out of the moment and transferring part of *your* memory to a device."

"So we shouldn't take videos and photos at birthday parties anymore?" Eleanor asks, gasping.

I try to hold my tongue. *At least not post them, so people who weren't invited can see!*

"No, I'm not saying that," Mrs. Carter says quickly. "But

maybe one of these days, do an experiment. Try not taking any photos and videos, just for a day—"

"Even if something cool happens?" Eleanor asks.

"If something cool happens, just take it in. Let your eyes and your skin and your ears remember it. Ditch your external memory drive," Mrs. Carter says. "Just for a day!"

"And your snow globe," I mutter.

Eleanor glances at me. "Huh?"

I pretend to examine my pencil case.

One by one, we all zip our phones into our backpacks—even Jon Butterkatz. As Eleanor turns back to the board, I bloom with pride that I actually said something. I didn't just stay quiet. I roll up the sleeves of my sweatshirt. My skin's growing thicker. I can feel it!

Chapter 28

I'm explaining to Carla later why I made the snow globe comment, but she doesn't seem to understand what the big deal is.

"So she had a trampoline party," Carla says later. "I wouldn't want to eat all that cake and jump up and down until I puke. No thanks."

We're walking to Rosa's taco truck, which is stationed at the park, just two blocks from school today. Mom texted and said she'd meet us there. I glance back at Millie and Finn, but they're still a whole block behind us, bopping their heads to "Hot in Herre."

"You don't understand. We weren't even invited!"

"You want to be invited to puke??" Carla asks, giving me a funny look.

"Okay, first of all, no one puked," I say. "Everyone had fun." The party was incredible! Clearly, my description of the party was not doing it justice. So I pull out my phone.

But before I can play it, Carla begs me to put it away.

"No no no!" she says. "I don't want to see it! I don't want to get transactive memory!"

"That's not how you get it!"

"Still, I don't want to see," Carla says, turning the corner to the park. "I can imagine it in my head: trampoline. Cake.

Eleanor! I'm activating my hippocampus and picturing it right now!"

"I promise you, any kind of chocolate cake you're picturing? This one's bigger. And look at the party bags!"

She stops walking. "Why's it so important to you?" And then, a second later, she looks sad. "Just because Eleanor's one of the popular girls?"

"Nooo," I insist. "That's not it!"

"Then what is it?"

I think hard. Why *is* it important? If I'm honest, it's not the gift bag or the cake. Or the jumping, though that does look super fun. It's the not being part of the club. (Again.)

"I guess . . . it just hurts that she didn't even think of me. I thought we had stuff in common. Like books." I look to the curb, shaking my head. Finally, I mumble, "My mom's always saying the internet's an equalizer, and I really thought that . . ."

"It's okay, you can say it," Carla urges. "You thought because you have a phone now . . ."

I nod slowly. "I'd finally feel like I was on the same level."

We both sit down on the curb.

Carla puts her arm over my shoulder and gives it a little squeeze. "We knew their lives are different," Carla whispers. "You see the cars their parents drive to pick them up. And the fifty thousand different scents of hand sanitizers from Bath & Body Works in their backpacks!"

I nod quietly. Still, it's one thing to imagine their home life and another to see it *up close*. It's not just fancy, it's next level. And Carla still has no idea what I'm talking about.

"Please, can I just show you?" I ask, my eyes pleading with her.

Before Carla can respond, I pull out my phone and press play on the video. As the sounds of the trampoline park blast from my phone, Carla tries to turn it off. I lift my arm to hold the phone away. Unfortunately, my finger accidentally taps *like* on the video.

"Duuuuude," Carla says as I let out a piercing cry.

We stare at my heart on Eleanor's post. *Noooooooo!* I picture Eleanor getting the notification that I *like* her trampoline party. I *like* being left out!

"What do I do?!" I ask, the anxiety jolting through me. "Should I un-heart it?"

"No! That'll make it even worse! Then she'll think you're trying to make a point or something!"

"But I can't leave it!"

"Just forget it," Carla urges. "Here."

Carla reaches for my phone, and before I can stop her, she sticks it in her pocket.

"I'll hold it for you," she says. "For the rest of the day."

"What?!" I gasp.

"Lina," Carla looks into my eyes. "As your director, I need you to focus. Forget Eleanor. We have a job to do. We owe it to Rosa and little Alfie to deliver. Now, are you in the moment? Or are you in a post?"

I swallow hard. As hard as it is to hear it, I know Carla's right. What's done is done. I've got to focus. I can't let my hippocampus get distracted today.

"I'm in the moment."

"Good!" Carla smiles. "Then let's do this!"

The two of us take off running to Rosa's truck.

Chapter 29

And . . . action!" Finn cries.

Carla smiles brightly into the camera, while I tug at the neck of my sweatshirt. It didn't hit me until Rosa put out all the Cheetos that I was filming a hot sauce contest *in a sweatshirt.* At least we're filming out in the park, not in Rosa's small truck.

"Today we're at Rosa's Tacos. Rosa here has been making tacos and proudly serving the community for the last fifteen years. Her tacos are *to die for.*" Carla pauses, turning to me.

"She says she has the best hot sauce in Winfield!" I exclaim. Rosa's turn.

"Sí!" Rosa says, waving at the camera. "Every day, I take the freshest hot peppers and I grind them up. I make fresh, not like other taco trucks—they just buy from the store! No good!"

Millie gives Rosa a thumbs-up from behind Finn's phone—she's doing great!

"We're going to put her recipe to the test!" Carla says. "My friend Lina and I are going to see how many Flamin' Hot Cheetos we can eat with *your* hot sauce, Rosa, versus with Red Russo's hot sauce."

Carla shows off two dipping containers. I reach for Red Russo's, while Carla places Rosa's in front of her. I can feel my forehead bubbling. I haven't even started yet, and I'm already sweating. Here's hoping Red Russo's is *actually* store-bought and mild.

"Ready?" Carla asks.

I nod.

Water? Check.

Big old stack of napkins? Check.

Even bigger stacks of napkins inside my sweatshirt? Check, check.

"Here we go!" I smile.

I grab my first Cheeto and start dipping. Thankfully, the sauce is mild, just like Rosa promised. I pop three more in my mouth. Soon I get into a rhythm. Dip, chew, water, dip, chew, water.

"C'mon, Lina!" Millie cheers.

"Go, Carla!" Rosa cheers.

Alfie barks excitedly for us. By my sixteenth Cheeto, I'm a volcano. I can't wipe my face with enough napkins. I hold and chug the water for dear life.

"Are you hot? Take off your sweatshirt!" Finn calls.

I shake my head, sweat dripping off my face.

No way. I don't care if I have to swim in hot sauce. This sweatshirt is staying ON.

Carla, turns to me, gasping. She sticks her bright red tongue out, as if trying to say something. But she can't get the words out. She needs more water. But we're all out. I jump up to get some more for her. As I'm getting up, a thick wad of napkins falls out of me. *Oh no!*

To make matters worse, the wind carries the napkins all over the park. Thankfully, Millie jumps into action, chasing after the napkins.

"I'll get it!" she exclaims.

I sit my butt down, hoping Finn didn't get that on camera, and lock my arms.

A few minutes later, Millie brings over more water bottles for us. As Carla drinks thirstily, I manage to get five more Cheetos down before Carla cries defeat.

"There you have it!" Finn declares, from behind the camera. I hold my arm up. "Rosa's Tacos for the win! Try it and let us know what you think!"

Rosa pops into the frame to add, "We're parked outside Meadow Park, City Hall, and across from Chevron, in Winfield, California!"

"And CUT!" Finn declares.

Carla falls into my arms as Millie pours water all over our faces with the water jug. I don't even care that the water pours down my neck and gets my sweatshirt wet—I'm just relieved it's over! We did it! Rosa runs over with Alfie, handing me and Carla sweet Horchatas she just made.

"That was beautiful! You girls made me feel *so* alive!" Rosa praises us as we drink the Horchatas gratefully.

Millie grabs a handful of Cheetos and throws them up in the air. As Alfie catches one in his mouth, he makes a funny yelp. We all laugh.

I walk over to Finn, on the grass, and lean over anxiously while he edits. I hope he didn't get any of the part when napkins were falling out of my sweatshirt. Jessica would make that her phone wallpaper. Luckily, it wasn't in the shot! I'm filled with relief.

"Are you done?" Rosa asks.

Millie runs over. She instructs Finn on what part of the

catchy tune to use. Finally, we're ready to show Rosa. As the video plays, Rosa picks up Alfie and kisses his furry ears.

"Perfecta!" Rosa says, reaching into her pocket and handing us fifty dollars.

I stare at the bill, wide-eyed.

"Do you want to do the honors?" Finn asks, holding out his phone. He points to the red post button.

Rosa does a little prayer.

With one single tap of her finger, she catapults her taco truck into the internet with the fire of a thousand habaneros!

Chapter 30

Hang in there, baby, I'll get you your surgery!" Rosa says to Alfie, her voice choking. "This is gonna work! I can feel it!"

"204 views so far!" Finn tells Rosa.

Carla peeks over Finn's shoulders and starts reading some of the comments aloud:

FIRE ME UP. Rosa's Tacos, do you deliver??

I'll take thirty bottles of this stuff. Rosa, what's your Venmo?

I know who's catering my daughter's quinceañera! ❤

Somebody give these girls some Gatorade! And a TV show!!!

#CheetosChallenge let's goooooo!!!

Love these girls supporting small businesses. I'll definitely be going to Rosa's Tacos!

Rosa gets so emotional reading all the comments. Alfie thinks *she* ate fifty thousand Cheetos and starts licking her face!

"We need to send this to the mayor!" Rosa says, clapping her hands. "He's got to see this! Then maybe he'll let me serve my tacos at the Concert at the Park next weekend!"

"Sure!" Finn says, looking up from his phone. "You have his number?"

Rosa starts shaking her head, then holds up a finger. "Actually . . . I might have it in the truck. It was from a while ago, when he stopped by. Come, help me find it!"

Finn hands me his phone.

"Here. Keep hearting comments!" Finn instructs as he goes with Rosa.

I take Finn's phone and continue liking the comments. The notifications pile up like an anthill, filling me with hope that maybe Eleanor won't see my one like. Maybe it'll all get buried in a giant smoke of internet love.

I feel better and better, reading all the wonderful comments, until my eyes land on one:

Didn't anyone tell you girls, spicy snacks give you pimples?

I immediately stop liking.

My fingertips reach for my forehead, instead, searching. But I don't *feel* anything.

Not that I even know what a pimple feels like. I start sweating again.

"Carla!" I call out to my friend.

I think of Mom's warning about haters. Is this a hater? But it almost feels too mean to be completely made-up.

Carla stops doing somersaults with Millie and runs over.

She laughs when I show her the comment. "That's nonsense. All I do at my house is eat spicy food. I *wish* I got a pimple!" She takes the phone in her hands. "Block!"

"Wait—what if they saw something on our sweaty faces? How do you know we don't have one?" I ask, taking the phone and holding the camera up to my face. But all I can see are my two worried eyes staring back at me.

"They didn't see anything! There's nothing to see!" Carla assures me.

"Are you sure?" I poke at my forehead some more. "What if it's *in* there, planning its grand entrance?"

Carla giggles.

"This is not a Taylor Swift concert!"

This might be funny for her, but a pimple is the last thing I need right now. I've already got way too many things to worry about. And there aren't sweatshirts for foreheads!

As I'm panicking, Finn's dad rolls up in a black SUV. "Finn! You ready?" Finn's dad calls. "I've got to meet Brooke at five!"

Finn jogs back, muttering, "See what I'm talking about?" He reaches for his phone. "Gotta go."

After Finn leaves, I turn and plead with Carla. "Please, can I have my phone back? I've got to search up this pimple thing! I need to do more research."

"You're fine, trust me," Carla says, lowering her hands to do another cartwheel.

"But I need it! It's a pimple emergency!"

"You know what you need? A nice, relaxing movie night. You want recommendations?"

I shake my head. I want my phone back. That's what I want! I rack my brain trying to come up with another reason. "But what about the comments? I've got to respond to them!"

"I'll respond to the comments tonight!" Carla assures me.

As Mom's car pulls up, Carla skips away with my phone. The entire ride, I sit with one hand over my forehead, hoping I don't have a humongous new friend waiting for me when I get home.

Chapter 31

Here goes.

I pick up the toothpaste. I can't believe I'm doing this. But after searching up *How to get rid of a pimple* on my laptop and watching a bazillion videos, I'm convinced I've got to do something.

According to the videos, a mint and yogurt mask is the best way to get rid of pimples. Since we don't have any yogurt or mint, I decide to go with the next best minty thing—toothpaste.

As I'm applying it all over my face, Mom knocks on the bathroom door.

"You almost done in there?" she asks. "I need my bra."

"Uhhhh. . . ." I glance over at her stringy jellyfish of a bra. "I'm kinda busy in here."

"Doing what?" she asks.

I blurt out the first thing I can think of. "Steaming my brain?" I smack my forehead at my ridiculous answer, accidentally getting toothpaste all over my hands. "Ugh!"

"What's wrong?" Mom asks.

"Nothing!" I tell her. "Everything's fine!" I quickly wipe my hands and grab her jellyfish. I open the door a tiny crack. "Here, take your bra."

Mom takes it and stuffs her phone in my hand.

"Talk to your lao lao," she says. "I gotta go help Rosa with something! Be right back!"

I hold the phone up before realizing it's a video call.

"AHHH!" Lao Lao shrieks. "What's that white stuff on your face??!"

I thrust a finger to my lip. "Shhhhh! Toothpaste," I whisper. Then I think I might as well ask her, now that she's seen. Holding the camera as close to my face as possible, I ask, "Does this look like a pimple to you?"

"No, that's just your nose!"

"Are you sure?"

Lao Lao studies me. "What's all this about?"

I groan, sitting down on the bathroom floor.

"I ate all this hot sauce today," I confess to Lao Lao. "And this person online said I might get pimples."

"See! It *is* too much! I knew it—"

"No, no." I try to calm Lao Lao down. I can't stop now! "I just made a video that helped a small business! It might even save a dog's life!"

I feel a swell of pride at our fantastic first job. I should be celebrating! Making dan dan noodles and bringing them to Dad's restaurant, so we can have another celebratory family meal! Instead, I'm sitting on the bathroom floor, with my face caked in toothpaste, wondering if I'm going to turn into a spotted owl.

Lao Lao's face softens.

"Well, that person is absolutely wrong. Spicy food doesn't cause pimples. If spicy food causes pimples, the whole of Sichuan would be covered in zits. And everybody knows, Sichuan girls have the *best* skin."

"Really?" I ask.

"They're famous for it!" Lao Lao says.

I breathe out a sigh of relief. Thank God, because I can't imagine giving up mapo tofu or hot and sour soup!

"Besides, everyone knows, the real cause of pimples is unexpressed anger. . . ."

The next thing I know, Lao Lao holds up *her* phone to *her* chin and shows me a tiny bump. "See that little guy right there? That's from everybody skipping my dance party."

"They didn't come?!"

Lao Lao shakes her head. "Only the cafeteria ladies showed up. I don't understand. I put up flyers everywhere and even asked the nurses to help me pass them out—I *know* everyone saw them. And it's not like there was anything else going on!"

"What about Li Ran and Wei and Ning?" I ask, referring to Lao Lao's friends that she plays mahjong with.

"They all said they were too tired," Lao Lao says, shaking her head. "Even though I saw them later in Wei's room, playing bridge. I don't understand. I worked so hard! I even got a disco ball!"

I put a minty hand to my heart. Immediately, I scramble up from the bathroom floor and reach for my laptop.

"Hey, let's have one right here," I suggest, searching up "Shake It Off" on YouTube.

Lao Lao starts saying no, but I insist. I may not know tai chi, but I know how to shake.

"C'mon, do it with me!" I urge as the song plays, shaking my butt.

Lao Lao gives me a small smile. She gets up from her bed reluctantly.

That afternoon, we shake, shake, shake. Even though it's terrifying to see my new body jiggle in the mirror, I pretend I'm in Beijing, dancing with my lao lao. I even roll my chest forward and back and lift my arms, taking off my sweatshirt, because I'm so hot. It feels so good to be free like this.

Millie comes barging into the bathroom.

"What are you guys doing?" she asks.

"Having a dance party! C'mon!" I toss my head around.

Millie screams as a tiny bit of toothpaste lands on her cheek. "What do you have on your face?"

Turning red, I quickly grab a towel. "Nothing!" I insist. "You going to stand there, or are you going to show us your moves?"

Never one to resist a good dance-off, Millie throws her arms up, grinning. As we give my grandmother the dance party she deserves, I think about how nice it would be to feel this way *all the time*. To not care what anyone thinks and just *move*. I wish I could bottle up the magic in that tiny bathroom, and slather *that* all over my face.

Chapter 32

The next morning, I flutter open my minty lashes and see Millie peering down at me.

Her entire face is covered with toothpaste.

I scream.

"What are you doing?" I ask.

"Nothing." Millie shrugs, as she puts a toothbrush to her eyebrow.

"No, Millie, you're not supposed to brush your face!" I wince, leaping out of my bunk bed and trying to grab the toothbrush from her before she gets fluoride in her eye.

"Why not? I want a facial too!" Millie protests.

I shake my head. "That's not—" I don't even know how to say it, it's so embarrassing. Instead, I charge toward the bathroom and return with a wet towel. "That's not what it's for."

"Then what's it for?" she asks, dabbing her face.

I hesitate for a second, debating whether to tell her. "Nothing," I finally say.

Thirty minutes later, and thankfully no longer dripping with fluoride, we climb into the car. Mom's quiet in the front, checking her messages, before starting the engine. She suddenly lets out a yelp.

"Guess what? The mayor's gonna let Rosa serve her tacos at the park!" she declares.

"REALLY?!" I put my hands on my cheeks.

"She just heard! Oh, and Mrs. Kim called too! You know Mrs. Kim, from bag store? She wants to know whether you guys can help her make a video!" Mom says. "She'll pay!"

"Absolutely!" I say, bouncing in my seat. I can't wait to tell my friends—we're a real business now!

Mom pauses. "But what's this about a mean pimple comment?" she asks, glancing at me in the mirror. "Your lao lao told me . . ."

Panic takes over.

"Nothing. It's nothing!"

"You have *pimples*??" Millie turns, her eyes widening.

I sneak a peek at the rearview mirror. "No! At least I don't think I do. . . ."

"You don't," Mom assures me. "That person was just trying to get a reaction out of you. Did you write anything back?"

I shake my head. "Carla deleted and blocked."

"Good," she says. She starts up the car. "And by the way, there's nothing wrong with pimples. You should have seen all the pimples I got."

"Really?" I ask.

Mom's skin is silky smooth. I crane my neck but can't see any blemishes. Just her glowing forehead and warm rose tea cheeks.

But Mom insists it's true. "So many that I even started naming them." My sister and I laugh. "Serious! There was Fang and Li, and Min, of course. I liked Fang because she was right under my nose, so when I smiled, you couldn't really see her. But Min! Min was a stubborn old goat."

I lean in. It's strangely comforting hearing Mom talk about her pimple days.

"What did Min do?" I ask.

"Oh, Min would always appear at the worst times, like right before a school photo day! Or on my birthday! And just be like, SURPRISE!"

Nervously, I ask, "When did you . . . uh . . . start getting them?"

"I believe I was thirteen . . . ," Mom says. "But it could happen at any time. Even babies get pimples."

"WHAT?!" I ask.

"Oh yeah, it's called baby acne. You had it when you were a baby. Both you girls."

Great. I was literally born with puberty.

"How'd you finally get rid of Min?" I ask. "Did you toothpaste him?"

Millie gasps. "Is that . . . ?"

I nod. I give her a sheepish look. *Now you know.*

"You wanna know how? I IGNORED him!" Mom tells me.

Funny, that wasn't in *any* of the videos I watched yesterday on my computer.

"I didn't see the point in all those cleansers and creams. So I decided . . . Come on out, Min. Bring it on! I will wear you proudly, because you are mine. And everything on my face, every eyelash and every blemish . . . is beautiful. Remember that, girls."

I picture a young Mom walking around school with her head held high, proudly displaying her Min. Bet she never bowed out on the chance to draw a brain in front of her class. I have to find my confidence again.

"Hey. Real talk. I know I gave you a phone but . . . ," Mom says, as she stops at a traffic light. "If any of this is getting to you, I can totally film the video for Mrs. Kim myself. Maybe we can do one together—bath bombs and bags!"

Fiercely, I shake my head. "No! I've got this."

"Because I don't want you being influenced by mean comments—"

"Mom! I'm not going to get influenced by random spammers!" I assure her.

"Well, what if *I* reply to all the comments from now on?" she suggests. "From my phone?"

"Or me!" Millie volunteers. "I can do it!"

"Oh no no no," Mom and I both blurt out.

"It's fine," I tell Mom. "I can handle it. I'm not going to get influenced or sidetracked."

Mom holds my gaze for a long time.

"Mom, you said you want to teach me not to be afraid and to grab on to my own future," I remind her. "Please. Let me do this. This is my small business, too. . . ."

Finally, she relents. "Okay . . . ," she says. "But if anyone says anything remotely mean ever again—"

"Don't worry!" I quickly say as we arrive at school. I'm desperate to get out of the car.

But Mom reaches out a hand. "You're my baby. . . . It's my job to worry."

Our fingertips touch briefly before I let go. I know Mom's trying to protect me, but she should know I'm not a baby anymore. I'm tough and strong, just like her.

Chapter 33

H ey! You have my phone?" I ask Carla first thing in the courtyard.

She smiles and takes it out from her pocket, lingering, hanging on to it for just a second longer—during which time every hair on the back of my neck stands, terrified she's not gonna give it back—before gently placing it in my palm.

I exhale in relief as my fingers grip the cold edges. To think, this morning I was so close to losing it forever!

"Guess what? We have our second customer, Mrs. Kim!" I tell Carla.

"Seriously?" Carla squeals. "YESSS!"

I glance down at my phone. "Did Eleanor write anything back? Did we get any more pimple comments?" I ask as we walk to class. I swipe open my phone and see a missed text from Dad.

Hi Lina! I brought you back some walnut shrimp🍤 from the restaurant last night! It's in the fridge! 🥡🍴 Just reheat, so Mom doesn't need to make dinner. 😄😄😄 She's been working so hard! Love, Dad

I smile. Another reason I can't give up my phone. How would I find out about the walnut shrimp?

"Nope! All good," Carla says. She stops walking for a second and whispers, "More than good! I met a boy!"

I look up. "What???"

"Yeah! He left us a comment! So we started talking!"

"Who?" I ask.

"Jake Evermoon," Carla says. "Even his name is beautiful!"

As Carla tells me all about the exciting new boy she met, and what he loves to read, and his super-clean pencil case, and their joint obsession over *You've Got Mail*, I get a strange, prickly feeling in my tummy. Like maybe my liking Eleanor's post is suddenly not my worst problem.

I tell myself it's going to be okay. Just because she thinks this Jake is the coolest thing since sweet potato fries doesn't mean she's going to stop being best friends with me. And I knew this was coming. She'd said she was ready for a crush. Still, I didn't think it would happen so soon. And through my phone.

As Carla tells me her plan to keep emailing Jake, I try to smile and be excited for her.

But deep down inside, it's harder than I thought to not be the one galloping ahead, for once.

In class, I search for the comment from Jake. Who is he? And what does he REALLY want with my best friend?

Luckily, Jon's giant backpack blocks my phone from view. Quickly, I wade through the deep pool of comments, but I can't find any from someone named Jake. Was it on one of Mom's? I tap over to her video from yesterday. Mom filmed it in Starbucks! She looks good! Her hair's pulled back in a sleek bun, her shirt's ironed, and she looks confident. I scroll through the new comments that Mom hasn't even had time to heart yet. As I'm hearting them, I see a comment:

Way too much eyeliner, honey.

What? I immediately zoom in on Mom's eyes. She looks great! What is this person talking about? Maybe it's her long lashes? *Maybe you've never seen an Asian person with naturally long lashes,* I want to write back. *But we exist!*

Instead, I tap on the video search bar. I delete the pimple search I made, walking to class. This time I write: *Eyeliner. Makeup. How much is too much eyeliner?*

One by one, videos start appearing on my screen. I watch lawyers, dentists, astronauts, paramedics, flight attendants, and custodians putting on makeup. Some use way more eye makeup than my mom. Phew. Mom's safe.

But the people in the videos don't stop with makeup. I watch as the women get dressed, throwing shirts, dresses, skirts on. I stare at their bodies.

Their mile-long legs.

Toned arms.

Pillow lips.

I glance over at my classmates, trying to discern who among us looks like that. Tonya, maybe? I once saw her wearing high heels to a music recital at school. Nora if she put lip gloss on. I put a finger to my lips. Could *I* look like that?

"All right, people!" Mrs. Carter claps. "Now that you know all about the pre-frontal cortex and what it does, let's get into small groups of three and see if you can label everything correctly!"

I lock eyes with Finn and Carla.

"Lina, get over here!" Finn invites. I stuff my phone into my pocket and take my pencil case.

"Dude! I thought we were gonna be a group!" Nate protests, frowning at Finn.

Jon Butterkatz immediately pounces on the opportunity. "I'll be in your group!" he volunteers. He scrambles to go and sit next to Preston and Nate.

Finn calls back apologetically, "Sorry, we just have a lot to talk about. Our new business is taking off!"

Jessica overhears. "What new business?"

"You didn't know? We're officially *paid* content creators," Carla beams at her. "Just got our second customer today!"

"Why on earth would *anyone* want to pay you three Cheetos-heads to make content for them?" Jessica asks, crossing her arms.

"For your information, we Cheetos-heads saved a business and a puppy," I tell her. "And we're going to keep going until every small business is heard."

"Oh, that's a great business name!" Finn exclaims. "*Be Heard!*"

I love that! Carla mouths.

"Be Heard??!" Jessica cries. "That's *my* line—*You heard it here first!* Can't believe you're copying my account!"

I've *never* heard Jessica use that. But when I pull up her account on my phone, I see it in the tiny font in her profile.

Jessica Scott. I make bestsellers. If it's worth reading, you'll hear it here first. For content sponsorship, contact my MOMager courtney-scott@courtneyscottmarketing.com.

"Enough chitchat!" Mrs. Carter says. "I know your prefrontal cortexes are still developing and won't fully mature until after you've grown. But we have got to get to our worksheets!"

"We're not copying you," I whisper to Jessica as we all take our seats. "We're not even doing the same thing! We're talking about tacos, and you're talking about books!"

But no matter what I say, Jessica stabs her paper with her pencil, drawing angry faces all over her worksheet.

"This isn't over!" she warns when the bell rings for recess.

Chapter 34

Should we go with another name?" I ask my friends in the library.

"No way," Carla says. "She can't copyright 'Heard'! Everyone can be heard. That's the whole point of our business!"

"I agree," Finn says. "Don't worry about Jess—she's just going to have to get over it."

But before we can shake on it, Finn's phone lights up on the table with an urgent message from Preston.

Bro, you gotta see this!!

Finn taps on the link. I expect it to be some prank video or meme of a talking skateboard. But it's a link to Jessica's page. Finn plays the video.

"You heard it here first," Jessica's bright cheery voice says. "I don't know how many authors have to deal with this. But today I found out that some of my classmates are ripping off *my* social media presence. It's called Be Heard. That's like having your title stolen. And it's just . . ." She starts fanning her eyes.

"Oh my God, is she going to cry?" Carla asks. Finn and I exchange a bewildered look.

A tear drops. Then another. And yup, Jessica is full-on crying.

"It's *beyond* devastating. Have you ever had something important of yours copied?" Jessica wails. Then just as quick as it started, her crying stops and she puts on a smile. "Let me know in the comments below!"

Wow, I mouth.

My friends and I look at each other.

"Rude," Carla says.

"At least she didn't name us?" Finn asks hopefully.

Still, the anxiety chokes in my throat. Could our small business be over before it even starts?

After recess, I sneak peeks at my desk, lifting my sleeve ever so slowly. I can't believe I'm using Jon's old tricks. But I need to know how Jessica's ridiculous video is doing!

I turn my arm and pinch my sleeve again. It moves an inch. And another inch. I peek at my phone, hidden inside.

259 views.

I tap refresh.

347. Every time the number rises, I feel my body temperature jump. By 567, my phone is fully in my palm. I wish I could tell all the people watching the video, she actually copied me first!

I glance over at Jessica. She's crouched over at her desk, also secretly checking her phone. No doubt she's loving the comments:

I'm sooo sorry!

I hate it when people copy omg why do people do this 😩

Be Heard? Such a rip off

They should be banned from this app!

HATE copycats!

"Lina!" Mrs. Carter calls out.

My head jerks up.

"That's it." Mrs. Carter walks over to me and holds out her hand. "Phone, please."

I break out in a cold sweat. *I can't lose it again!*

"I'm so sorry, Mrs. Carter. I won't do it again, I promise." I search Mrs. Carter's eyes.

"I've warned the whole class, multiple times," Mrs. Carter says, gesturing for me to hand it over.

Tears brim in my eyes. We have a business to run! Videos to make! Today was not supposed to go like this! "I really . . . really need this phone!"

"You know the school policy—"

"I know. And I feel awful," I say to Mrs. Carter. I plunge my head down. Jon glances at me like, *Dude, haven't I taught you anything? Keep it IN your sleeve.* I try to find the words to explain my behavior, but my throat is dust. I'm so ashamed. I shouldn't have even had it out to begin with. Mrs. Carter deserves better than this. "I don't know what happened. . . ."

"I'll tell you what happened if you really want to know," she says.

"We want to know!" my classmates all call out. They throw their pencils down, grateful for this blessed distraction from math. We're learning about coordinate planes. Mrs. Carter leans in, uttering a word I'd never heard before.

"It's called dopamine, friends," she whispers.

The classroom goes still. Dopa-what?

"It's a feel-good chemical in our brain. Whenever we do something good, like score a goal in soccer or get an A on a test, we get a little hit of it," Mrs. Carter says.

"Sounds . . . like a drug." Nate giggles.

"Oh, it's very addictive," Mrs. Carter says. "It's specifically designed that way, to reward our brains, so we keep making good decisions."

"So it's a good thing?" Finn asks.

"Yes! Dopamine's what got us to where we are now. Helped us learn what predators to avoid, share how to make tools, and eventually develop language—all of that is fueled by dopamine."

"So what does that have to do with Lina checking her phone?" Jessica asks.

I glare at her. *Thanks a lot for reminding Mrs. Carter!*

"Well, it turns out, when we get likes or comments on our phones? That gives our brains a *flood* of dopamine." Mrs. Carter glances around the room. "How many of you have continued to stare at your phone even after you've gotten a bunch of likes?"

A few awkward hands go up, including mine. The night our first video went up, I stared for hours. Even my toes were anxious.

"Because it feels *good!* You're getting MASSIVE dopamine. And your brain's going, *Ooh that was easy; give me more!!!* It's just DOPAMINE, DOPAMINE, DOPAMINE all rushing into your prefrontal cortex," Mrs. Carter explains.

"I *love* that feeling," Preston says, grinning.

"Me too," Jessica adds.

"Oh, it's so powerful!" Mrs. Carter says. "And your brain will do just about *anything* to keep it going. That's why it's so hard for you all to stop checking."

She walks around the room, kneeling and collecting

phones off textbooks, desks, even shoes. My classmates howl when she takes the phones away. They hold out their hands, begging, clamoring, jumping for her to give them back. But Mrs. Carter keeps walking ahead.

"Because you're trying to get that rush of dopamine, you're on your phone more, trying to get extra dopamine, checking and refreshing to get all those likes. That's what's called a dopamine loop," She makes a circle in the air with her finger. "Except social media is not predictable, is it? Who knows exactly how many likes you'll get on your next post?"

I look around the room. No one raises their hand.

"Could be one or could be a hundred! You don't know!" Mrs. Carter says. "That's what makes it so exciting and infuriating. But also, *addictive.*"

Out of the corner of my eye, I spy Jessica back on her phone, hitting refresh. And smiling.

"You know what else is like that?" Mrs. Carter asks. "A slot machine."

"They have those in Vegas!" Finn calls out. "Isn't it for gambling?"

"Exactly. You pull on this lever. You don't know if you're going to win, but the reason people keep playing is there's a *chance* they might win," Mrs. Carter says. "It turns out, that element of unpredictability is what keeps people addicted."

She walks back to her desk and projects a website onto the whiteboard. "In 1930, a psychologist named B. F. Skinner discovered that when you reward mice randomly and the mice can't predict *when* they're going to get rewarded, the mice will constantly check in to see if they're gonna be rewarded."

She looks up at us. "Turns out, we're no different. If we

think there's a chance we'll get rewarded for something . . ."

She gets up from her desk and heads toward Jessica. "Like say, for instance, maybe a whole bunch of people will like our new post. . . ." Mrs. Carter taps Jessica on the shoulder.

"Fine," Jessica mumbles, putting her phone down.

"Then we'll constantly check it. And I mean *constantly.* It's no surprise that anxiety and depression are both through the roof!"

I raise my hand. "But Mrs. Carter, what about all the good sides of social media?"

"Yeah! Like helping small businesses?" Carla asks.

"Connecting with people!" Finn adds.

"You're absolutely right!" Mrs. Carter says. "From Greta Thunberg to X González, young people are using social media every day to change the world. But . . . that doesn't make it any less addictive, is my point. Which is why Jessica is, *once again,* checking her phone. Jessica, are you serious right now?"

Jessica snaps her head up from her phone.

"I'm sorry! But I think Catherine Wang just liked my video!" Jessica exclaims.

"WHAT!?" I shout. I grab my phone.

All self-control goes out the window. My favorite author *cannot* like the video of me being a copycat!

"Lina! Jessica! Give me your phones!" Mrs. Carter says, holding out her hand.

But I can't! It's like my fingers are possessed! I scroll and scroll, the anxiety pounding in me until I see it.

"You mean this person?" I ask, holding up my phone. "That's not *the* Catherine Wang! She's a real estate agent in Texas!"

"Oh," Jessica says, slightly embarrassed.

I throw up my arms in triumph. Until I see the look on Mrs. Carter's face.

"Hand 'em over," she says, confiscating both our phones. I gulp as she takes mine. "I'll be holding on to these for the rest of the day," she says. "*And* you're both staying in at recess tomorrow."

As Jessica gives me an *it's all your fault* scowl, I sink back in my chair. I've never gotten detention before. Not even in China when I put sticky fly tape on this boy's backpack because he kept making fun of me for not having "real parents" at Parents' Day. Jon sticks his lower lip out. Even *he* feels bad for me.

I never get in trouble! Why couldn't I have just put the phone down, like Mrs. Carter asked? I curse the dopamine in my brain, feeling like a real dope . . . and shuddering at the thought of being stuck with Jessica tomorrow.

Chapter 35

That night, I write Mrs. Carter a letter.

Dear Mrs. Carter,
I am so sorry for checking my phone while in your
class. It was irresponsible of me, and I am very
ashamed.

From now on, I will bring my phone to school
in a Ziploc bag and leave it zipped up inside my
backpack. You're right, it is too tempting and I just
want to check. Even when you were telling me to
stop, my fingers kept moving. It's like they weren't
even my fingers! Maybe because of the dopamine
you were talking about.

By the way, I really appreciate you talking to us
about our brains. I think it is my favorite unit of
the year, even though I didn't show it today. I will
try harder. I'm sorry again.

Thank you for being a kind and amazing teacher.
Your student,
Lina

I'm putting the letter in my backpack when Lao Lao calls
me. I stare at my phone. At least I got it back. I chew the inside

of my cheeks, trying to decide if I should tell her. I want to tell her, and then she might tell my mom, just like she did with the pimple comment. And Mom will *definitely* take away my phone.

"Hi, Lao Lao," I answer, smiling as sweetly as I can.

"Hi, seashell! What are you doing?" she asks.

"Nothing. Just finishing the walnut shrimp Dad got us from the restaurant," I say innocently. I hold up a piece from my plate to show her. I was going to wait for Mom, but I got too hungry. She's still at the UPS store, dropping off packages.

"Guess what? I *finally* mustered up the courage to ask my buddies here why they didn't come to my dance party."

"And?"

"Turns out, they were intimidated! Wei was worried about her knees. Li Ran's been feeling a little stiff in his hips, even though he had his operation years ago. They just didn't think they could move as well as they used to."

"See? It wasn't that they didn't want to dance!"

Lao Lao's face beams.

"I know," Lao Lao says. "I'm so glad I asked. I would have never known if I hadn't had a heart-to-heart with them."

I nod, wishing I had stayed and apologized to Mrs. Carter in person after school. Or better yet, at recess, when I first saw Jessica's video. I wish I'd talked to her about how much it hurt.

"What's wrong?" Lao Lao asks, studying me. "Someone on the internet again? You're not still putting toothpaste on your face, are you?"

"No," I quickly say. Thankfully, instead of showing me gross pimple videos, now when I open my phone, I get a bazillion makeup videos.

Tinted moisturizer! Glow stick! Concealer! Flawless finish foundation! Instant age-rewind eraser!

Everything sounds so fascinating and grown-up. I don't know how many of them I'll need, but one thing's for sure— I'm going to need something. The way I look, right now, is not enough.

"Then what is it?" she asks.

I bite the inside of my cheeks. *Don't say it. . . . Don't say it!*

My grandma holds the phone right up to her eyeball. The sight of her giant pupils freaks me out, and I blurt out, "All right, I got in trouble today, for being on my phone in class. And now I have to sit in at recess, with Jessica!"

"*The* Jessica?" Lao Lao asks.

I nod slowly. Even Lao Lao remembers Jessica. As I tell her about her latest video, she frowns.

"I'm so sorry, sweetheart. Did you tell your teacher?"

I shake my head. "I just want no more drama with this girl. I told her that at the end of last term. But every day she finds new ways to create problems with me!"

"Sounds like your mom needs to have a conversation with her mom—"

"*No,*" I insist. "Her mom's terrifying . . . and filled with broccoli water."

"What?"

"Never mind."

"Well, if you don't want the moms involved, you'll just need to be honest and direct with her. Like I was with my friends. Have a real heart-to-heart. You might be surprised!"

A real heart-to-heart? With Jessica?

I shudder.

"I'd rather have a heart-to-heart with my future pimple."

"Hey," Lao Lao says gently. "Sometimes those who don't deserve our kindness need it the most."

I let out a sigh. I know she's right, but it sure feels hard. When I think of Jessica gleefully reminding Mrs. Carter that I was on my phone, it makes me want to grab an On-the-Glow blush stick and dot her whole face with it.

"Maybe I can just send her a text," I suggest.

Lao Lao shakes her head. "For this kind of thing? Talking in person is better."

"Why?"

"Because when you talk to people face-to-face, you can see their body language. You can see their emotion."

"Oh, I doubt she's gonna show me her emotion," I quickly say.

"No. But maybe she can see yours."

I nod reluctantly, hoping Lao Lao's right. It'll take every ounce of grown-up willpower for me to try tomorrow.

Chapter 36

Time moves like molasses when your phone is zipped up in your backpack. By the time recess finally rolls around, I'm about Lao Lao's age, with Jell-O legs that nearly give in when I try to stand.

Step by step, I march to the front of the room to give my letter to Mrs. Carter. As I'm walking back, I offer Jessica a small smile.

She winces, like I've just flown a paper airplane into her eye.

I sit back down and wait while Mrs. Carter reads my letter. By this point, almost everyone else in the classroom has piled out. I catch Carla's eyes, *good luck!* I'm so sad to be missing out on our brainstorming for Mrs. Kim's video.

Mrs. Carter looks up from the letter.

"Thank you for this, Lina," she says. "I appreciate you writing this beautiful letter, and I want you to know I'm not mad at you. I know how hard this is on you and so many kids. In fact, we're thinking of putting on a Dangers of Social Media night."

"That's a great idea!" Jessica says.

I'm encouraged by Jessica's bright and positive response. Maybe she's had some time to reflect, and she wants to turn a new page too!

But as soon as Mrs. Carter turns back to her grading, Jessica whispers to me, "A letter, really? You're such a Goody Two-shoes!"

I'm confused. "What shoes?"

I glance down at my Vans—they look perfectly good to me!

Mrs. Carter takes off her reading glasses and announces, "Girls . . . I need to go make some copies. I'll be right back. Can I trust you two to stay nice and quiet while I'm gone?"

We both nod.

As soon as Mrs. Carter leaves the classroom, Jessica immediately reaches into her desk for her phone. Enviously, I watch as she scrolls. It feels so unfair to be sitting here with all my thoughts, while she gets to tap and like.

Still, I made a promise to Mrs. Carter.

I remember I have headphones in my backpack. What if I grab my headphones and *pretend* to be listening to music? As I'm reaching for my headphones, my Ziploc bag with my phone in it falls out. I quickly grab the bag off the floor before Jessica sees. I hide it in my hands, turning it over. My phone glows to life. I smile at a message from Finn—we're by the oak tree, if you get out early!

K, I text back.

I look over at Jessica. She's totally engrossed in her phone. I wonder what new thing my classmates have posted that's so fascinating. Cotton candy armchair? Flying TV? Talking shower? I'm tempted to check.

But I also don't want to check, afraid of the mustardy-green feelings it might stir up, like last time. Which is why I've been avoiding their Stories.

Instead, I tap on the app that I've been watching all the makeup videos on.

In the search bar, I type in *goody too shoes*.

Within seconds, all kinds of videos on shoes populate. Cowboy boots, shiny pumps, thin stilettos, tall gladiators. I sit back, watching supermodels stomp down the runway in four-inch platforms, wondering, *How do they do that?*

Not just walk in those shoes but look like that. In their dainty jackets and their clunky bracelets, their skin gleaming, perfect, glossy like glazed donuts.

I tap on the camera app and hold it up to my face.

Why don't I look like a glazed donut?

I suddenly fret not just about pimples but about the very texture of my face. What if it's all wrong? Lao Lao once said that my skin was soft like fluffy mantou. But where does that fit in the American beauty standard of pastries?

I watch more and more videos. I'm deeply engrossed in *Glazed Donut Skin—Tried and True Beauty Tips from a Model*, when Jessica laughs.

"*You* want to look like a model?" she asks.

"No!" I immediately put my phone away, embarrassed. "I was just watching."

"Pro-tip, it's not the makeup. You're either born with glazed donut skin, or you're not."

I'm so sick of her trying to put me down. Trying to convince me she's better than me, that I'll never catch up. "Anyone can be a glazed donut! The internet is an equalizer!"

"Right, that's why we're both here. Even though you copied me."

I squeeze my eyes shut, telling myself to stay calm. I

think of Lao Lao's words. "Listen, can we just have a truth?"

"It's called truce, dummy. And no, we can't have one. My mom's threatening to put Screen Time on my phone because you got me in trouble!"

"It's not my fault!" I tell her. "You were on your phone too!"

"Because you stole my name—"

"Actually, you copied me first." I can almost hear my lao lao's voice: *Stop, no! Tone it down!* This isn't going the way I imagined. But it's too late. I'm already here. I have to keep going. I have to say it. "The first video you made. You copied my words. I mean, it's not a big deal, but it happened."

I brace for Jessica's response, half expecting tears. Half expecting an apology. But nothing prepares me for her next words.

"See, this is exactly why you weren't invited to Eleanor's party."

What???

"I don't know what you're talking about," I pretend.

"Oh sure, that's why you liked her post," Jessica says. "*Everyone's* talking about it on Discord."

The air in my lungs freezes as the doorknob turns. Mrs. Carter walks back in.

"Everything okay while I was gone?" Mrs. Carter asks.

Jessica smiles sweetly, shoving her phone into her desk.

"Totes!" Jessica replies.

Mrs. Carter hands us each a copy of her freshly printed flyer.

"As discussed, the Dangers of Social Media night," Mrs. Carter says. "I'll be expecting both of your families there!"

I look down at the flyer in my scorching hot hands.

Dangers of Social Media Evening
Winfield Elementary School Auditorium
Next Saturday, 6:30 p.m.
Parents Encouraged to Attend

"It'll be great! We'll have cookies!" Mrs. Carter says, look-ing at me.

I put on my bravest smile. "Yay, cookies!"

All the while, I'm trying not to crumble at the thought—everyone's talking about me online!

Chapter 37

----

need to see your Discord." I run up to Finn at lunch. He's already sitting down with his sack lunch. I slide next to him, empty-handed. I don't have time to wait in line for my free hot lunch. I have to know now.

"Discord?" Finn asks, suddenly looking worried. "Why? What's going on?"

"Jessica said . . ." I try to push out the words. Try to still my panicking heart. "Can I just see?"

Finn hesitates, reaching for his phone. He holds it tight in his hands. I don't know why he's not showing me. If it were me, I'd show him in two seconds.

"I can't."

I stare at Finn, stunned. "What?"

"You'll never look at me the same again," Finn says, lowering his head. "There are things on there . . . things I've said." He lowers his voice. "It's not just me. Everyone's said stuff on there. But it's not real. It's more like a video game!"

I don't understand. "So it's a game?"

"No! But . . . it feels like one! You can say whatever you want. There are confessions. Secrets. Language. Dumb jokes. A *lot* of dumb jokes," Finn says. "Trust me, you're better off not seeing it." He starts putting his phone away.

"No!" I reach out a hand. "I have to see it."

"Why??"

I hide behind his lunch sack and tell him my embarrassing like of Eleanor's trampoline birthday party. It's bad enough to be on the outside of the snow globe, looking in. Now my accidental like is possibly the subject of even more inside jokes!

"I'm so sorry," Finn says. "Lina, you gotta know. I didn't know you weren't going to be at that party! I wanted to tell you. I felt bad for days!"

"Just . . . let me see the Discord," I beg.

Finn relents. As my friend loads the app, I start reading:

My snitch sister ratted me out for having my phone on at
night!
🟢 Bro, tell ur parents to send her to the wilderness survival
camp my brother went to this summer. It's BRUTAL. They
have NO toilet paper!
❤️ 5
🟢 Perfect!
😇 2

Dude, who stole my phone and posted the pic of me falling
off my skateboard? I went to the bathroom for 5 mins! When I
got back, there were 87 likes! NOT COOL!
🙃 2
🟢 My money's on Finny!
😵 1
🟢 It wasn't me, I promise!
🟢 Yeah, you're probably too busy shushing people at the
library!
😂 2

🅖 Why don't you admit it? You can't skate for ****!

😩 2

🅖 Shut up, library nerd!

🅖 Woodpusher!

🤮 1

I look up at Finn. Whoa.

"Woodpusher?" I ask.

"He's the one who called me library nerd!" Finn says. He reaches for his phone back. "See! This is why I didn't want you to see it. Now you're going to judge me—"

"No!" I take his phone back. "I promise I won't."

I keep reading.

Speaking of the library, who thinks the website that Mrs. Hollins started looks like my grandma's hot pink hair?

❤ 3

🅖 It's almost as ugly as Principal Bennett's lego tie.

🅖 OMG I saw Principal Bennett in Palm Springs over spring break. He was there with his wife! At the same hotel!

❤ 6

🅖 Which one?

🅖 The Royal Palm! Wanna see pics? [Pics]

❤ 7

🅖 You should have gone to the Princess Palm—it's way better.

🅖 Wait, I think I have a picture of Principal Bennett at the pool!

😳 7

🅖 You saw the principal swimming?? Did he have his lego tie on??!

🌀 No, but he had a chest tattoo!

😱 7

🌀 WHAT?!

🌀 What'd it say??

🌀 LOVE YOU, MOM!

😂 6

🌀 GO WINFIELD!

🌀 SCHOOL'S NOT OVER TILL I SAY IT'S OVER!

🌀 No, it was just an owl, sitting on a tree! With HUGE eyes!

💀 5

🌀 Even when he's swimming, he's watching! No wonder he's the principal.

❤ 7

[GIF] Mrs. Carter railing against social media, then sitting at her desk to check Instagram.

🌀 How many phones do u think she's confiscated? She's probably selling them on eBay!

🌀 We're her retirement fund.

❤ 2

[GIF] Mrs. Corso, every time someone asks for more tater tots.

🌀 5 bucks if you can get her to eat the corn dog.

🌀 Bruh, the most disgusting thing is Mystery Meat Friday. They literally don't know what's in there!

🤮 5

🌀 I once found a button in my sloppy joe.

🤢 3

🌀 Guys, I think my mac n cheese moved. I think it's alive.

😈 It's just your eyeballs sweating from all that broccoli water.

💀 1

😈 Shut up, you dehydrated poser!

☠ 1

"Geez, is it always like this?" I ask. I look across the room at Mrs. Corso, the cafeteria lady, feeling bad. She works so hard to make sure all of us are fed. She'd be so sad to know my classmates are making fun of her.

"Pretty much—but we don't talk like this in real life!" Finn quickly says.

That's true. I've *never* heard Finn talk like this before. Not even Preston and Nate are like this in class.

"Then why are you like this online?" I ask.

Finn shrugs.

"Because it's funny?" Finn asks. Then he covers his face with his hands. "I don't even know. But I can't leave the group chat. I'm in too deep. This is all I have with Preston and Nate—I don't even hang out with them in real life much anymore. If I leave, they might get mad and tell all my secrets to everyone! Or worse, call me a library nerd in class."

"So you're in a mean group chat because you're too scared to leave?"

"It's not *only* mean. We talk about our problems, too."

"Like where?"

Finn scrolls down and shows me.

Is it weird that I just flew my new drone that my dad got me
over to my mom's house? And hovered in her window?

❤ 6

163

🅒 No it's not weird bro.

🅒 I just wish she could see it! It's so cool!

🅒 Can you FaceTime her?

🅒 My dad says this is his day. He doesn't want me on the phone with her. Why can't they just GET ALONG??

😔 4

🅒 When my parents broke up, they fought for months over a stupid coffee machine. Finally, my mom got it. She never even uses it.

😞 2

🅒 I asked my dad the other day, what does Brooke have that my mom doesn't have?

🅒 What'd he say?

🅒 He says one day, you'll understand. 😔

😭 1

🅒 I'm sorry man

❤ 2

I look up at Finn, who pulls his baseball cap down over his eyes.

"I left out a word, by the way," he says. "What he actually said was 'one day when you're a *real* man, you'll understand.'"

I shake my head.

"First of all, you are a real man," I tell him.

"No, I'm not," he says, pushing up his glasses. He flexes his thin arms. "That's all I got, no matter how many protein shakes I drink."

I stare at Finn, stunned. I'd never even thought about boys and puberty before.

"It's not about protein shakes," I assure him with a smile.

"It's your heart. The fact that you flew a drone all the way over to your Mom's, so she could see it . . . That's the biggest muscle right here."

"I just wish my dad were real with me, you know? Just tell me the truth already. My mom may not be super makeup-y or have blinding white teeth, but she loved him before his cool jeans."

Sometimes when Finn says things like that, I feel a surge of hope. Not in the I-have-a-crush-on-him hopeful way, but in a maybe-at-the-end-of-this-fast-train, nothing's-really-going-to-change way. We're going to emerge as our same old selves. Only bigger and with more capacity for love.

"Anyway," Finn says, reaching for his phone. "Now you know what's on Discord. Jessica's full of cap. No one said anything about your liking Eleanor's video on *Balloon Powered Car Challenge*."

"Balloon Powered Car Challenge?" I ask, giving him a funny look.

"That's the name of the chat," Finn explains, pointing to the title of the group. "It was Preston's idea. He said that if our parents ever saw it, we could say we're working on a science project."

I have to admit, it's kind of genius.

"Let me guess, Preston's MemeLord248?" I ask.

"Yup!"

"And Jessica's QueenBee805?"

"For the record, I think Nate invited her. It was just me and Preston in the beginning, and we really *were* just talking about video games. That's the only reason I joined. I thought I was going to talk about Minecraft."

I believe him. I gaze down at the chat, giving it one last scroll. That's when I suddenly see my name.

"Here it is! I found it!" I exclaim.

> OMG did Lina just LIKE Eleanor's bday post??
>
> 😵 4
>
> 😬 Noooooooooo!
>
> 😬 LOOK! 👀 [Link]
>
> 💜 3
>
> 😬 I feel bad. Should I say something?
>
> 😬 No, don't say anything! It was YOUR party. You get to invite whoever you want at YOUR party! And remember, you would have had to invite Carla, too.

My fingers freeze. What about Carla?

> 😬 It would have been totally lame. Who still carries a unicorn backpack? What are we, in 3rd grade?
>
> 🦄 2
>
> 😬 AND plays with Pop-It!

So what??!, I want to scream. Who doesn't love Pop-Its? They're amazing! They instantly reduce stress. I could use one right now, reading this chat!

> 😬 They're such babies, the two of them.
>
> 😬 If Carla wears that backpack in middle school, I'm gonna scream!
>
> 😬 Def the right move not to invite them.

I feel like I'm gonna be sick. I hand the phone back to Finn. I've seen enough.

From across the cafeteria, Carla waves at us. She's wearing her unicorn backpack, loading her plate up with nachos, totally oblivious. I feel *terrible* knowing what they've said about her. How could my classmates say that? Carla can *never* know about this. My eyes slide over to Eleanor and Nora, the fury bubbling inside me.

I can't believe I even wanted to go to her party. *We're not babies,* I want to scream. Carla's practically a Hollywood director. And I've got *b* double-*o b*s hidden under my sweatshirt!

"I'm so sorry, Lina," Finn says. "It's just the way people trash-talk on Discord. Like I said, not real."

"But it *is* real," I argue back. "They're making fun of us, and it *really* hurts."

Finn blinks at me. Several seconds pass. Then Finn does something incredible. He grabs his phone and starts typing.

"What are you doing?" I ask.

"Doing what I should have done a long time ago. Telling them to cut it out!" Finn says. I glance over Finn's shoulder at the reply he's adding: *Delete all this, you butt clowns!*

He pounds on the send button.

I marvel at his unflinching courage.

"I should have said that when Nate first called me a library nerd," he says. "You're right. Just because it's online doesn't mean it's not real."

He looks earnestly at me.

"I'm sorry, Lina. I should have told you earlier about the party. From now on, I've got you. They can't talk about my friends that way, or me."

My eyes mist as I take in Finn's words. I'm so moved and inspired by my friend, I throw my arms around him. There in front of everyone in the cafeteria, in my sweaty and lumpy sweatshirt, I hug Finn.

I have witnessed real bravery today.

I'm done being scared too.

----

ina! That hug!" Carla gushes that afternoon. We're sitting on the stoop outside Mrs. Kim's purse repair store, waiting for Mrs. Kim to get her shop ready, so we can film the idea Carla and Finn came up with at recess. Finn couldn't come. He had to help his mom with something after school, which is just as well, because Carla's eyebrows jump up and down at me, like a pogo stick.

"What?" I pretend to not know what she's talking about.

Carla pulls her pineapple sunglasses down an inch. "Um. Cafeteria? Long hug? Over velvety Jell-O pudding?"

"There was no velvety Jell-O pudding. You're adding props in your head!"

"Fine! But what was it for?"

"I was just upset. . . ." I tell Carla.

"Over what Jessica said?" Carla asks.

I couldn't keep *everything* from Carla, so I told her about the Discord. But just about my liking Eleanor's post. I didn't mention anything about her backpack or the Pop-It.

"Forget about that!" Carla says. "Don't give her an audience!"

"But I saw it. I can't just forget about it! Eleanor said she felt bad for not inviting me, and Jessica said that it was definitely the right move!"

I pick up a tiny branch and throw it on the ground. I'm so annoyed. How can I go from having *b* double-*o bs* to being babyish? In just a week?

Am I growing too fast or not fast enough? Which is it?

I blink back the tears.

"You know what Jake says? Focus on the things that you can control." She bumps her shoulders with mine. "Let go of everything else."

"You still talking to him?" I ask, surprised.

"'Course! On email! You know, he asked for my address, so he can send me a bottle of his grandmother's hot sauce. Apparently, it's even spicier than Rosa's!"

"Did you give it to him?" I ask, suddenly alarmed.

I don't know why I'm alarmed. But I am. It seems odd to ask someone you've just met online for their address. What if he's a kidnapper?

But then Carla pulls up a picture of him on her laptop.

"Relax, I didn't give it to him," Carla says. "But look how cute he is!"

I glance at Carla's laptop. Jake's definitely our age. He's in a newspaper hat, smiling shyly at the camera. He has a wool vest on over his flannel shirt. He's giving serious bookstore-manager-in-training vibes. I could see why she'd like him.

As Carla swoons over the picture, I get a funny feeling in my tummy again. Like my best friend cares more about her new bookstore manager than our *real* problems.

"Maybe I should just give it to him," Carla says.

"No, you shouldn't!"

"But, Lina, you don't understand. We have a bond! He wants to send me *the* ultimate Bajan Pepper Sauce—" Carla says.

"Are you even listening to me about Discord?" I ask.

"Yes, I am!"

"No, you're not. You're trying to figure out how to smuggle hot sauce from a stranger—"

"He's not a stranger! He lives right here in Ventura! You know the bowling alley over by Second Street? Right around the corner from Los Romas Elementary? Which is the school we *would* have gone to, if we hadn't been admitted to Winfield," Carla says. "That's where he lives. He's practically our classmate!"

But I'm *actually* your classmate, I want to point out as Mrs. Kim walks out of her shop, in her bright yellow dress, announcing she's ready for us.

I wait for Carla to look away, then quickly wipe the wet corners of my eyes.

Get it together!

The last thing I want is a video proving Jessica's right.

Chapter 39

Mrs. Kim shows us around her shop, in her sunny dress and all-leather apron. I've never seen an all-leather apron before. But given how much leather there is in Mrs. Kim's shop, it fits right in.

"This way, girls! Here is where the magic happens!" Mrs. Kim says, showing off her workstation. Her cat Bo Bo hops off the desk and hides underneath. There are a million tools all along her desk. I walk over and pick up what looks like the world's tiniest toothbrush.

Now, *this* is babyish. And it's adorable.

"What does this do?" I ask.

"I use that to stain and polish the leather!" she says.

She points to a whole row of bags behind her. Next to each restored bag, Mrs. Kim has a picture of the original bag's condition.

"Wow," I say, waving Carla over. The difference in the before-and-after pictures is stunning!

I take a picture of Mrs. Kim's shop and text it to Mom and Dad.

WOW. Nice 👜👜👜! 💶 💶 💶 ✳ ✳ ✳ 🏅 🏅 🏅 Dad texts back.

I smile. Dad always overdoes it with emojis.

I knew you would like Mrs. Kim! Can't wait to see the video! Mom writes.

Bo Bo walks over, brushing up against my leg. She purrs when I pet her.

Carla points to a beautiful leather messenger bag. "How did you restore this?"

"Lots of polish and patience," Mrs. Kim says. "It wasn't easy finding the exact kind of brass buttons! I had to go to swap meets on the weekends."

"Someone found a button in a sloppy joe at my school," I volunteer.

"What?" Carla asks.

"Discord," I say, shrugging.

"Well, I've never found one there!" Mrs. Kim chuckles. "But I am always keeping an eye out. I learned that from my father. He was in the Korean army. My mother, she was a seamstress."

She points to an old black-and-white photo of her parents.

"They look so in love!" Carla says, smiling.

"Oh, they were! My mother asked him to write to her every day. My father would search for every possible piece of paper. But you know, in war, you can't just mail letters all the time. You need to wait until there's opportunity. So my mother, she made my dad a leather satchel, strong enough to last in the rain, in the snow, and strong enough to hold all their letters. Strong enough to hold their love."

Awwwww. Carla and I both look at each other and smile.

"Did it work? Were the letters safe?" I ask.

"Yes!" Mrs. Kim's eyes twinkle. "Every single one."

"Do you still have the bag??" I ask. Carla squeals as Mrs. Kim rummages around her shop. Finally, she holds up a dusty box.

She opens it. I peer at the leather satchel inside, richly brown and aged with love.

Mrs. Kim was saving more than just bags—she was saving *stories*.

I knew instantly what we needed to make a video on.

"Action!" Carla calls out. She hits record on my phone.

I walk along the parking lot, proudly carrying a nice leather backpack that Mrs. Kim loaned me. We didn't want to mess up her priceless leather satchel, so we're using a new backpack instead.

Carla comes along and asks, "Where'd you get that backpack?"

"This?" I ask. "My grandmother got it for me. I used to take it to the market to buy groceries. Every weekend, we'd make a new dish together." I take the backpack off to show Carla. "And even though she now lives in Beijing and I live here, whenever I wear this bag—"

All of a sudden, the backpack slips out of Carla's hand and lands in a puddle of water. Carla grabs the phone from the tree and gets a close-up of the backpack sitting in the puddle. I fall to my knees, reaching for my backpack. Carla closes in on my devastated face.

"My bag!" I cry. "All those memories!"

Mrs. Kim walks out of her shop, right on cue. She rushes over to me and helps me up. Taking the wet backpack in her hand, she smiles into the camera. "Don't you worry. I'll save your bag. And your memories! Just come to my shop—Mrs. Kim's Bag Restoration, on the corner of Spring Street and Acorn!"

I open my leather bag, to reveal a whole bunch of envelopes with hearts doodled on them.

"And CUT!" Carla exclaims.

"Brava!" Mrs. Kim says, clapping. "That was fantastic, girls!"

"Wait till you see the finished video!" I tell her, handing her the backpack before I run over to the bench by the tree.

I work as fast as I can, splicing and cutting, just like Finn showed me. Carla sits next to me, watching me work.

"Let me try!" Carla says.

She takes my phone. Unfortunately, she zooms *all the way* in on my face. I gulp. It's so hard to see my giant pores, after watching all those beautiful people on my phone all week. Jessica's harsh words creep into my mind. *You're either born with glazed donut skin, or you're not.*

I definitely do NOT look like I was born with it, in this video.

I flip the phone facedown.

"We're not going to keep editing?" Carla asks.

I fall quiet. I don't know how to explain it. I just know I can't look at my skin for another second.

"What's the matter?"

"I look horrible. I don't have glazed donut skin," I finally mutter.

"Donut skin? What are you talking about?" Carla starts giggling. "You're *not* a donut!"

As Carla laughs, I suddenly remember something. There's a filter for Glazed Donut Skin! I saw a video on it! I turn my phone back around and try to find the filter.

Holy mother of donuts! I almost drop my phone when I see

175

my reflection with the filter on. I look *so* much better. Undeniably better. Even *Jessica couldn't argue with it* better!

"We gotta shoot it again, with the filter!" I urge.

"We are not reshooting! Our video's *great*!"

"But it'll be even more amazing, with this filter!" I promise. I plead with Carla. "I need this. I've had such a bad day. Don't you want to have perfect Krispy Kreme skin?"

"Nope! I don't want Krispy Kreme skin, or Dunkin' Donuts skin," Carla jokes. "Or Kentucky Fried Chicken skin, or Chipotle skin . . ."

I don't laugh.

"C'mon, that's funny!"

"It's not funny," I tell her. "Just like it's not funny what they said on Discord."

I look down at my knees.

Gently, Carla puts a hand on my shoulder. "Fine. We'll shoot it again," she says.

"Really?" I ask.

Carla chuckles. I know she probably thinks I'm being a silly maple bar. But she doesn't know what it's like to have a million people on my phone telling me I don't stand a chance at being beautiful unless I buy this serum or that tinted moisturizer. Or have elbows as smooth as milk. And cheekbones that point to the stars.

With one tap, I can *have* all that. I can see! I can feel! I can know what it's like to be the *real* me, even if it's not . . . real.

Chapter 40

ina! Your skin! It looks *so shiny!*" Millie gushes in the car when I show her the video. "Did you use a filter?"

My face reddens. Is it that obvious?

"No!"

"You should use the puppy one next time! Mallory tried it once! Let me find it!" Millie says, trying on different filters. "See how cute it is?"

"It's cute," I admit. But I don't want my sister spending all her time trying to find the one I used, so I redirect her to Spotify. "Help me find a song!"

As she searches, Mom talks with Aunt Jing on WeChat.

"Hey, sis, did you hear about Ma's dance party?" Mom asks Aunt Jing.

"I know. . . . She told me. Such a shame," Aunt Jing says. I can hear the sound of her typing in the background. Aunt Jing is always typing. Lao Lao once said if Aunt Jing could bring her computer into the shower with her, she would.

"You think you could visit her sometime? Maybe take her on the town? Sounds like she could really use a night out."

"I wish. I've got this major project due. My boss is breathing down my neck—"

"Really? Because I saw you in Sanya sitting on the beach on WeChat . . . ," Mom mutters.

"That was a tech conference! Seven hours in a hotel," Aunt Jing says. "The *one* time I stepped out of the room—just for a minute, to get some air—my colleague posted a pic."

"Oh."

"Why don't you bring her over to America for a visit?" Aunt Jing asks. "I saw all *your* posts. You're a mega internet star now."

"Hardly!" Mom says. "Every time I put up a video, it's unpredictable. Sometimes I'll work really really hard on something, and it'll get, like, thirty views. And other times, I'll put up a random video of me doing yoga with a bath bomb, and it'll get three thousand views."

I lean forward. "My teacher taught us about that! It's called the dopamine loop! It's unpredictable for a reason, to keep us interested!"

"She's not wrong," Aunt Jing says. "You have to be really careful with your mental health, sis."

"My health is fine," Mom insists. "So I'm a little tired. And my back hurts from being hunched over editing the videos. But still, to have this platform? I know how lucky I am."

"I've seen a lot of good people get sucked dry by the machine, and they all thought they were lucky," Aunt Jing says. "Why don't you take a break?"

"I did," Mom says. "That day when we posted my friend Rosa's video, I took a break."

"And?"

"It was so great. I did the laundry. I took a walk. But the next day, my orders went down. I need to keep posting!"

"Remember Narcissus?" Aunt Jing asks gently.

"The Greek god?" Mom asks. "What does he have to do with it?"

"He died because he was unable to stop staring at his reflection in the water. Well . . ." Aunt Jing lowers her voice to a whisper. "Social media's the water. That's what I've realized, working in the industry."

I furrow my eyebrows. *What?*

"I've got to go," Aunt Jing says, signing off. "Please take care of yourself."

Aunt Jing's words buzz in my head the whole next day. I think about them as I put up Mrs. Kim's video. I think about them when I'm at school, debating whether to delete some videos on my phone, so I can download Discord and see what my classmates are talking about now.

In the end I decide not to.

There are way more interesting things to stare at in the lake.

Millie comes strutting in wearing her fuzzy pink robe, a toothbrush sticking out of her mouth.

"You want to play the stuffed animal game?" she asks.

"Sure." I shrug.

I reach for our animals while Millie goes to rinse out her mouth. I set them all up in a circle. I expect it to be a celebratory game—Mrs. Kim's video's at 2,300 views already! And it's only been a few hours!—but instead, Millie reaches for Rabbity and asks worriedly, "What are we going to do about Mom?"

We both glance toward the door. Mom's still out there replying to comments.

"You don't think she's . . . going to fall into a lake, do you?"

I pick up Snowy and say, "No way. Mom's got the thickest skin. I think it also doubles as a flotation device."

"But what if it's a really deep lake?" Millie asks.

I plop on my belly. I agree Mom should take a break. I think about the weekend. Saturday's out. Dad's still working. But maybe on Sunday? We *should* do something. It's been so long since we went somewhere as a family.

"Let's drag them somewhere on Sunday!" I suggest.

"Somewhere with no reception?" Millie asks.

I immediately reach for my own phone, clutching it tightly. NO WAY!

"I know! How about we just hide *her* phone and go to the Concert at the Park? Didn't Rosa say she's going to be there?" I ask.

"Yeah!" Millie says. "And Mallory said there's going to be a live band! I can scope out more songs!"

"Perfect!" I grin.

"Good game!" Millie says, petting each one of the stuffies on the head. "Thank you all for your contributions!"

As Millie hands out her surveys and puts them all back, I curl into bed, planning how I'm going to hide Mom's phone. It won't be easy, since it's with her all the time. But maybe if I do it at the very last minute. . . . I reach for my own phone, getting cozy under my blanket.

I wait for Millie to get comfortable. It always takes her a long time to find the perfect spot. When she's finally still, I swipe open my phone. As the soft, incandescent glow of the screen washes over me, I relax. I love this time at night, when it's just me and them.

Strangers from all corners of the world, telling me about *their* day.

They're not real strangers, I remind myself. I've been watching them for a whole week now.

I *know* them.

"Don't you stay up too late looking at the lake too . . . ," Millie mumbles, from the top bunk.

"I'm *not* even checking it!" I tell Millie.

I throw the covers over my head and switch the volume off. Tucked under my blanket, I watch and scroll. A thousand secret videos transforming my dull, small bed. Rocking me to sleep. Each one telling me something special. Something secret. I watch and watch, until my eyelids are too heavy to lift.

Even then I keep scrolling.

Chapter 41

Winfield Park is buzzing with excitement as families arrive with picnic baskets, folding chairs, and coolers filled with snacks. Lao Lao told us to take lots of pictures, so I snap them with my phone.

It's incredible how they transformed the front part of the lush green lawn into a stage. As a local band plays "Fly Me to the Moon," Mom sings along, swaying to the music.

"Isn't this wonderful?" Mom asks Dad.

Dad puts an arm around her. "Just wonderful!"

I take a picture of the two of them. I'm so glad we came. It's so rare to see them relaxing, not hunched over bills.

"I'm going to go find Mallory!" Millie says. "Can I get a taco?"

"'Course," Mom says, reaching into her purse. She starts digging around for some cash, only to look up, panicked. "Where's my phone?"

"Are you sure it's not in your hand?" I joke.

She stares at her hand. "No, it's not here!"

I resist the urge to high-five my sister. Just seconds before we left the house, I hid it inside Mom's slipper on the shoe rack.

"You probably left it on the counter," Dad says. "Happens to me all the time."

"We've got to go back for it!" Mom says. "I was texting

with Mr. Li, the foot massage guy! He says he wants the girls to make a video for his salon. I need to text him back—"

"He can wait. You saw how hard it was to get parking," Dad says. "We're *staying*. For the whole night!"

"Yay!" my sister cheers.

Dad puts his hand on Mom's shoulder and gives her a gentle shoulder rub. "Besides, you could use a night off. You deserve it." With a twinkle in his eye, he holds out his hand. "May I have this dance?"

Mom's eyes melt into a smile.

As my parents dance on the grass, I take another picture of them, then nudge my sister with my elbow. "How about that taco?" I pull out some cash from my pocket. "C'mon, let's go say hi to Rosa!"

We speed-walk toward the food trucks. I keep hoping I'd bump into Mrs. Kim. Her leather backpack video racked up more views than Jessica's latest "10 Most Overrated Books" video! But instead, I see Finn bouncing over to me.

"Hey!" he says. "Did you see the mayor over at Rosa's truck? Apparently, he stood in line for twenty minutes for her hot sauce!"

"No way!" I lean closer to him and whisper, "So did Jessica or Eleanor say anything after you posted on Discord?"

I finally cracked and checked their Snapchat last night. But there wasn't anything weird. Just the usual carousel of puppy and pedicure pictures.

"No," Finn says distractedly, gazing over at Rosa's truck.

"Are you sure?"

"Don't worry. I'll let you know if they do," he says, tossing me a grin before he jets over to Rosa's.

Millie and I follow him, nearly crashing into the line for Rosa's Tacos. It stretches all the way down the block!

"Lina! Millie! Finn!" Rosa pokes her head out from inside her taco truck and waves us over. "Isn't this amazing? Look at this line! And it's all because of you! You kids are total geniuses!"

We grin. I snap a picture of Rosa with my phone, to email it to Carla later. She couldn't come because she had to help her mom at the flower shop.

"Where's Alfie?" Finn asks.

"My sister's watching him. I want him to relax. His big surgery's tomorrow! He's gotta rest up!" Rosa says, handing us a giant plate of tacos, chips, and salsa.

I put down twenty dollars, but Rosa insists it's on the house.

"Can we visit him after the surgery?" I ask, taking the food. I hand a taco to Millie.

"You sure can!" Rosa says. "Tell you what, after the surgery, together we'll whip up his favorite—my abuela's chicken mole!"

We fist-bump with Rosa. As Rosa turns to her next customer, Finn and I carry the food to a nearby table. Millie ditches us to find Mallory.

Finn digs in.

"You want some?" Finn asks, holding up the basket of chips.

I eye the chips hungrily. I'd love some. But last night I saw this video from this girl Amber. She said if you want to have glazed donut skin without all these products and serums, you've got to stay away from white foods. Not white people food. Just white food. Anything white. Maybe it's the flour content? I don't really know. But Amber looked like someone I could really trust. She had a fancy-looking college degree behind her. She also had a huge bookshelf, and I spotted *Because of Winn-Dixie* on it. Anyone who likes Kate DiCamillo is a friend of mine.

So I shake my head, trusting Amber.

Even though a tortilla chip is not really white—it's more beige—but I don't want to take any chances.

"No thanks. I'm good," I say to Finn.

Finn takes another scoop of salsa with his chip. "You sure?" he asks, tempting me.

My stomach growls. I step away from the stuff.

I turn around and scan the crowd. I see Finn's dad, over by a tree. He's wearing his ripped jeans and cool shades. A tall blond woman is talking to him. I look closely. Is she . . . leaning against him?

Finn follows my eyes. "That's Brooke," he groans, putting his chip down.

We watch them for a while.

"Maybe they're discussing work stuff?" I ask.

But when his dad casually drapes an arm around Brooke, Finn grabs his face.

"No! What are you doing? Stop that!" Finn blurts out. But Brooke holds up a camera. She snaps a selfie of them. Finn panics and starts running toward them.

I run after him. "Why are we running?" I ask.

"I have to get her phone away from her and delete it," Finn says. "If she posts that on Instagram, it's over! My mom will be up all night singing Alanis Morrissette."

"Who's Alanis Morrissette?" I ask, hopping over picnic blankets.

"She sings loud, angry mom music!" Finn shouts back.

We run too fast and get stuck in a tangle of golden retrievers and leashes and lawn chairs. As we wait for the family to untangle us, I scan the lawn for Finn's mom. "She's not here, is she?"

"No, but Brooke posts everything online. *Everything!*" Finn says. "We've got to delete that selfie!"

"But what if they take another one tomorrow?" I ask Finn.

Finn sinks to the ground. I feel terrible for putting the possibility in his head that *more* selfies might happen. I think back to how I felt seeing Eleanor's post. We can't let his mom look into the snow globe. There's got to be something we can do.

Suddenly, I remember what Carla did when we got that mean pimple comment. "What if we block Brooke from your mom's phone?"

"That could work!" Finn says, jumping up. But then, his face falls a little. "We're going to have to pry it away from her first. . . . That *won't* be easy."

I point a thumb at my chest. "Luckily, I am an expert prier. How do you think I got my mom to take the night off?"

Finn grins. "So you'll help me?"

"Sure!"

"Thanks, Lina," Finn says. As the golden retrievers do another lap around us, retying us with their leashes, Finn surprises me with another hug. "You really are the best."

I smile into his hair as the band plays.

Chapter 42

Finn answers his door after school.

"Thanks so much for coming!" Finn says.

"Of course! Where's your mom?" I walk inside, eager to get Operation Secretly Block underway. Finn's mom's house is a one-story ranch house, with a beach-cottage theme.

"She's just on the phone . . . ," Finn says.

I walk into the living room and pick up one of the seashells lying on the coffee table. "I love seashells!"

Finn grins. "You and my mom both."

I sit down on the couch and examine the pearly shimmer inside. I snap a pic, so I can show it to Lao Lao later. We didn't get a chance to talk after the concert, since we got home so late, but I sent her the pictures. She texted back this morning: Wish I could be there! Enjoy every moment! 🖤

"That one's from Maine," Finn says, pointing to the one I'm holding. "We used to go every summer, to Goose Rocks Beach."

That's a funny name for a beach. "Were there lots of geese?"

"Surprisingly, no. But I saw an octopus there once! It was in the sand! Oh, and this place had the *best* sand. One time my dad and I built the biggest sandcastle. It was massive! An architectural marvel!"

I smile, imagining what a marvel looks like to Finn. Glow-in-the-dark bookshelves and fish-tank walls?

"And my mom, she even decorated it with sand furniture," Finn's face is full of nostalgia. I put the shell down and listen with my hands under my chin. His shoulders sag. "I wish I had a picture of it. . . ."

I think about what Mrs. Carter told us in class.

"Bet you remember it so well though, even without a picture," I say.

"Maybe." Finn gives me a lopsided grin.

His Mom walks out of her bedroom, still talking on the phone.

"No, Lorene. It was just a single emoji, that's it. A walking man. Do you think it means he wants to take a walk with me? Or does it mean, *I'm walking away because I'm not interested?* It's all so confusing, this whole online dating thing!" Finn's mom says.

Ms. Wright waves at me. "Oh hi, Lina! I'm sorry. I didn't see you there!" She holds up a finger to say, *Give me a sec,* and turns back to her conversation. "Or maybe it means he's moving out of Ventura?"

I see Finn chewing nervously on his finger.

I jump up from the couch, gesturing to my friend to meet me in the kitchen. We have to strategize.

"Let's create a diversion," I whisper to Finn when he walks over.

"Okay!" He reaches for the blender, opening up the fridge. "I'm gonna make us some protein shakes while we brainstorm."

He grabs some ice. I look over, slightly concerned, as he

reaches for the bananas. Is banana a white food? Technically it's yellow on the outside.

"What's wrong? You don't like bananas?" he asks.

"Ummm . . ." I chew my lip, trying to decide.

This whole challenge is so impossible. I wish I'd never seen the video.

"How about matcha green tea powder?" Finn asks, reaching for a bag.

I nod eagerly. "Yes! Love green! Lots and lots of green!"

"Okay!" Finn smiles, scooping out a generous spoonful. He presses blend.

As we wait, I rack my brain.

"We've got to get her off the phone. What if I pretended to see, I don't know, a giant roach or something?"

"She hates roaches," Finn says. "Plus, we have a bug guy. She'll never believe it."

He pours me a glass, and I drink hungrily from it.

Finn opens a box of crackers and offers me some. They're some sort of healthy purple yam crackers.

I don't even care what they taste like. I take the box from him, shoving as many purple crackers as I can in my mouth.

"I've got the perfect diversion!" Finn announces. "What if I get a nosebleed?"

"That's brilliant!"

"I need ketchup!" Finn says. We poke around in the kitchen, while Finn's mom continues gabbing with her friend.

"Honestly, sometimes I think, you get to a certain age, and you just don't have the energy to put yourself out there again. You don't want to have to rehash all the jokes, the movies, the stories. . . . I'm sure it's the same for Jon."

At the mention of Jon, Finn's dad, Finn stops searching. He runs into the living room, pinching his nose and waving his arms to get his mom's attention. "Help! Mom!"

But Ms. Wright's too distracted by her conversation. "You saw him at the Concert at the Park, with a girl?" She sits up, taking her feet off the ottoman.

Uh-oh. Finn flings his head back dramatically, screaming, "MOM!" He walks around the living room with his arms out, like a zombie. "I have a nosebleed!"

"A nosebleed? I don't see anything," Finn's mom says, looking over at Finn. I rush over and stand next to Finn's mom, ready to grab her phone.

"Well, it's UP in my nose!"

"Hang on, honey!" Finn's mom starts getting up, but her butt plunges right back down a second later. "There's a picture of *them* on Instagram?"

"Mom! I'm BLEEDING!" Finn shrieks.

"Put a tissue up it!" Finn's mom says distractedly. She continues with her friend. "Can you screenshot it for me? 'Course I want to see! Send it to me!"

"I'm DYING!" Finn pleads, as his mom's phone explodes with incoming pictures. "Will you just put your phone down and help me? *Please?*"

I walk over to Mrs. Wright, ready to snatch her phone. *Just put it down for a second, woman!*

"MOM!" Finn screams again.

Ms. Wright gazes at Finn. Finally, she sticks her phone in her pocket and starts getting up. The whole time she's walking, her friend's sending pics. After the eighth ding, her curiosity gets the better of her and she reaches for a peek.

Finn and I both lunge toward her. "Nooooo!"

But it's too late.

"Oh my God," Finn's Mom gasps at the image.

I almost hear the crack of the snow globe in her hand.

Chapter 43

Tiny little specs of dust float off Finn's computer monitor and land on the edge of our protein shakes. Finn stays as still as a rock, not taking a single sip. He's listening to his parents' conversation. It's hard not to overhear. His parents are louder than blue whales.

"Who's the blond?" Finn's mom yells at his dad on speakerphone. "And when were you going to tell me about her?"

"Her name is Brooke."

"Do you know how embarrassing it is for me to find out about *Brooke* from *Instagram?*" Finn's mom asks.

I feel so bad for Mrs. Wright. It stinks to find out this way. I wish I had just grabbed the phone from her when she first walked out of her bedroom.

Finn reaches into his desk drawer and pulls out a half bucket of leftover Halloween candy.

"Want one?" Finn asks.

I peer at the candy curiously.

"Why do you still have so much?" I ask. Halloween was *months* ago. My mind takes me back to my first American one. Dad took me and Millie around the apartment complex. Some people gave us pens instead of candies. But it was still fun.

"I'm saving it," he says.

He digs through his stash until he finds the last full-size Snickers bar he has left. He hands it to me. My taste buds salivate. *It's not white!* I frantically start to unwrap it. But as I'm lifting it to my mouth, I suddenly remember *another* video I watched this morning.

This one talked about round foods—avocados, tomatoes, meatballs, and quiches—and how they're so much better for your hair than rectangular foods. I remember laughing at first, thinking it was a joke.

But the guy saying it had a white coat on and really shiny hair. It looked almost like a window on his head. He sounded nice too, like Po from *Kung Fu Panda*.

I hold up my own dry tips. My hair does *not* look like a window. It looks more like the inside of an air fryer. I think about all the videos of leave-in hair masks and protectors and treatments people use. I'm not sure how I got all those videos, but I know I can't afford any of that stuff.

I move the Snickers away.

But I can't bring myself to hand it back either, so I just hold it in my hand while his parents argue.

"She's a nice, kind, highly intelligent woman, who *actually* likes going to the Rams games with me!" his dad cries.

"No, she doesn't!" Finn's mom replies. "She's just saying that. She doesn't like going to the Rams games."

"Oh, like you know her so well."

"Lorene did a forensic analysis of her entire Instagram. And guess what? She's superficial. She hates cheese. And she hasn't liked her best friend's posts for a week!"

"A forensic analysis of her Instagram—how classy!"

"I am classy. I'm the same person I've always been. You're the one wearing ripped jeans, looking like a backup singer for Justin Bieber!"

I look over at Finn, whose head is crouched so low, he's practically underneath his desk.

"Finn?" I say gently. "Are you okay?"

He shakes his head. "This is all my fault. If I'd just found the ketchup, she would have believed me—"

I crawl under his desk too.

"It's not your fault. Even if we could have blocked Brooke's Instagram on your mom's phone, we couldn't have blocked her from Lorene!"

"But she would have gotten off the phone earlier—"

"Lorene would have just told her tomorrow," I say gently.

"That's one less day that she's hurting," Finn says.

My chest squeezes tight. I put my hand on Finn's back. Is this what Carla means by having a crush on someone? I listen for the pitter-patter of my heart. But it's just my stomach rumbling for the Snickers bar.

Suddenly, Finn's parents' voices grow louder. Finn cowers lower. He's pressing down so hard on his Kit Kat, it's all smooshed.

"Tell me more about Maine," I say, trying to distract him.

Finn hesitates for a second. Against the earsplitting screaming outside, Finn tries to re-create the scene.

"We used to go to this place, Moxie Falls. They had these amazing waterfalls. We'd go swimming in the lake in the summer. My mom would pack this huge picnic dinner."

I close my eyes, imagining it.

"And at night, the frogs would come out. They'd sing all

night long. And my mom and dad, they'd make up what they were saying." He smiles. "They did these great frog voices. We'd pretend all night—"

"I do that with my sister!" I tell Finn. "Except with stuffed animals." I blush, embarrassed. "It's . . . kind of silly, I know."

"I don't think it's silly," Finn says.

I tell him all about our hilarious group therapy sessions.

"That sounds awesome," Finn says. He looks around. "I wish I had some here, but my mom donated all my stuffed guys to Goodwill."

"That's okay! We can just close our eyes and pretend we're listening to frogs!"

Finn gives me a funny look. "You mean . . . ?" He points out his open door, toward the sound of his parents fighting.

"I'll start," I say. Closing my eyes, I put on my deepest frog voice and translate what Finn's mom is saying into frog. "I love your new ripped jeans. They are beautiful."

Finn laughs. Replying as the dad frog, he croaks, "Thank you. I almost fell putting them on this morning. But they were worth it, because now I have air-conditioned knees."

I giggle.

"I am proud of you for trying them. It takes guts to put on jeans that could lead to injury."

"Thank you. But I do miss my old jeans sometimes. Even if on Instagram it looks like I am fully happy with my new jeans."

"I know. I miss them too. But we will always have those memories of the old jeans. And the old sandcastle we built."

We both open our eyes. Finn's voice returns to normal. "See? Why couldn't they have said that to each other . . . ?"

"They will. It just takes a little while sometimes."

"Thanks, Lina." Finn points to my Snickers bar. "You going to eat that? You've been staring at it like it's a remote."

I look down at the Snickers in my hand. It's practically melted by now. I consider tossing it inside my sweatshirt. I'm so embarrassed. Instead, I tell him the truth. "I'm sorry. I've been watching all these random videos on my phone—"

"What kind of videos?"

"Well, according to this girl who likes Winn-Dixie, I can't eat anything white, which stinks because I LOVE rice. And then yesterday, this guy who sounds like Po from *Kung Fu Panda* said that rectangular-shaped foods are bad."

"What?" Finn asks.

"You know, like hot dogs, chocolate fingers, spam," I say.

"Technically, hot dogs are elongated cylinder capsules," Finn points out.

Leave it to Finn, who has his geometric shapes down. Mrs. Carter would be proud.

"When did you start watching all this?" he asks.

"I don't know, since I did a search on pimples and eyeliner," I tell him.

"Pimples?" Finn asks.

I cover my embarrassed face with my melted Snickers. Gently, Finn reaches to pull my hand down.

"You don't have any pimples," Finn tells me. "And even if you did, they'd probably look cool on you."

What? I give him a funny look.

Finn blushes. "I mean! Not that I'm saying you need pimples. But if you had them, you would rock them. Okay, I'm going to stop talking now."

The doorbell rings. It's my mom, here to pick me up. Finn

gives me a fist bump and climbs out from under his desk to go let my mom in. I crawl out too. As I'm getting ready to go, I see a notification on his computer.

> New Discord group message:
> Did you see Lina's latest vid?

I instantly drop the Snickers in my hand and tap on the screen. I sit down at Finn's computer to read.

> 🌀 Yeah! I saw the leather backpack! Who do you think all those love letters are for??
> 👀 5
> 🌀 Finn?? 🔪 Did you get one?
> 🌀 Dear Finny Finn, please write to me in my war-time leather satchel. I will accept only invisible ink written by feather.
> Yours, Lina.
> ♥ 4

I roll my eyes. They were for my grandma, you feather-heads! I keep reading.

> 🌀 I think the leather satchel looks kind of cool!
> 🌀 ME TOO. I SO WANT A LEATHER SATCHEL LIKE THAT!
> ♥ 2
> 🌀 It's giving international spy girl vibes!
> 🕵 2

Ooooh, now I have vibes! I'm liking this group chat more! I bounce on Finn's computer chair, grinning as I keep reading:

🅖 Her skin looks extra glowy too. Is that a filter? She looks
SO good!

🅖 Love how her skin's all shimmery.

🅖 😍😍😍

My heart swells. I can't believe it! I did it! I got all those sour grumps to admit that I look good! I take out my phone and snap a pic of the Discord thread, so I can reread it later.

I dance to "We Are Family" all the way home. Mom's singing as she drives. Millie's got both arms up, swaying to the music.

But my eyes are glued to an app. I put on the filter and grin at the new me. I can't tear my eyes away. The girl in the app smiles back. Her confident eyes assure me: *I see you. I've got you.* I love this girl. She never has to worry about what to eat. Or what to wear. She didn't accidentally like Eleanor's post. Or have her ideas ripped off by Jessica. She can show up to school with her phone wrapped in a leaf, and people would think it's cool. Because *she's* cool.

She's perfect.

I would do *anything* to be that girl—and not just online.

Chapter 44

There's *got* to be a way to look like the filter. I lean against our bathroom sink, searching through the medicine cabinet. Where's all of Mom's makeup?

I pull up a selfie of me with the filter on. I took fifteen in the car, but deleted fourteen of them because they were lame. But one of them looks halfway decent. I compare the selfie to my actual face in the mirror.

My eyes immediately jolt away. It's *so* depressing to see real-me, after staring at filter-me.

I'm going to need bronzer. A *lot* of bronzer.

I find a compact in the drawer that looks like it's not been used in eighty-five years. The powder inside looks like a mound of eraser shavings. And, of course, my mom doesn't have any brushes.

Still, I take a finger and dip it into the powder. I trace it along my nose, just like in all the videos I've watched. I stand back, prepared to be transformed into a glowy queen.

But I just look dustier.

I open up more drawers, looking for foundation. Ideally, I'd want something with a hydrating moisture lock and a soft, matte, airbrushed finish. But I'll settle for just a primer. Or even a sheer skin tint. Anything.

But the only thing my mom has looks like a chewed-up

piece of cheese. I frown at Mom's sad sad concealer. My glue stick is in better shape, honestly.

At the thought of my glittery glue stick, the gears in my brain start turning. *That could work. . . .*

The next morning, I slide into the backseat of the car with my shimmery, sticky face, as casually as I can. I keep my face positioned to the window so Mom and Millie don't notice. Thankfully, Mom's too busy dealing with the responses to her latest video.

"These people are all upset! I just said it's good to invite kids to be part of the conversation on rules. I didn't say let them go to bed whenever they want!" Mom says, shaking her head.

"Let me see the video," I say, reaching for my phone.

In the second that it takes my phone to load, Millie points to my face.

"Why's your face so shiny?" she asks.

"It's not," I insist.

I turn my head away. But she scoots closer toward me, studying me with her razor-sharp eyes. I hold up my phone, like a shield, distracting her with Mom's video. In it, Mom's sitting in a lush lawn.

"Where'd you film this?" I ask her.

"At the community college," she says. "I couldn't keep filming at Starbucks! They were saying I was distracting all the people who went there to write. So I found a nice lawn at the community college, and I made a deal with the college kids—I bring them dumplings, and they don't come into my shot!"

"That's a good deal," I say. A *delicious* deal. My stomach

growls at the thought of dumplings. But that's white, too. ALL the best foods are. Lychee, congee, cookies, coconuts! I'm missing out on everything good!

I watch Mom's video. She's right. At no point does she say kids should control their own bedtimes. But the number of people who take the video the wrong way is astounding.

"Should I make another video? Saying I'm sorry?" Mom asks.

"But you didn't do anything wrong," I remind her.

I replay her *actual* remarks in English. "A lot of people want magic answer for household rules. When to go to bed? When to get phone for your kid? I think it vary from child to child. My older daughter, for instance, I completely trust. I know she going to use the internet responsibly. And if something's not sitting well with her, she going to talk to me about it. Just like I know she's going to go to bed at decent hour. So I think instead of rules, rules, rules, it's important we invite kids to be part of the conversation."

Millie gives Mom a double thumbs-up.

"Great answer, Mommy!" Millie says.

"Dad thought so, too," Mom says. She chews her nail worriedly. "But . . ."

I flash her a reassuring smile, then quickly look away when our eyes meet in the mirror. Not just because I don't want her seeing my glittery-glue face. But because there are a *lot* of things I've watched that don't sit well with me, that I haven't told her.

So many that I don't know where to start.

At school, I wave and smile at my classmates, in my new golden tint. Carla walks over to my desk. Eleanor and Nora wave back, but their eyes don't linger on me. I tell myself it's a good thing. I've transformed myself so naturally, no one can even tell!

Carla and I start chatting about what video to make for Mr. Li after school, when Mrs. Carter turns on the fan.

Uh-oh.

The breeze sends my hair flying in a bazillion directions . . . and landing flat on my sticky face.

"Help!" I whisper to Carla, under my mop of hair. I tug at the strands, but it's useless. They're all glued to my face. I look like a hairy It!

"Why's it stuck?" Carla asks, trying to yank on my hair.

"I put glue all over my face," I whisper back.

"What?"

We try to tug my hair free. We manage to get one section off my face, but it stands straight up, flat as a glittery STOP sign, sprouting right out of my head.

Jessica starts giggling. "What's wrong with your hair?" she asks, pointing.

"Nothing! Just this extra-strong shampoo I used," I lie.

"More like an extra-strong mohawk!" Jessica snorts.

Out of the corner of my eye, I spy Nate snapping a pic.

"This is *gold*!" He grins.

"Don't you dare post that!" I warn.

But he keeps right on snapping. He's *definitely* going to put this up on Discord. The thought sends me into full-on panic mode. I grab my water bottle from my backpack. Maybe if I put some water on my hair, it'll flatten? I squirt frantically. Unfortunately, the water makes it worse. Now my whole face looks like it's peeling!

"OMG, Lina's peeling!" Tonya yells.

"She's disappearing like an onion!" someone else says, giggling.

I dump the whole bottle of water over my head. As water gushes all over my desk and Mrs. Carter turns to me hopping mad, asking "Why did you do that?"—I shake my head. I wish I knew.

I wish I could explain what's going on with me.

I wish I could just be happy.

I wish I could stop.

Chapter 45

'm crying my eyes out in front of Mr. Li's Happy Feet salon. Carla tries to cheer me up as Mr. Li tidies up his empty salon for us to film.

"It wasn't *that* bad," Carla says.

"It was that bad," I mumble to the cement, wiping my face. I hate that I'm crying. I know it dehydrates your skin, and I'm going to need puffy eye cream, which I definitely don't have. I shake my head. I should have known better than to use glitter glue on my face.

Now there are probably eighty-five memes of me floating around on Discord.

"No one's even going to remember tomorrow," Carla assures me.

"They will on Discord," I tell her. I'm tempted to text Finn. *Are* there eighty-five memes of me? But he's at the Rams game with his dad and Brooke.

"Hey, speaking of Discord. What exactly did they say, again?"

"That I looked glowy and shimmery—"

"No, before that," Carla says. "The first thing they said about us."

"About us?" I dab my eyes and look up, confused. I'm pretty sure I told her they were only talking about me. "Just that they didn't want to invite me to the party."

"That's it? That's all they said?"

I nod, hesitantly. Why's Carla asking me so many questions?

"They could have said more. . . . I didn't scroll that far. This thing goes back for *weeks*."

"But the part you read. About the party. That's all they said. 'Good thing we didn't invite Lina.' Nothing else?"

I flush, looking over at her unicorn backpack. I absolutely hate that I'm keeping things from Carla. But I remind myself I have to. She'd be crushed if she knew what they said, just like I'm crushed right now . . . *thinking* about what they're saying.

Mr. Li walks out of his salon. "All right, I'm ready!" he announces. Then he sees my tears. "Oh, Lina! Are you okay?"

I nod, embarrassed. I wipe the last of my tears with the back of my hand as I scramble up.

"Here, I get you warm towel!" Mr. Li says. His English reminds me of Mom, and I give him a small smile. We follow him inside the salon. There's a row of massage chairs, and Carla climbs on one of them as Mr. Li goes to fetch the towel.

I take the warm towel from Mr. Li and put it over my face.

"Thanks," I say gratefully. I hold the steamy towel over my eyes for a minute to reduce the swelling, like in some of the videos I've seen.

As I'm thinking this, I start crying even more. It's because of those ridiculous videos that I'm in this situation to begin with!

"I'm sorry," I sob.

"It's okay! We make video another time," Mr. Li offers. "We all have bad day sometimes. That's my business: make people feel better after bad day. I want you to feel better. Then we make video!"

"No, it's fine!" I quickly say. "I want to make the video."

"Are you sure?" Mr. Li asks.

I nod, putting on my most professional face. I'm determined to not let what happened ruin my work. Besides, there's gotta be a filter to hide my crying.

Carla climbs down from the massage chairs and gazes at me. "Really, Lina?"

"We're here. Let's just do it," I say. "We're mostly gonna shoot the salon anyway."

"And our feet. Don't forget our *baby* toes," Carla replies, looking right at me.

She says *baby* a little funny, and I furrow my eyebrows.

"All right! Okay! Let's do this!" Mr. Li claps, smiling.

Chapter 46

F eet the most important part of the body," Mr. Li explains to the camera as I record. "They carry all our problems. All our worries. Most people think brain have most pressure, but we don't walk with our brains. Our brains up here, our feet down there."

I turn the camera to face me, grateful I picked an extra-strong filter—Starry Light.

"But do we give them the attention they deserve?" I ask. "No! We stuff them into tight, stinky shoes! Then we make them walk for miles and miles!"

"Hike through forests!" Carla adds.

"Jog marathons!" I jump in.

"Surf ten-feet waves!" Mr. Li adds.

"Run through airports!" Carla tosses out.

I jump back to Mr. Li. "All without giving them a break. But what if . . . once a week, you can come here and get this?"

As Mr. Li starts massaging Carla's feet, I zoom in with my phone. I record in slow motion as Mr. Li works every single one of Carla's stress points, from her big toe to her pinkie, while Carla reminds everyone where to find his salon.

"CUT!" I exclaim. "That was great!"

"Better than great! It was magnificent!" Mr. Li grins, drying Carla's feet with a towel. "Hope it works!" He glances around at his empty salon. "If business not pick up soon, I be out on *my* feet!"

"Don't worry, Mr. Li," I assure him. "You can count on us!"

He takes two twenty-dollar bills and a ten-dollar bill, then squeezes the bills into our hands.

Later, I stare at the cash on my desk, stress-eating Wheat Thins.

"I don't understand. We put up the video an hour ago. It's so good! Why's it only at forty-five views?" I ask Millie, disappointed.

"Forty-five hundred?" Millie asks, walking over.

"No, forty-five."

"That's it?" she asks. I offer her a Wheat Thin, but she shakes her head. I don't blame her. They taste like cardboard. I know it's ridiculous. But I still haven't found the guts to break the white-food challenge, not even when Dad texted me earlier:

BBQ Pork Buns in the fridge! Just steam! 🍲 And tell your mom I'm getting her more dumpling wrappers, so she doesn't have to make all from scratch for the university students!

I'd steamed the white buns perfectly. But when it came to eating it, I picked the buns apart and only ate the pork inside. Mom was too busy making dumplings to notice. Thankfully, Dad wasn't here to see it, or he would have been so sad.

My tummy churns, in protest. *I know, tummy. I'm sad too.*

"You think it was the song I picked?" Millie asks.

"No no, it wasn't the song," I say. I mutter to myself, "Was it the filter?"

"I knew it!" Millie says, grinning.

I turn away, embarrassed. "Fine, I used a filter! But only because . . . I'd been scratching my eye. Allergies."

I look back at the screen. "How do we get these views up? Mr. Li's counting on us!"

My phone rings. It's Lao Lao.

"Hey, Lao Lao!" I smile into the screen.

"I'm sorry I missed your call the other day," Lao Lao says. "But I'm so glad you got a chance to go to a *real* dance concert at the park, and not just our little bathroom bash!"

"I loved our bathroom bash," I tell her, propping her up against a book, so Millie and I can both see her.

"Me too," Millie says, smiling.

"But the concert was amazing, too!" I tell Lao Lao. "Mom and Dad danced all night!"

"I saw! And you know what else I saw? Seniors sitting on a blanket on the grass—just enjoying the music! That got me thinking, maybe I could try something like that for my dance party. Take a survey of what people need and want and see if we can make accommodations for everyone," Lao Lao says.

"I love surveys!" Millie runs and grabs her stuffed-animal feedback cards. She shows Lao Lao. "Look! These are some of mine!"

Lao Lao leans into the camera. "Send me that, will you?" she asks. "I'm excited to try it! Everyone should get a say!"

We both nod and give Lao Lao a double thumbs-up on her great plan.

"How are the videos going?" she asks.

The smile vanishes from my face.

"What's wrong?" Lao Lao asks.

I shake my head. "It's this video we just made. . . ." I send it over to her. Forty-eight views now. *What's going on? Why isn't it going up?*

"Oh, this is delightful! I love foot massages!" Lao Lao says. "Ask him if he'll open up a salon in a retirement home in Beijing!"

"He might have to if these views don't go up," I lament. I tell her the low number. It makes no sense. We had a great hook, a great story!

"It'll pick up. The video's wonderful," Lao Lao says. "Except . . . why do the colors look so different?"

"Oh, that's the filter!" Millie tells her.

"A filter?" Lao Lao asks, making a weird face.

I flush. "It's just this thing," I quickly say. "It makes everything look better! Do you not like it?"

"It's fine. But it doesn't make everything look *better*," Lao Lao says. "You look great just the way you are. I hope you know that."

Easy for her to say. She's my grandmother. Besides, I probably look like an ant on her tiny screen.

"I still think the most wonderful video you ever did was the one about the book," Lao Lao says. "You were real, and you spoke from your heart."

"I still put my heart into every video," I say in my defense. "Which is why I'm so stumped. . . ." I tap back to Mr. Li's video one more time, but it's still stuck at forty-eight. I sigh, disappointed in myself.

"Does he know?" Millie asks nervously.

I shake my head.

"Should I text him?" I ask.

Lao Lao chimes in, "In my experience, bad news is best delivered in person. Preferably with golden pineapple cakes!"

Golden pineapple cakes! My mouth salivates. I tell Lao Lao to send me the recipe, then run out to get Mom. Time to start baking!

Chapter 47

I hold up the tiny golden pineapple squares to Mr. Li after school. Mom helped me and Millie bake them yesterday. I was careful to shape them into squares, not rectangles. They were so delicious, I snarfed down five. Lao Lao was right; everything's better with pineapples! Even disappointment, I hope.

"I'm so sorry, Mr. Li," I tell him, giving him the squares. Carla hands him back the fifty dollars. "We don't know why it didn't work."

"We even tried reposting it," Carla says.

I nod, thinking about our second attempt last night.

"But for some reason . . . we just couldn't get past fifty views on it. We're sorry we failed."

To our surprise, Mr. Li shakes his head and raises a finger. "Not failure!"

He sets the pineapple squares down and climbs onto a massage chair. He tells us to sit. We get up on the chairs next to him.

"Let me tell you a story. I have customer. She sixty-seven years old. Working at a Chinese restaurant. Always on her feet. Once a week, she come in here, and I massage her feet. One day, she told me she has cancer. Liver, stage three," Mr. Li says, shaking his head. "She came to say goodbye, because she can't come to salon anymore. She need get chemo."

My heart lurches, hearing this story.

"I tell her I go to your house. Every week, I go. I massage her feet, even she throw up. She argue with me, *no use, cancer spread, go home*. But you know what? I keep going. Because that's what my customer need. Real care. Real kindness. I there for them for *real times*, not just good times."

"Oh, Mr. Li," Carla says, her chin quivering.

"And you know what? She survive!" Mr. Li says, beaming as he dabbed his own eyes. "She beat the cancer! Chemo worked! And now she's back to work! Every Thursday, she come in here."

"It wasn't just the chemo," I tell Mr. Li. "It was also *you*."

"My point is, fifty is not a failure. Even *one* is not a failure," he tells us, patting my hand. "Social media is not only way. Social kindness . . . is another way!"

While I'm listening to Mr. Li, my eyes grow misty.

"You're right," I say.

Social kindness. I hadn't known that's what I was longing for or even what to call it, before Mr. Li said it. But as soon as he said that, I know. That's what I *really* want, more than videos telling me what I need to be wearing, eating, and doing. Even more than Jessica and Eleanor occasionally saying something nice about my video on Discord.

I want a world in which we're kind to each other online, all the time. Where we think before we speak. Where we cheer each other on. Where we spread joy, not meanness.

Carla turns to me as we're sitting on the curb later, waiting for my mom to pick us up.

"There's something I have to tell you," she says.

She peers down at her backpack. I wait and wait. Finally, she says, "I saw what they said on Discord."

I feel the tips of my ears get hot. *No.*

"I peeked at Tonya's phone while she was in the bathroom the other day. Why didn't you tell me?"

"I'm so sorry. I wanted to tell you!"

"Then why didn't you?" she asks.

I look down, embarrassed.

"You heard Mr. Li," Carla continues. "You're my friend. You're supposed to be there for me during the *real* times, not just the good times!"

"I know and I'm sorry. I was just trying to protect you!" I say.

"I don't need you to protect me." Carla sniffles. "I need you to be honest with me."

"I know," I reply, reaching out an arm and hugging Carla. "I messed up."

"We have to turn it in to Principal Bennett," she suddenly says.

I immediately shake my head. "No! We can't! Finn's on it!"

"So?"

"So if we turn it in, everyone on the thread is going to get in trouble. Did you read that thing? It's so mean!"

"Exactly. That's why we have to turn it in!" Carla insists. "That stuff about Mrs. Corso. What has she ever done to any of those kids? All she ever does is try to give everyone a meal, even to those kids who can't afford it, like me." Carla's voice shakes. "Kids who have to buy their backpacks at a garage sale! And I'm sorry it's not the latest color or trend, and it has a fuzzy unicorn on it, but it's all my mom can afford!"

"It's beautiful!" I reach over and hug her unicorn. "It's my favorite backpack of all backpacks! And I love the fuzzy unicorn!"

Carla wipes her eyes with her hand.

"You do?" she asks, sniffling.

I nod, reaching over to stroke the unicorn's rainbow horn. I unzip my own backpack and offer her a tissue. "And I bought my backpack from a secondhand shop, too, remember? I know it hurts."

Carla blows her nose. "You were right, it *really* hurts. And it's so much harder to get over once you see it."

I put a hand over her back and give it a squeeze. I guess even the thickest of skin sometimes can't protect you fully.

"But we just have to ignore it. What's that thing Jake said? Focus on what we can control?"

Carla dabs her eyes. "You know he offered to send me a new backpack?"

"Really?"

Carla nods. "I was so upset last night, I tried to call him."

"He gave you his number?" I ask, surprised.

"Yeah, but it didn't work for some reason. So then I tried to email him. He must have been out of town, because when he emailed back, he wrote *good morning* even though it was, like, night," she says, blowing again into the tissue. "But it was such a nice email, Lina. He tried to make me feel better, even offered to buy me one of those black Lululemon backpacks."

"Oh," I squeak.

I crouch into a ball, waiting for Carla to announce she'll soon be joining the black Lululemon army. I wouldn't blame her for it if she did. But I'd be sad.

Carla hugs her knees.

"But I *like* my backpack. I don't want another one," she finally whispers. Tearfully, she turns to me. "How am I supposed to carry it to school every day, knowing what they said about me?"

I sit up with resolve. "We'll do it together. We'll start our own thread."

"What kind of thread?" she asks, rubbing her eyes.

I think of Mr. Li's words.

"A thread of kindness!" I declare.

Chapter 48

Carla's face blooms into a smile when she sees me at school the next day. I turn to show off my sister's unicorn backpack, bouncing behind me. I dug it out of the closet this morning.

"You like it?" I ask.

Carla grins. "You didn't have to," she says, blushing.

"Oh, I had to," I tell her. I lock arms with her and walk toward the hallways. "And that's not all."

When we get to the hallways, I unzip my backpack and reveal my colorful posters. I'd stayed up till eleven decorating them with my sister. They said:

Just be kind!

Words matter! Kindness starts here!

Let's Make Kindness Go Viral!

It only takes one nice comment to make someone's day!

Kinder Together!

Carla hugs me when I show her. The two of us run around in our unicorn backpacks, putting them up all over school.

As we're putting them up, Mrs. Sanchez, the counselor, stops to admire them.

"What's all this? Did something happen?" Mrs. Sanchez asks.

Carla and I exchange a glance.

"Because if something happened, even if it's outside of school, you can tell me," Mrs. Sanchez says. She points to the Let's Make Kindness Go Viral! poster. "Did someone say something to you . . . online?"

I hold my breath, waiting for Carla to respond.

"No," Carla says, her eyes on Finn in the courtyard. "We just think everyone needs a boost of kindness."

"I agree!" Mrs. Sanchez says. "We'll be sure to bring that up in the Dangers of Social Media Night this Saturday. You two coming?"

"Yeah!" I tell Mrs. Sanchez. "We'll be there."

"Me and my mom too," Carla says.

As Mrs. Sanchez helps us tape up the rest of the posters, I spy Millie hopping along in the hallway.

Her face is glistening. I look closely. That's when I see the unmistakable spark of glitter glue. *Oh nooooo.*

"I'll be right back . . . ," I tell Carla and Mrs. Sanchez. Running over, I call out, "Millie!" I reach out an arm, asking, "Did you . . . ? Is that . . . ?"

She giggles.

I should have known better than to leave my glitter glue at home.

"Millie, you have to wash that stuff off!" I order my sister. "Right now."

"Why?" she asks.

There's no time to explain. Any minute now, a gust of wind might blow, and I won't have my sister being a hairy It too. So I drag her by her wrist to the nearest bathroom.

"Where are we going?" Millie complains. "It's not fair! I

can handle makeup! Why do you get to wear it?"

"I don't!" I say. "And it's *not* makeup!"

"I saw you!" Millie says. "You just don't want to share!"

I ignore her. We're almost there. We get into the bathroom, and I take a paper towel, soak it in water, and hand it to her.

"Here, wipe your face with this," I tell her.

Reluctantly, Millie starts dabbing. She takes her time, going so slow I glance at the clock in the bathroom. The bell's going to ring for class any second. I take the paper towel and start dabbing for her.

"Stop! That hurts!" Millie complains.

I ignore her and keep dabbing. "Do you know what can happen if we don't get this off?" I ask.

But before I can tell my sister, Eleanor walks out of a stall.

"Hi, Lina," she says.

"Oh hey!" I say, blushing. I immediately hide the wet paper towel wads behind my back.

"Well? What can happen if I put glitter glue—" Millie starts to ask. I reach over and put my hand over Millie's mouth.

"Nothing!" I say. "I don't know what you're talking about."

Eleanor gives us a funny look as she washes her hands. "Hey, did you put those kindness posters up?" she asks.

"Yeah!" I say.

"They're nice," Eleanor says, smiling.

Millie wriggles free after Eleanor leaves, glaring at me as she says, "You should try following your own posters!"

I emerge from the bathroom, red-faced but mostly relieved that Millie won't look like Chewbacca from *Star Wars*.

"Lina!" Finn calls, waving at me.

I walk over to him. He pulls a surprise out of his backpack.

"Here, I got this for you," Finn says.

I stare at the dark chocolate bar, with caramel and matcha green tea inside, wrapped in golden fancy paper. The best part, it's a *ROUND* chocolate bar. I smile.

"I got it at a specialty store, with my dad, in LA. And I thought of you. I think it's from Canada!" he says. Bouncing on the balls of his feet, he asks, "Maybe we can eat it at lunch, together?"

"Sure." I grin, equally excited.

A few kids start singing "OoooooooOooooOO," smirking at me and Finn, but I ignore them.

Talk about the ultimate gesture of kindness!

Chapter 49

My mouth's a swimming pool as I count the minutes until lunch. Carla sneaks peeks over at my chocolate coin. I showed her right before class.

"You're so lucky!" she had said. "I wish I got a chocolate coin from Jake!"

"I'll give you a piece," I had promised.

She shook her head. "You should eat the whole thing. It's from your crush."

I gave her a funny look, wanting to laugh. We didn't have time to talk more about it, because Mrs. Carter quickly ushered us inside. She said she had an important lesson on the brain and there was no time to waste. Now I'm sitting at my desk, turning the coin over in my hand, wondering.

Does Finn have a crush on me?

Mrs. Carter scribbles *Oxytocin* on the board.

"Today, we're going to talk about oxytocin, otherwise known as the *love hormone*."

The whole back row starts giggling. Carla sits up and gives Mrs. Carter her full attention. Several people look at me and Finn funny. I stuff the chocolate coin back into my desk. People are making way too big of a deal out of it!

"Now, I won't have my kids being silly about their brain. This hormone is *important*," Mrs. Carter says, quieting us. "It plays two very important roles—helping us *bond* and helping us *trust*." She writes down those words on the board.

Eleanor's hand goes up. "Trust? Like checking credible sources?"

Mrs. Hollins had given the entire fifth grade a talk a few months back about how to evaluate sources for reliability. We learned that .com and .net websites are less credible than .gov and .edu websites. It was a really interesting talk, and to this day, when I search up websites, I always go through a mental checklist.

"Exactly!" Mrs. Carter says.

"What does that have to do with love?" Nora asks.

"A lot actually! We tend to trust information from people we love. People who we think are part of our pack. Now, why do you think that is, from an evolutionary perspective?" Mrs. Carter asks.

"So we can watch out for each other?" Finn asks, smiling at me.

I blush. Did Finn just call me a part of his pack? Jon Butterkatz catches Finn smiling at me and starts hooting, "Ooooooh." I elbow him to stop it.

"That's exactly right, Finn!" Mrs. Carter says. "Our ancestors relied on this hormone to form communities, so they could protect each other. So they could know how to avoid predators. What information to trust."

She holds up a finger.

"Information is essential to our survival. But what happens when we're bombarded with information? What happens when our trust circle expands to every stranger in the whole world?" she asks, holding up her phone. "Suddenly every post, every video, feels so immediately important. Something you need to *trust*."

I lean in. Mrs. Carter has my full attention.

"Who has ever watched a video that is clearly ridiculous, but still, a part of you thinks . . . maybe that makes sense?" Mrs. Carter asks, raising her own hand.

Several hands shoot up.

"I did the soda water and vinegar challenge. It did *not* taste like Coca-Cola," Preston lamented.

"I put lemon in my dog's ear, and it gave him an ear infection," Nora mutters.

I feel a lot better, knowing that I'm not the only one wondering about these videos. I raise my own hand.

"Wait, why's our brain telling us to trust these videos?" I ask.

Mrs. Carter explains, "Because your brain's releasing oxytocin when we're on social media, something Professor Paul Zak discovered. He did this experiment, measuring people's blood before and after they go on Twitter—in just ten minutes of being on the app, oxytocin rose 13.2 percent."

"Is that a lot?" Finn asks.

"That's as much as the oxytocin release levels measured for *grooms on their wedding day*!"

Our class erupts in chaos.

"What??" Jon Butterkatz shrieks. "So we're all getting married?"

"No, but our feeling of trust is that high!" Mrs. Carter says.

"No wonder my mom bought that musical toilet seat!" Jon says.

Nate nearly spits out his water.

"Mine threw away all our kitchen rags because a video said they breed mold. Then she had to buy them all over again when she saw another video saying they're fine," Finn adds, shaking his head.

"My sister put *clay* in her hair instead of shampoo! Her hair almost turned into a vase!" Eleanor says.

As we all gasp, Mrs. Carter writes the word MISINFORMATION on the board.

"So what's happening," Mrs. Carter says, "is that our brains are not wired to have this many social interactions! We're all releasing oxytocin, without these strangers really earning our trust. Some of them can be straight up delivering us misinformation, but we still *feel* like it's real."

My stomach knots, thinking of all the lovely bowls of rice that I've been missing out on! And lychee! And ice cream sandwiches!

"So what do we do?" I ask.

"We have to be much more discerning," Mrs. Carter says. "Just like with articles online, when you watch a video, ask yourself, what makes this person an expert? Do they have credentials? Or are they just trying to sell me something? Because that's a red flag."

I think back to that original video that got me all confused. What else was on Amber's bookshelf besides the Winn-Dixie book and her fancy diploma? Come to think of it, there were a lot of books. Nonfiction books. On sales strategies.

"Are they citing their sources in the description or the comments of the video?" Mrs. Carter continues. "Can you verify the information or their sources by doing an independent search on it?"

"But they always say what they're telling you is top secret!" Eleanor adds.

"Oh, I know! There's nothing more exciting than being in on a secret," Mrs. Carter says, her beautiful black curls moving up and down.

We all nod with her.

"But in order for a secret to matter, it has to be *real*. We have to resist the urge to auto-trust. Our trust has to be *earned*. That goes for social media." Mrs. Carter's eyes smile. "That goes for love. And it goes for life."

As soon as the bell rings, I bolt out the door. I can't wait a second longer. I gotta make up for all the delicious white food I've been missing out on!

I run into the cafeteria. Mrs. Corso looks up from salting the French fries.

"Not lunchtime yet, hun," she says. "Come back in two hours!"

"Please . . . I just . . . I really need white food!" I plead with her.

"Excuse me?" she asks.

Quickly, I explain to her about the absurd video I watched. And how I haven't had rice in days! When Mrs. Corso hears that, she waves me over.

"Oh, you poor girl, come back here," she says. "You want a burrito rice bowl?"

"Yes, please." I nod eagerly.

She hops into the back and returns a few minutes later with a tray.

"Thank you!" I take it from her and give Mrs. Corso a hug. She really is the best cafeteria worker ever.

As I wolf down the rice, I can't believe I thought about giving up this amazing food that my people have been eating for literally *thousands of years*. To think I trusted Amber over my ancestors! All because of one video! I reach for my phone to text Mom, can we have Yangzhou fried rice tonight?

Just as I send it, I get a notification from Finn.

Jess's new video . . . you might want to look at this.

Chapter 50

"Hey, guys! It's me, your girl Jessica. I want to tell you about a new book that I got a sneak peek of this morning. It's called *Chocolate Crush*, and just as you've probably guessed, it's about two kids who have a crush on each other. It all starts with a chocolate coin," Jessica says, smiling at the camera.

The fork falls out of my hand. *Are you kidding me?* I pause the video, stuff the last two bites of the burrito bowl into my mouth, thank Mrs. Corso, and dash out to find Finn.

No fewer than eight kids are playing Jessica's video in the courtyard, and they're all giggling. I glance back at my phone and push play.

"It's the story of this boy, Sfinn . . . from, er, Norway. . . ."

Sfinn?

"And this girl Bina. . . ."

OH, THAT'S IT! I gaze around the courtyard, looking for Jessica. Finn comes running over to me.

"Have you seen it?" he asks.

"I'm watching it right now!" I say, turning back to the video.

"So the book starts with Sfinn giving Bina this chocolate bar. Not just any chocolate bar, but a round chocolate bar. Which, personally, I don't get why it's such a big deal. But Bina was like, *OMG, Sfinn, you got me a round chocolate bar? You are my forever hero. I love you. You're the best!*"

My jaw drops to the ground. I did not say that! I look around at all my classmates hearing *I love you.* They're all going to believe her video! I have to stop this! I put my phone down and start marching across the courtyard.

"Lina!" Finn chases after me. "Where are you going?"

"I've had it with her!" I shout back. "First my book video, then the copycat thing, and now this?"

"But if we make a big deal out of it, everyone will know it's *us.* Right now at least people online think it's a book!"

To our horror, a few kids walk over and start chanting at us, "Chocolate crush! Chocolate crush!"

"It's not like that! We don't have a chocolate crush! It's misinformation!" I cry back.

But it's useless. Everyone keeps giggling and pointing to my chocolate coin, peeking out from my pocket.

I turn and sprint across the field, covering my red face. I can't believe Jessica took a nice, kind, private gesture and made it *content.* Not even real content. Misleading content! And it's impossible to argue back because of all the oxytocin coursing through my classmates.

There's only one thing to do.

Chapter 51

I feel awful about what I'm about to do. But as eyeballs bounce between me and Finn, as I walk up to him in the cafeteria, I know I have no choice.

I hold out the chocolate coin in my hand.

"You brought it!" Finn smiles, putting down his tuna sandwich. "Now we can finally eat it!"

He keeps his eyes locked on me. It's like he doesn't even see all the people staring at us.

"Should I just cut it?" Finn asks, reaching for a plastic knife. "Right down the middle—"

Someone behind me coos, "Awww, he's cutting it for his girlfriend!"

My mind starts blaring, *DO IT. ACT NOW!*

"No! You can have the whole thing," I tell Finn, handing him the chocolate bar. "I don't like chocolate. Round or rectangular! I don't want it."

Finn's eyes flash with hurt. As the whole cafeteria turns back to their Lunchables, Finn doesn't say a word. He just stares at his sandwich. He can't even bring himself to look at the chocolate coin.

"I'm sorry," I whisper. I know I've hurt him terribly.

Finn jumps up, stuffing his lunch in his sack and grabbing his backpack. "It's okay. I don't really like chocolate either," he says, heading to the door. On his way out, he chucks the chocolate coin. I watch as the loveliest, most thoughtful gift anyone's ever given me lands on top of the trash. I fight the urge to run over and save it.

But it's too late.

As Finn hustles out of the cafeteria, I am filled with regret that I squashed his kindness.

Guilt collects in my throat as I eat the Yangzhou fried rice that night. Dad came home early and cooked a whole wok for us.

"Whoa, slow down." He chuckles. "Plenty more where that came from!"

I polish off the rest of the rice.

"Are there any more dumplings?" I ask, trying to stuff the guilt out of me.

Mom gets up and goes to the fridge to look. "No more," she says. She tells us she gave them all to the college kids. But the crowd was so big, the dean had to come out and have a word with her.

"What'd he say?" Dad asks.

"He said I couldn't swap dumplings for lawn space anymore," Mom says. "Something about food and permits. They let me make one last video, but I was so nervous, I think I botched it."

"I'm sure you did fine," Dad says, clearing the dishes.

Mom shakes her head, taking a long sip of her soy milk. "I told my followers I didn't think six was too young to be in charge of the family dog's social media account."

My phone rings. I lunge for it, hoping it's Finn. But it's Lao Lao calling.

"You're eating," Lao Lao says when she sees us. "I'll call back!"

"No, we're finishing up!" Mom says, nodding to Dad as she takes the phone from me and heads over to the sofa.

"Don't worry. I got the dishes," Dad offers.

Millie and I join Mom on the couch.

"How's your dance planning going?" Mom asks.

"Did you make the survey?" Millie asks.

"I did! And I just got them all back! Guess what? We're going to have a wheelchair dance party!" Lao Lao announces, beaming with excitement.

"That sounds *awesome*!" I say.

Millie starts dancing in celebration.

"How was your day?" Lao Lao asks.

Before I can say anything, Millie stops dancing and crosses her arms. "Lina was very unposterly."

Hey! I give Millie a look. But she sticks her tongue out at me, which I suppose I sorta deserve.

"You were unkind to your sister?" Mom asks, concerned. I forgot that she'd helped us fold the posters into my tiny unicorn backpack last night, so she knows all about them.

"No . . . ," I start saying.

"Yes, you were!"

"Okay, maybe a little, but I was really unkind to Finn," I confess. "He gave me a chocolate bar . . . and I think I hurt his feelings."

"Lina has a boyfriend! Lina has a boyfriend!" Millie immediately starts singing.

"No, I *don't.*" I shoot her a look.

"But he gave you a chocolate bar?" Mom smiles. "That's sweet!"

Oh, for crying out loud!

"What kind of chocolate bar was it?" Lao Lao asks. "Expensive one?"

"I don't know the *price* of it! That's not the point!"

"Well, was it a Butterfinger? A Cadbury? A Ferrero Rocher?" Millie asks.

"It's from Canada. He got it at a specialty store."

"A *special* one from *Canada*?" Millie gushes.

Clearly she's enjoying this. I shoot her a look—*stop*.

"He was just trying to be nice," I tell Mom and Lao Lao. "But then Jessica made a video about it." I roll my eyes. "And everyone wouldn't stop staring at us . . . so I gave the chocolate bar back, and now I feel really bad."

I stare at my empty hands, wishing things had turned out differently.

"Awwww . . . ," Lao Lao says. "These things happen. I remember your mom's first crush. What was his name again?"

A nostalgic smile settles over Mom.

"Kang," Mom says.

"Sweet boy," Lao Lao says.

"Great sense of humor."

"He had the loveliest nose!" Lao Lao adds.

My sister and I giggle at this random outburst from Lao Lao.

"We both liked climbing trees. All the other girls wanted to stand around and talk, but I wanted to do stuff! Go look for frogs in the river! Find a corn maze and get lost!" Mom says.

"Your mama and this boy were inseparable!" Lao Lao says.

"Oh, those were the days . . . ," Mom says.

Dad pokes his head out from the kitchen. "Just so you know, we can still go look for frogs! Anytime! Just saying."

Mom chuckles.

"So what happened?" Millie asks.

"Well, one day he told me he liked me. Out of nowhere," Mom says. "I was shocked. I thought he'd like one of the other girls who were always staring at him in class. What, with his fine nose. I didn't think he'd have a crush on *me*."

"You didn't like him back?" I ask.

Mom shakes her head. "I just wanted to keep climbing trees! But he was my friend, and I didn't want to hurt him."

I nod, knowing the feeling. It'd crossed my mind when I gave back the chocolate, and Finn looked so hurt. I gaze guiltily down at my hands.

"So your mother made up an imaginary boyfriend!" Lao Lao says.

"WHAT?" Millie and I blurt out.

"Muchen Li." Mom nods.

"Muchen?? That's your imaginary boyfriend?" Millie giggles.

I can't resist, so I elbow my sister, joking, "Hey what's up? Not Muchen!"

Millie laughs so hard, the sofa squeaks.

"Hey!" Mom crosses her arms. "I'll have you two know, Muchen was a sensitive, tall piano player who took meticulous care of his pet lizard, who he kept in his pencil case, at all times, even at school, okay?"

My sister and I are *dying*.

"And Kang never figured it out?" I ask.

"'Course he did, but by that time, we were already in high school, and he had a steady girlfriend," Mom says, beaming.

"Pretty clever!" Lao Lao praises.

"Sometimes, with a friend, you have to be creatively kind," Mom says.

Creatively kind. I like that.

"It's part of growing up," Mom says.

Speaking of growing up, shyly, I ask, "So when did you know that you were ready to have a crush? Is there . . . a sign?"

"You'll know when you're ready. Just remember the first rule of love—"

"Always keep a pet lizard in your pencil box?!" Millie asks.

"Be gentle and respectful, with your heart and theirs," Mom says, patting my hand.

As she gets up to go and help Dad with the dishes, I swallow hard, thinking of Finn and how I am going to make it up to him.

Chapter 52

I look into the camera. It's just me this time. No filters. No script.

"Hi, Finn, it's me," I say. "I just want to say I'm so sorry about the chocolate today."

I take a deep breath. I consider blaming it on the Jessica video. But I know that's not the whole truth.

"Lately, I care so much about how people see me online. What they're thinking about me. What they're saying about me. And I don't know why."

I get quiet for a second.

"I thought when I got a phone that, finally, I'd have what everyone else has. But every time I open up an app, I see new things. Clothes I don't have. Places I can't go." I pause before confessing, "Problems about myself I never even cared about before. But now they're on my mind all the time!"

I look down, embarrassed.

"Maybe it's the dopamine. Or the oxytocin. I wish I knew the answer. But I *know* I messed up today." I gaze into the camera timidly. "Will you forgive me? You're my real friend. In real life. I care about you so much. Will you give me another chance?"

Millie walks in as I'm finishing up my video. "Oh, sorry."

"No, it's okay. Stay," I tell her. "I'm done anyway." I quickly send the video to Finn. "Hey, I'm sorry I was unposterly to you today."

"Why'd you make me wash all that good glitter off?" she asks, climbing into her bunk.

"Because I didn't want you to have your hair glued to your face when the teacher turned on the fan, which is what happened to me."

"Oh."

I take off my sweatshirt and climb into my own bed. We lie in silence.

"Well, why'd you put it on your face to begin with?"

"Good question . . . ," I mutter. I consider making up a reason—some sort of internet challenge. But I've already lied to a friend today. And it didn't turn out so great. "Because I tried out a filter. Then I wanted to *be* the filter."

"Why?" Millie asks again, turning onto her tummy. She gazes down at me.

"Because I didn't think I looked good enough just as me," I say in a tiny voice.

Millie gasps.

"You? Not good enough?" she says. "With your sunny smile and your belly laugh? And all your *amazing* stuffed-animal voices?"

My lips curl into a smile. I guess I'd been so busy focusing on all the things about me that are changing that I haven't thought about all the things about me that *aren't*.

"Thanks." My voice chokes.

"You're the most beautiful big sister in the world," she assures me. "Right, Rabbity?"

She thrusts Rabbity down at me and makes her nod.

"Thanks, guys." My eyes mist. "I guess . . . sometimes I just get a little confused."

"It's okay."

"I'm sorry I didn't explain all this to you in the bathroom."

Millie reaches out a hand. "I know your friend was there."

I shake my head. "She's not my real friend. I only have three real friends in the world. Finn, Carla . . ."

"And who's the third one?" Millie asks, curious.

I reach out and touch her fingertips. "You."

I think about how good it feels to be honest and brave with my sister about what I'm going through even though I don't have everything all figured out just yet.

Chapter 53

F inn!" I call out.

Finn looks up from his phone with a smile.

"Lina! I just saw your video—"

"I'm so sorry for all the texts," I say, sitting down next to him. I'd sent him a whole bunch in the middle of the night when I didn't hear back from him:

Did you get my video?? 😫😫😫

I'M SO SORRY!!!

It's ok if you're mad at me, but I really am sorry. 😩

Are u going to stay mad at me forever?

I hope not.

I will be really sad.

WRITE BACK IF YOU'LL BE SAD TOO.

"No! My phone died, and my mom took away my charger because she wanted me to go with her on a 'digital fast.' Anyway, I just texted you back!"

I smile, relieved.

"I appreciated what you said. But Jessica shouldn't have made that video. That chocolate coin was ours," Finn says, putting his phone back in his pocket.

"Exactly."

"It was something just between us, and she took it and made a fake book out of it!"

"Didn't even bother to come up with better names for us!" I add with a chuckle.

"Or at least a better title! *Chocolate Crush*? That's so cliché!"

I nod in full agreement.

"Titles have to have some mystery to it! Or irony!" Finn says, "Like *New from Here*!"

"Or *Elie Engle Saves Herself*!" I add.

"Or *Doodles from the Boogie Down*!" Finn tosses out.

"Exactly." I giggle.

"They have to make you wonder. They can't be right on the nose," Finn says. "*Especially* if they're accurate."

I stop giggling.

"What do you mean, accurate?" I ask.

The bell rings. Finn gets up, swinging his backpack over his shoulder. "We don't have to talk about it here."

"No—"

"Check your messages!"

Chapter 54

I open my phone to find four new text messages from Finn waiting for me:

'Course I'm not mad! 🐮🖤🐸

Want to eat chocolate some other time? 😊🍫

Seriously, don't let Jessica or anyone else get you down.

I hope you know, Lina, you are the most special girl in the world. When u came over the other day, and we listened to frogs together . . . it was like . . . getting Wi-Fi after a long car trip. 😎😎😎

WHOA. Did Finn just call me Wi-Fi? And that's a lot of heart eyes!

I think of Carla's joking words yesterday. What if she's right . . . and Finn has a crush on me?

"Carla!" I call out.

But she's not on the field. I scroll up to see my own emojis to Finn last night:

I gulp when I see the red heart. Why'd I have to throw that in there? And how do I fix this without putting my big foot in my mouth again?

"Carla!" I call her on the phone after school. "You've got to help me!"

I tried to talk about it with her at school, but Finn glued himself to me all day, like he was my hair.

"I need your help too!" Carla wails.

She sounds frantic, so I let her go first.

"I told my mom about Jake, and she started asking a whole bunch of weird questions," Carla says. "She made me email Jake asking him to hold up a sign with his ID and today's date, like some sort of robot test!"

"What??" I ask.

"And now he's not responding!" Carla says. "I sent him five emails—no response!"

"When's the last time you heard from him?" I ask.

"Tuesday night!" she says. "And he *knew* how upset I was over the whole Discord thing! This is so unlike him."

"Maybe he's just busy?" I offer.

"I shouldn't have sent him that email asking him for his ID. Now he probably thinks we're trying to steal his identity!"

"No, you weren't wrong to email him. Remember what Mrs. Carter says?" I ask her. "We can't trust everything we see?"

"Well, I can trust him. I *do* trust him," Carla says. "I know everything about him! I know his favorite color is teal blue. I know he also lost his dad—"

I try to wrap my mind around this earthshaking coincidence, a fact so big I can't believe Carla's just telling me this now. "Wait, he *also* lost his dad?" I ask. "When?"

"When he was five," Carla says. "Apparently, it happened in his sleep. He just didn't—"

"No, when did he tell you?" I ask.

"On Tuesday," Carla admits.

She's been talking to him for weeks, and he only just told her? I fall quiet.

"Carla . . . ," I start saying.

"You're missing the whole point!" Carla says. "Someone else in the universe gets what I'm going through, knows what it's like to click through streets on Google Maps that I used to walk down with my dad. Knows *why* I still play with the Pop-It my dad gave me—because it's hard." Her voice quivers with emotion. "And my mom, she won't talk about it. So I have to try to piece together how they first met from a million rom-coms. . . ."

My heart breaks for my friend. "Oh, Carla . . ."

"Finally, I found someone who gets it, Lina. And I scared him away," Carla says. I can hear her crying softly. "I scared him away with my questions!"

"You didn't scare him away," I promise my friend.

"Then where'd he go?" Carla asks.

"He could be . . . on a trip!" I rack my brain, trying to come up with a logical explanation.

Carla stops sniffling. "Maybe he went to visit his dad's grave!" she suddenly says.

"Or maybe he went to get more spicy hot peppers for his hot sauce."

"Why would that take him three days?" Carla asks.

"Maybe they're grown in . . ." I scratch my head. "Chile?"

"Chile does have great peppers!" Excitedly, she adds, "Or maybe while he's there, he lost his phone. And he can't borrow his mom's because she lost hers too. . . ." As my friend tosses out more and more maybes, I wait for her breathing to return to normal before reminding her of something very important.

"When he finally emails you back," I tell Carla, "remember, your heart gets to ask him questions, too. It's like Mrs. Carter says. Our trust has to be *earned*."

I hope Carla knows that's just as important as their bond.

Chapter 55

I f having a crush is as intense as Carla's describing, I've *got* to tell Finn the truth. I can't let him go the entire weekend thinking that I like him. I pick up my phone. But before I can call him, I get a text from Finn.

Nate just called me a wuss. 😔

I don't know what a wuss is, but judging from the emoji, it's not good. How dare Nate!

I'm sorry!! You are not a wuss!

Thanks. He's just mad at me for not going to Camp Arrowstone this summer.

What's Camp Arrowstone?

Just some dumb camp that him, me, and Preston have been going to since we were seven. Three dots appear. He adds, Actually it's not that dumb.

What do they have?

Lots of stuff. Zip-lining and go-karting. And there's ATV dirt biking, which we can finally do this year! 🏍 We've been waiting and waiting to be old enough!

Sounds fun!

It'd be fun if you came too! ⛺

I read the last sentence a few times in my head. The first time with a hopeful, romantic voice. The second time with a serious, sheriff voice.

Can't. I don't think we have money for camp. I delete the words, embarrassed. Instead, I type, I have to help my mom with videos, probably.

That's what I thought. I'd rather just hang out here with you and Carla. I kinda want to see if I can write a movie script too, like Carla!

Great idea!

But then Nate got all mad! He thinks I'm too chicken to go on the ATV dirt bikes. That's when he called me a wuss. 😒

NOT COOL.

Maybe we are drifting apart. My dad says all his elementary school friends drifted apart in middle school.

Gosh, I hope that doesn't happen! I'd drown without Carla and Finn. *Not all, I hope.*

Definitely not me and you! he types.

No way! I assure him.

😊☠️🥤🍫👀🎬

I tap on a bunch of emojis back, including a cute smiley face drinking a boba.

☠️📄🎶✨😌

Finn sends back:

❤️📄❤️

There are the hearts again. Sandwiched, this time, in a chocolate bar! Oh no! I just tapped on the chocolate. It didn't mean anything. I quickly sprinkle back a bunch of random emojis:

🧠🥤🐼☠️🌵🎹

Thankfully, Finn continues typing:

Maybe I'll write a thriller! Boy goes to summer camp and there's no camp counselors. Just a speaker with a creepy voice, giving out instructions.

Oooooh!

So everyone ignores the voice. But then mysterious things start happening!

That's so good! I'd watch that!

Really? Nate thinks it's horrible.

Forget Nate.

He says I'd be a lame writer because I never do anything. All I do is read.

My fingers fly as I type my response. You, lame? I type. The boy who gave me the confidence to speak English? Who taught me to draw graphic novels? Who told me I could make videos? Who stood up for me on that Discord thread? YOU'RE NOT LAME. You're the opposite of lame.

LINA. That is the nicest thing you've ever said about me 😲😳 🥹❤️😍😊

My eyes widen at the heart eyes. And the emoji after it. I look more carefully. What if that smiley face drinking a boba . . . is not drinking a boba?

I've got to go! I type quickly.

Me too! 🍱🥢😊

Eek! There it is again! I've got to stop this madness, before it gets any worse!

But how do I tell him this was all a big misunderstanding? I don't Wi-Fi him—I'm more like a school-issued Chromebook. Always there for him! But not in the special way he thinks . . .

I remember what Mom did with her crush. *Be creatively kind.*

If only there was an anonymous way to suggest to him there's someone else I like. . . . That's when my eyes slide over to my computer.

Discord.

Chapter 56

I try to choose a username.

>*LinaGao10*
>*SeashellGirl714*
>*Beheard13*
>*Bookworm5*
>*SparklySpecialGirl1000*

None of these will do. It's gotta be something totally anonymous and untraceable to me. A username *any* of my classmates can have. Finally, I settle on:

>*TaterTots2930*

Because who doesn't like tater tots?

My plan is simple, to pop into the group chat anonymously and write one thing:

I was walking by Lina's desk, and this letter fell out with a heart on it! And it had Chinese characters—maybe it's someone she used to go to school with in China? 😍

Then, when Finn asks me about it later, I'm going to tell him the truth. That I don't like Muchen or him *or anyone*, because I'm just not there yet.

BOOM. Done. No feelings hurt. Back to normal.

It's total genius. Except for one problem.

I can't get in.

I tap and click on the dizzying buffet of servers, threads, and topics in Discord. When I search up Balloon Powered Car Challenge, nothing comes up.

I drop my forehead to my keyboard.

Why. Can't. I. Find. Them?

On the third keyboard pound, I suddenly remember— MemeLord248! Preston's screen name!

I search him up. Sure enough, there he is. SEND FRIEND REQUEST.

It takes Preston only two minutes to respond. He sends me a direct message:

WHO ARE YOU, FOOL?

I try to channel my inner bro in an equally rude response:

IT'S ME, FOOL! I CREATED A NEW ACCOUNT. NOW ADD ME BACK TO BALLOON NOW!

To my shock, Preston buys it. As my computer dings with an invitation to join Balloon, I laugh out loud! I'm *in*!

My fingers work quickly, scrolling all the way to the bottom. I start typing out my two sentences. Somewhere in between the first one and the second one, I see Finn's name pop up. He's on! Right now! I pause to read what he says.

> Stop calling me a wuss! I am NOT too chicken to go on the
> ATV dirt bikes! That was MY idea!
> ⊙ Then why don't u want to do it w us anymore??
> ⊙ Cuz I want to write a script! I told u!
> ⫿ 2

Ⓖ Dude, we've never tried the ATV thing! We gotta do it!

Ⓖ Just admit it, u wanna hang out with ur girlfriend. 🤮

Whoa! I know I came on here to say I'm not Finn's girl-friend, but still . . . a vomit emoji?!

Ⓖ She uses so many filters and she's always overacting!

Ⓖ Jess is right, can't even tell it's her anymore

Ⓖ She looks like a cartoon.

🤡 1

My jaw drops. *A cartoon???* I stare at the clown-face reaction. "Because of YOU!" I scream at the computer. "You said I looked good! You said my skin was all glowy! That's why I became obsessed with filters!"

I blink back the tears. Over and over again, I stare at my classmates' mean words. Finally, I type a new sentence:

Only a wimp says mean things online.

I press post.

I get out of there so fast, jumping into bed, heart pound-ing. I tell myself I'm never going back in there again. First thing tomorrow, I'm logging out of Discord. I'm throwing away the password to TaterTots2930, along with everything bad they ever said about me.

Then the morning comes.

Chapter 57

I just need to know one thing. One tiny thing.

Did they figure out it was me?

By nine thirty, I can't stand it anymore. I reach for my laptop and climb into my bed with it. I throw the covers over my head, and I open up the site.

Who posted that??

🌀 Reveal urself, or we'll report u to Discord!

🌀 Ur the wimp, hiding behind a screen name!

🌀 We're going to find u, TaterTots2930!

🌀 I bet ur ugly!

"No, I'm not!" I cry out. I hide under my blanket, reading:

🌀 Stop being mean! TaterTots2930's right—that stuff u said about Lina? It was NOT COOL!

🌀 It's a private chat, we can say what we want!

🌀 What's not cool is having TaterTots2930 in here!

🌀 Get out!

🌀 What a lame screen name anyway!

🌀 Yeah! No one even likes tater tots!

☺ 4

Before I know it, I'm typing a response: ⓒ Not true! Everyone likes tater tots! I write.

ⓒ Well, well, well! Look everybody, it's the spy herself!

Uh-oh. ⓒ How do u know I'm a girl? I ask.

ⓒ U just confirmed it! 😁
ⓒ Hi Lina!
😶 3

Nooooooooo. I try my best to throw them off my identity.
ⓒ Bruh, it's not Lina! U think if I was Lina, I'd come back in here, after what u said about her? I ask.
ⓒ It's not her, all right?? Finn adds.

ⓒ Look, library nerd's defending the intruder!

UGH! I want to shake the computer. Instead, I type: ⓒ Stop calling him that!!!

ⓒ Then tell us! Who are u??

I hesitate. I've already gone this far, I might as well continue: ⓒ Someone who is SICK and tired of u making mean comments about everyone! I write.

ⓒ GET OUT OF HERE, u slimy, sneaky, crow-faced, Mystery Meat, stinky-breath snake!
🐍 4

Oh, that does it!

🌀 U get out of here, u gross, cowardly, pathetic half hot dog bun! I type.

🌀 Ur so dumb u can't even spell ur own name. U have to use a breakfast food for ur screen name!

🥜 5

🌀 Ur so mean, when u look into the mirror, it breaks, I write back.

🌀 Ur so fake, u make bots look real.

My fingers pound on the keyboard. Before I know it, I'm in an intense insult-a-thon with these clowns. I hurl out things I would never say offline. But I can't stop. It's too hard to stop!

🌀 You have hairy eyeballs! I type.

🌀 Your breath stinks and you blink too slow!

My jaw drops. I do NOT blink too slow. Suddenly, I remember the book I read on beetles and how it said that some of them are extremely toxic. I start typing the biggest burn of all time:

🌀 Ur as toxic as the gas that comes shooting out of a toad when he swallows a bombardier beetle! Because he can't handle it! He was just going about his day when all of a sudden, he sees a beetle out of nowhere. And it's so small and tiny, and it seems totally harmless. But it really

really hurts! Now he has to flip his stomach inside out from his mouth, before the toxic beetle kills him! YOU'RE THE BEETLE!

☺ 2

Ⓒ WHOA man! Not cool! That was WAY too harsh! And u say WE'RE mean??!

I yank my fingers away from the keyboard. My ears turn scorching hot. I look at all the things I wrote, horrified at all the insults that came from *me*. How could they have come from me? I think about Mr. Li and what he said about social kindness. I shrink under the covers, embarrassed. Finally, I type one last thing. A plea. The reason I came back in here to begin with:

Ⓒ Just be kind, and I'll go away!

Only after hitting send, do I realize the mistake I made. I used the same exact words as in my posters! Jessica jumps on it immediately:

Ⓒ Lina! I knew it! You're SO going down for this!

☻ 4

I slam my laptop shut, my pulse racing. I poke my head out from under the covers, gasping for air. *Where's the phone? I gotta call Finn!*

I look everywhere, but the phone's not in my room. Millie must have taken it. I walk out in my pajamas. Mom's making congee, bouncing to the catchy beat of Aretha

Franklin's "Respect." She smiles at me, but I lower my face. If she knew the things I typed, she wouldn't be smiling.

I remind myself of the words Finn once told me.

It's not real. It's just Discord.

Then why do I feel . . . as small as a beetle?

Chapter 58

Welcome to the Dangers of Social Media evening," Mrs. Carter says. "I'm Mrs. Carter, one of the fifth-grade teachers here. I'm joined tonight by Mrs. Sanchez, our school counselor, and our principal, Mr. Bennett."

The gym's packed. Almost everyone came out with their parents. Little brothers and sisters nibble on chocolate chip cookies, while moms and dads chitchat. Dad takes Millie to go and get some cookies. I look around for Finn. He and Carla are sitting together. They wave at me.

"Lina!" Finn smiles.

I relax, seeing his smile. *Maybe it's not that bad. Maybe after I left, they all moved on!*

I hustle across the gym to join them. Mom and I squeeze by other moms. One of them gives my mom a once-over as she passes by, commenting, "Look, it's Modern Mama." Another woman, in a red shirt, leans over and adds, "Thought you didn't believe in the dangers of social media."

Mom flushes. Luckily, the auditorium lights dim and we hurry to our seats, as Dad and Millie come over with cookies.

"We're so glad you can join us tonight," Mrs. Carter says. "If you're here, chances are you're concerned about how social media impacts your kids. And so are we. We'd like to start tonight with a short video."

As music fills the darkened room, Finn turns to me.

"Are you okay?" he asks.

"Yeah, what'd everyone say after I left?" I ask.

"Oh, you know, the usual," Finn says. He leans closer to me and whispers, "I thought it was so brave. You're right—people who say mean things online are wimps. And you know what?"

"What?"

"You inspired me. I logged out after you left."

I smile. Good for Finn. We both watch the video. It's about a girl our age texting with some kid named Sam. At first it seems pretty innocent. They're goofing around, telling jokes. Then Sam asks the girl to send him a photo of her. So the girl sends him a pic of her at the park. The next thing I know, a dark van pulls up next to the park *and the girl disappears*!

WHOA. That got scary FAST.

I glance over at Carla, watching with her mouth hanging open.

The lights turn on. Everyone's aghast. Cookie crumbs are hanging off shirts. Moms are frozen, mid–lipstick reapplication. Dads are fuming in Patagonia vests. Mrs. Sanchez, the school counselor, steps to the front.

"As you can see from the video, when it comes to social media, Stranger Danger is very real." Mrs. Sanchez says. "Now, you might be asking why we're calling this meeting when most of your kids aren't on social media yet."

"My Eleanor would *never*," says Eleanor's mother, a tall brunette wearing a blazer and gold hoops in the front row. I glance over at Eleanor sitting next to her, shrinking in her hoodie.

"First of all, what you think is happening and what's actually happening . . . ," Mrs. Sanchez says, "are not always the same. Most social media sites are thirteen and above. But that doesn't mean your kids haven't figured out a way around it."

I look around at the many guilty faces, legs sliding lower in their chairs.

"We need to have these conversations with them early, so they understand all the risks. Here are just basic explanatory sheets for parents, to help you understand the landscape," Mrs. Sanchez walks around the room in her leather pumps and blue blazer, passing out printouts.

On the first page, it lists all the social media apps. The second page has a Family Plan, which people can fill out. The third page is a giant chart of emojis, with a list of *hidden meanings* next to them. I stare at the chart, fascinated.

Mrs. Sanchez flashes to a PowerPoint slide showing social media apps.

"For those of you wondering, what are the chances my kid's going to be on social media eventually? The answer is very high. A recent study on tweens—kids between ages eight to twelve—showed that thirty-eight percent use social media," Mrs. Sanchez says. "By thirteen, that number goes up to ninety percent. That's a lot of kids chatting, sharing pictures, videos, possibly getting into cyberbullying. We're going to focus on cyberbullying tonight."

The parents instantly sit up. Mrs. Sanchez hands it over to Mrs. Carter, who walks up to the front.

"It used to be that bullying, if it happened, would stop at three in the afternoon. Kids would go home, and they'd get to have a whole other life," Mrs. Carter says. "But now, thanks to the internet, whatever drama unfolds in school follows kids home after school. Into the weekend. The summer. There is no break!"

She taps on the next slide—showing statistics on anxiety and depression. Mothers reach for their kids, hugging them tightly.

"You can imagine what that does to a child," Mrs. Carter says.

The mom in the red shirt, sitting five seats over, turns to my mom. "And you wanna let six-year-olds have social media!"

Mom whispers back, "I didn't mean that!"

"But that's what you said! Isn't that what you said?" the mom asks.

As the mom in red gets into a side argument with my mom, a dad wearing a Lakers hat in the front row asks Mrs. Carter, "So is there cyberbullying going on at this school? Have you seen it?"

"We honestly don't know," Mrs. Carter confesses. "But we're seeing a lot of kids unable to focus in class. Glued to their phones at recess. Not engaging the way they used to. Clearly, something's amiss, and we're *concerned.*"

"Something's amiss?" a mom in pearls asks. "What do you mean?"

"Well, I see their faces when they're looking at their phones sometimes," Mrs. Carter says. "And I can just see something's wrong. We suspect it may have to do with the way the kids are talking to each other on some of these apps. The other day, we had kids putting up kindness posters. No one asked them to do that. They did it themselves."

I look at Carla. She beams back proudly.

"But can't you *tell* through the school Wi-Fi?" a parent asks.

Principal Bennett walks up to the front and explains to the parents that, unfortunately, the school Wi-Fi does not allow the school to look at every message their kids send.

"Well, it *should*!" the Lakers dad hollers. "Maybe you should get a better Wi-Fi system!"

"Yeah!" the other parents agree.

"Please, everyone. Even if we could do that legally, which I doubt," Principal Bennett reminds the parents, "so much of this is happening *outside* of school. By the time they get to school, the message might be gone."

"What do you mean, the message might be gone?" the mom in pearls asks.

"Some of these apps have disappearing messages," Mrs. Sanchez explains, telling us to turn to the first page of the handout. She points out which ones.

There's an outcry among the parents.

"Who would make such a thing?" they ask.

Parents clutch their faces, muttering to each other, "Couple months ago, these kids were still braiding bracelets. Now they're sending disappearing messages?!"

The Lakers dad stands up and demands, "Who's the bad egg that started all this? I want to know!"

"There's no bad egg!" Mrs. Carter assures him. "They're just kids. Now, I *know* your kids. They're good kids. But the thing about the internet is, because there's a screen, it feels anonymous. It *feels* like you can do and say anything."

She taps on a slide and explains.

"It's called the online disinhibition effect. When we're

259

online, we act differently, in part because we can't see the people we're hurting. According to research by Stanford University, nearly two-thirds of Americans admit to being cruel to someone on the internet. *Two-thirds*."

My eyes jump to Jessica sitting in the back with her mom. *Is she listening to this?*

Principal Bennett steps up to the front again.

"We don't want it to be two-thirds at Winfield Elementary. We don't want it to be *any third*. We have a zero-tolerance policy when it comes to bullying here at this school, and if we find anyone engaging in cyberbullying, there will be drastic consequences," he says. "To that end, we've asked a special guest tonight to join the conversation."

The back door opens. To our surprise, the sheriff walks in. As he takes the stage in full uniform, no one looks more bewildered than Jessica. She finally puts her phone in her pocket and gives him her full attention.

Chapter 59

Good evening, everyone." The sheriff smiles. "I'm Sheriff Dan Stormhammer, here to chat safety with you. Our state has very strong laws on cyberbullying and cyberstalking. I want to remind everyone, cyberbullying is a crime."

He walks around the room.

"It is illegal for anyone to use an electronic device to contact another person, intending to intimidate, annoy, harass, or threaten that other person," he says. "This could take the form of text messages. It could take the form of emails. Chats. Posts. Threads. Pictures and videos."

He stops walking and looks intensely at all of us students.

"By the way, kids. I want to remind all of you that it is illegal to send or solicit inappropriate photos and videos of a minor, even if it's between two minors. It's still illegal."

We nod. He continues walking.

"Parents, you have my word that if something is happening in Winfield, I'm not going to rest until I get to the bottom of it. We are not joking around in our department. Cyberbullying is despicable because you know what it takes away? The feeling of safety. Every child deserves to feel safe in their school and their home. Make no mistake: words hurt. They hurt offline. They hurt online. Sometimes online, they hurt even more, because they can be forwarded and liked a bunch of times. And every time that happens, not only does it hurt the individual, but it hurts all of us, as a community. So how do we stop it? Well, that's why I'm here today."

He points to a slide with an email address on it:

cyberbullyingtips@winfieldpolice.org

"This is an email address for anonymous tips," Sheriff Stormhammer says. "If you see something, say something. If you come across something, take a screenshot of it and send it to me. I promise we will take every lead seriously."

As parents furiously write the email address down, I feel hope expand. Maybe, just maybe, everything we wished for in the posters *can* come true!

"In closing, I want to say, it takes a village. I know the internet can be a scary place. I've seen families navigate it well. And others . . . not so well," he says. "The key is communication. Which is why I'm so glad to see you all here tonight. I hope you talk to your kids early and often about digital safety. *Before* they hit middle school. Before they download these apps. We see too many kids get completely in over their heads in middle school and high school. And it doesn't have to be that way. We *can* set kids up for success!"

The room erupts in applause for the sheriff.

"Stay safe, everybody." He smiles. "And remember, email me with tips!"

As I jot down the email address, Jessica glances at me. She looks scared. She should be scared. I'm done being mocked by her online.

Chapter 60

A t school on Monday, all my classmates are still talking about the event. The boys jump around the room, pretending to be Sheriff Stormhammer, busting random people for cyberbullying. The girls chitchat about the poor girl in the video. And *everyone* frets about the all-powerful Wi-Fi our parents want to install to spy on us.

"I wouldn't worry about it," Mrs. Carter is quick to comfort us. "I think your parents are just concerned. They don't want you guys getting hurt online. Speaking of which . . ." Her soft brown eyes shift around the room. "I know we talked about this a lot on Saturday night, but has anyone actually experienced cyberbullying?"

I gaze up from the Hidden Meanings of Emojis page. I've been studying it ever since Mrs. Sanchez passed it out. Who knew that the frog emoji meant ugly? And the avocado emoji meant basic? I've been using these emojis all *wrong!*

Mrs. Carter takes her chair and wheels it toward us. "I guess I'll start."

Mrs. Carter's been cyberbullied?

"Last year, I joined a teacher's group on Facebook. The whole point of it was a place for us to share lesson plan ideas. It started off positive and wonderful. But it quickly turned into a place for people to vent. I get that. We as teachers have to deal with *a lot*. But it reached a point where the venting was ninety percent of the posts, and the lesson plan sharing was only ten percent. So I said something to the group."

"What'd you say?" Eleanor asks.

"Just like, 'Hey, guys, I know that we're all struggling. But I gotta say, these negative posts are starting to affect me. Today I told a kid he wasn't allowed to staple any more things because he'd borrowed my stapler for the eighteenth time and forgot to return it.'"

"Did that really happen?" Finn asks.

Mrs. Carter nods. "Yes. And I felt awful about it afterward. That wasn't nice of me."

I know Mrs. Carter didn't mean it. She's the nicest, most patient teacher I've ever had.

"I told the group, 'I'm so embarrassed. This is not why I got into teaching, to ban kids from stapling. I just want to ask everyone here if we can keep it more positive in this group. Cheer each other on. Celebrate the good stuff when it happens.'"

"That's a great post!" I say.

"I thought so, too, but you know what? I started getting replies."

"What kind of replies?"

"Nasty ones like—*don't blame us if you lost it with a kid!*"
We gasp.

"It made me feel *terrible*. All these people thought I was a bad teacher! And they kept saying it, over and over again. I started to believe it. I almost thought about quitting teaching!"

"Noooooo!" we cry.

"Thankfully, my principal saw I was struggling and had a good talk with me," Mrs. Carter says. "But it was still very difficult to recover from."

She looks around the room. "Anyone else?"

"Well . . . ," I mutter.

Jessica whips her head around to give me the death stare. *Don't you dare.*

I turn my eyes back to my Hidden Meanings handout. A surprising hand goes up.

"My mom sorta got cyberbullied on Nextdoor," Eleanor says. "She let our puppy go into the community pool once, and he had an accident. Everybody was furious at her for *months.*"

"And that's tough, because it's all your neighbors," Mrs. Carter says.

Eleanor nods. "She was so mortified, she couldn't even walk him anymore. My dad and I had to walk him. They posted pictures of her and Max. And the comments, they kept getting angrier and angrier."

Mrs. Carter holds up a finger. "That reminds me."

She goes up to the board and writes down, *The Algorithm and How It Changes Us.*

"We didn't get to talk about this on Saturday, but it's very important."

"What's an algorithm?" Nate asks.

I try to repeat it in my mouth. Al-go-ri-thm. It sounds like an alligator, with rhythm.

"An algorithm is the technology that the big tech companies use to decide what to put in front of us. Think of it as a super-fancy sorting hat," Mrs. Carter says.

"So it's a machine that decides? Not a person?" Jon asks.

Mrs. Carter nods. She holds up a finger. "It has one job. To keep us watching for as long as possible. How's it going to do that?"

"By showing us cool videos?" Finn asks.

"By showing us what it *knows* we're going to have a strong reaction to," Mrs. Carter answers.

A hand shoots up. "How does it know that?"

"Because it's constantly watching us," Mrs. Carter says. "Every video we watch, how long we watch for, when we scroll away, what we save. It *knows* everything about us!"

"Sounds like the scary Wi-Fi our parents want to install!" We gasp.

"I hate to say this, but it is! Every time we use one of the apps, the big tech companies are already watching and tracking us!"

Preston holds up his phone. "Is that why I'm getting so many videos on purple toes?"

My classmates all laugh, but for once Preston's not kidding around.

"I looked up bunion *once*, okay! My feet were hurting from all the skateboarding. Ever since then, I've been getting a million videos on foot corns and calluses!" Preston shudders. "I've SEEN TOES that should NEVER BE SEEN!"

"Same thing happened to me when I looked up muscles!" Finn admits. "Now I can't stop getting all these videos on protein shakes!"

OMG. Is *that* why I got all those nonstop makeup and skincare videos? Because the algorithm thought I wanted them? I didn't want them! I did one little search. I didn't want five thousand videos! In my face! All the time!

"How do we make it stop?" I ask.

"Well," Mrs. Carter says, getting up and going to the board. She draws a graph. "We have to start watching like we're being watched. But no one does that."

Mrs. Carter begins labeling her graph. In the X axis, she writes, "time on social media." In the Y axis, she writes, "how intensely you feel about something." She draws a steep diagonal line in her graph. And even though she's drawing *math*, we've never been more interested.

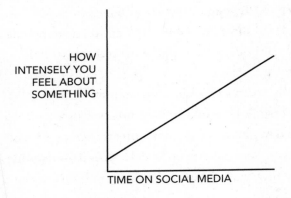

"Let's say you're like my husband, and you're slightly concerned about losing your hair. You might start off searching up some videos about thickening shampoo. Or maybe you don't even search it, but when it comes on your feed, you sit up. You pay attention."

She points to the bottom of the steep diagonal line. "That's where you are in the beginning. Worried a little about your hair, but not all that worried."

We nod.

"Now the app notices this. It *knows* you're worried about

going bald. And it's thinking, GREAT! I know what this guy's into. I've got him! I'm going to show him more hair-loss videos!"

Her finger moves an inch up on the diagonal line.

"Now you're watching them twice a day. Then five times a day. Shampoos, conditioners. Hair masks. Now it's showing you supplements. Things you can eat! And you're getting more worried! You're thinking about it constantly!"

Our eyes follow her finger sliding up and up and up on the diagonal line.

"You're spending money trying to fix a problem you're convinced you have! Buying pills you can take! Soups you can drink! Pillows! Hats! Blow dryers! You're hearing from people who are either bald or about to go bald. And they're telling you their struggle. . . ."

"And your oxytocin's kicking in!" we chime in.

Mrs. Carter smiles, snapping her fingers, *BINGO.* "Six hours of that a day, and by Christmas, you are *fully* convinced you are bald. And you will do *anything* to stop it—including dropping three thousand dollars on a laser comb that doesn't even work!"

As she moves her finger to the top of the diagonal line, the *TIPPY-TOP of INTENSE FEELING,* I gulp.

"And how do I know this?" Mrs. Carter declares. "Because it happened to my family! Not to my husband—but to my *mother!*"

"Your mother's bald??!" we cry out. Preston looks like he's about to faint.

Mrs. Carter pulls up a picture of her mama on her phone. A lovely Black woman with the most beautiful, voluminous head of hair. We look at the picture, confused.

"She's got *gorgeous hair*! And lots of it! But she was worried about losing it . . . and that *tiny* drop of a worry was enough for the algorithm to get her."

I sit back in my seat, mind blown. Now everything makes so much sense.

"Always keep that in mind, when you're online," Mrs. Carter reminds us as she walks back to the board and underlines the words: *Algorithm and How It Changes Us.* "It might surprise you how much we're all being shaped by what we see."

The bell rings. As we all pile out for recess, I think about Mrs. Carter's words. All this time, I thought I was in control. But when I think about what I typed on Saturday—the cruel words coming out of my fingers that I wrote without even flinching—I know. Mrs. Carter's right. I was totally influenced by what I saw.

Jessica starts walking over to me.

"Lina, can I talk to you?" she asks.

Her eyes plead with mine, and I follow her reluctantly out to the shaded wall behind the arts center.

----

wanted to clear the air," she says.

"Clear the air?" I ask, confused. What's wrong with the air? It's a lot less polluted than in Beijing!

"No, not the actual air. It's just something my mom says whenever she wants to apologize for something but doesn't really . . . apologize," Jessica says.

I suck in a breath. "So you want to . . . apologize?" I ask.

She doesn't answer that. Instead, she says, "For the record, all of us are still EXTREMELY mad at you for hacking into our chat."

"I didn't hack, but okay," I mutter.

"Lied, then. Tricked your way in. Deceived—"

"I get it!"

"Well, it was rude and humiliating and totally disturbing!"

"OKAY, OKAY!" I admit, my ears turning red.

"But, after hearing Officer Stormhammer talk about cyberbullying last night, I realize . . ." Jessica takes an extremely long time getting out the next part, like there's a gigantic pine cone stuck in her throat.

"Realize . . . ?" I ask, leaning in.

"Maybe we haven't always been the nicest to you," she finally coughs up.

She says it so faintly, I almost fall over, trying to hear. But then my eyes are dancing, smiling at Jessica. *How easy was that? That's all you had to say!*

Jessica reiterates, "Maybe."

"Well, I maybe agree with your maybe," I say. Then . . . just as quietly, I add, "And I maybe said some stuff too."

"How about this? From now on, if you promise never to go into Balloon, I won't say anything bad about you on there again."

Relief sweeps over me. I can't believe my ears! And I didn't even have to write an email to the anonymous tip site! Jessica holds up a hand. "Deal?" she asks.

I smile, then glance over across the courtyard at Carla. Any deal needs to include my best friend. "And you can't say anything bad about Carla either," I add.

"Fine."

"Or Finn."

"I won't. But Nate and Preston? I can't control those two. He's going to have to talk to the boys himself. This is between *us*."

That's fair. I take her hand and shake it firmly.

"Deal."

I flash Jessica a smile, which she doesn't return. Still, it was more than I ever thought I'd get from her, and I run off to find Carla to tell her the exciting news of our peace treaty!

Chapter 62

Carla and I celebrate by eating Cheetos from the vending machine with Mrs. Corso's hot sauce! It's such a relief not having to worry about Discord anymore. It's also a relief not having to worry about what to eat.

Now that I understand how the videos are appearing, I feel so much more empowered. On the way to school, when a new video appeared in my feed about puffy eyes and avoiding salt, I immediately scrolled away and searched for videos about body positivity instead.

I'm on cloud nine walking into school, when I see a police car parked in front of the office.

That's odd.

I look around for Carla. We'd planned to meet by the posters to add the anonymous tip email address to all of the kindness posters before school. But I don't see her anywhere. I start writing the email address on the first poster myself.

By 7:55, Carla still hasn't arrived yet. But all my other classmates have, and they're all gossiping about the police car.

"Maybe someone got arrested!" a fifth grader with gelled hair from Mrs. Anderson's class says.

"Can't arrest a kid!" his friend protests. "We're in elementary school!"

"Not true! My cousin's neighbor says he knows some kid who got arrested for stealing a bike!"

As they bicker back and forth, I try to think of the last time I saw a police car at my school. I don't think it's ever happened. Whatever's going on in the office, it's serious. I wonder if it's the anonymous email tip—did someone say something? As I'm adding the email address to the second poster, Jessica walks up to me.

"You know why the police are here?" she asks.

I shake my head. "No idea!" I reply.

"You didn't . . . email the . . . ?"

"No!" I immediately say.

"Then why are you writing it on every poster?" She points to my hand.

I put my hand down awkwardly. "So everyone knows it? In case they need it . . ."

A crowd gathers. Everyone's looking at me suspiciously.

"I thought we had a deal," Jessica says. She shakes her head at me, like I betrayed her.

"We do have a deal!" I insist.

Before I can say anything more, Principal Bennett walks out of the main office. He scans the courtyard, like he's urgently looking for someone. To my shock, he calls out my name.

"Lina?" he asks. "We need to have a word with you in the office. Right now!"

"But I have class. . . ."

"Don't worry. We'll tell Mrs. Carter. The sheriff's waiting," he says. "C'mon, there's no time!"

As Principal Bennett says *sheriff*, all the kids around me

273

take one step away from me. As I hustle over to the office, Jessica calls out to me.

"The deal's off!" she yells.

"I didn't do anything," I call back.

"You're going to pay for this!"

I try my best to drown out her voice as I pick up the pace. *It's going to be okay.* Still, the fear pounds in my chest as I open the door to the principal's office.

What could they possibly want with *me*?

Chapter 63

P lease take a seat. I'm Sheriff Stormhammer, and this is Lieutenant Jones," the sheriff tells me, introducing me to his partner, a Black police officer with a beard. Besides them, Principal Bennett is in the room, and Mrs. Sanchez, the counselor, is sitting in the corner taking notes. They point to a seat for me.

I sit down nervously.

"We just wanted to ask you a couple of questions. No need to be scared. You're not in any kind of trouble," Lieutenant Jones assures me.

I try to take comfort in their words, but I've watched too much TV to know they say that to everyone. Gently, they hold up a picture of an old man.

"Have you ever seen this man?" Sheriff Stormhammer asks.

I shake my head. It's a mug shot of a white man, about Dad's age. He has a salt-and-pepper mustache and stringy, long dark brown hair. He looks kind of mean.

"No."

"Are you sure?" they ask. "Look closely. . . ."

I take the picture from them and study it.

I shake my head again. "I'm sure. What's his name?"

"Maddox Reed," Sheriff Stormhammer says. "Though he

likely would have used a different name. He's a credit-card thief. Our associates in Chicago have been following him for some time. He likes to befriend kids online and get to know them and earn their trust before he attempts to send them something."

As soon as he says that, I'm filled with dread. *Oh noooo.*

"Then he'll say there was a problem at the post office, and that's when he'll ask them for their parents' credit card. We just found out that he's been in contact with a student at this school. He went by the name of . . ."

Please don't let it be who I think it is!

"Jake Evermoon."

I sink in my seat. My eyes flit to the office window. *Does Carla know yet? Is she here?*

"I know who he is. Is Carla okay??" I ask.

"Yes! She's just in the next room with her mother," Sheriff Stormhammer says. "We're sorry. We didn't mean to scare you. We just wanted to respect your privacy and get your statement separately, in case you've also heard from Jake."

I shake my head.

"No, never," I tell them.

"Are you sure?" Lieutenant Jones asks. "He didn't try to reach out to you by direct message? Or try to email you . . . ?"

"No, I only know about him from Carla."

Sheriff Stormhammer looks over at Lieutenant Jones and nods. Lieutenant Jones hands me his card.

"Just in case he does, here's our information."

I look down at the card. "You're going to find him, right?" I ask, thinking of how cruel it was for him to do this to Carla and how badly she must be hurting. "You're going to make sure he never tricks another kid again, right?"

Sheriff Stormhammer looks into my eyes. "We're going to do everything we can. Thanks to your friend's mother, now we have all the emails. And we can trace his IP address."

Mrs. Sanchez offers to take me back to class. But I look up at her and ask, "Can I see Carla?"

Principal Bennett nods.

The conference room door opens, and Carla scrambles up from a chair. She runs over and falls into my arms. Her eyes are pink from crying.

"I'm so sorry," I say, giving her a hug.

"I'm going to leave you two for a minute, to get more tissues," Mrs. Munoz says. She tosses me a grateful smile. "Thank you for being here for Carla."

"Of course," I say. I walk Carla over to one of the seats.

Mrs. Munoz steps out, and I turn back to my friend.

"He just lied, Lina! Can you believe it? He made up his whole identity! Thankfully, my mom called the police last night!" Carla wails. She twists, like there's a vomiting worm inside her. "I'm the biggest idiot in the world!"

"No, you're not," I tell her. "This could have happened to anyone."

"But it didn't happen to anyone. It happened to *me.*" Carla shakes her head, like she's disgusted with herself.

"I would have believed it too! He sent you a picture of that boy, and he told you all these details about Los Romas! What were you supposed to think?"

"I was supposed to be smarter," Carla says. "To check! To not be duped." Leaning closer, she confesses, "You know I *had* this suspicious feeling, deep down inside. But I just ignored it.

All because he said he also lost his dad. He used everything I told him about me against me, Lina."

"He's awful! I'm so sorry," I tell Carla, hugging her again.

Carla swallows hard. "You know what the scary part is?"

I shake my head.

"I *almost* gave him my address," she says, holding up her thumb and index finger. She pinches them real small. "I was this close."

"But you didn't," I remind her.

"I shouldn't have even talked to him to begin with. I would never do that in real life! Trust some stranger and almost give them my address!" she says. "But online, it's like I'm not even me! I'm this whole other person!"

"Well, you wouldn't be the only one . . . ," I confess.

Carla stops crying for a second and looks up.

"What do you mean?"

Cringing, I tell her how I snuck into the Discord group and wrote a whole bunch of mean messages. I didn't tell her the other day *that's* the reason Jessica called a truce.

"What'd you write?" Carla asks.

"Oh, I said some things," I confess. "Terrible things. About hairy eyeballs and beetles!"

"Hairy eyeballs?" Carla asks, giving me a funny look.

"I just wrote them! I don't know why! It's like you said. It's so easy to be a different version of yourself online," Slowly, I pull out the Hidden Meanings of Emojis handout. "And this doesn't help."

I point to all the wrong emojis I've been sending Finn. "Look! This smiley face drinking a boba? It's NOT drinking a boba! And the cute octopus? It means to CUDDLE! I used it

TWICE in our texts! No wonder he thinks I have a crush on him!"

I cover my embarrassed face with the handout.

"Wait, Lina, you *don't* have a crush on Finn?" she asks me, point-blank.

"No!"

"Then you've got to tell him," Carla says.

"I can't," I insist, shaking my head behind the paper. "It's too hard! I've sent way too many emojis! Plus he's my friend, and I don't want to hurt him. . . ."

"Take it from me," Carla says. "The longer you wait, the more it hurts. *Especially* if he's your friend."

The door opens. It's Mrs. Munoz, back with the tissues. Carla takes them from her mom gratefully.

"Thanks, Mom."

"Just so you know, when you're ready, Principal Bennett says we can take the staff exit out, so no one will even see you," Mrs. Munoz says.

"You're not coming back to class?" I ask Carla.

Carla shakes her head.

"I need to just lie in bed," she says. "For a day or two."

I nod. I can't imagine how awful this must be for her.

Mrs. Munoz puts her arms around her daughter. "Take all the time you need in the world, sweetie. Maybe we can watch some romantic comedies together."

Carla's face brightens.

"Really?" she asks.

I glance at the clock. It's nearly ten.

"I better get back to class," I tell Carla. "You going to be okay?"

Carla nods. "Hey, Lina? About this whole thing . . ."

She doesn't even have to say it. I put my hand to my mouth and zip it firmly across my lips.

"I won't tell a soul. Not even Finn."

I carry her secret deep in my pocket all the way back to class. Opening the classroom door, I brace for curious glances and prying eyes.

But what actually awaits me . . . is way worse.

Chapter 64

‑‑‑

D id you talk to the cops?" Nate demands. "What'd they want with you?"

"Just admit it! You snitched," Jessica says.

I look to Mrs. Carter, but she's too busy dealing with a jammed printer situation. I keep my lips sealed tight as I hustle back to my desk.

"I'll bet she sent them the whole thread," Jessica says to Nate.

"Leave her alone!" Finn calls out.

But Jessica ignores Finn, turning to face me. "You're gonna get us all in trouble, you know that!"

"I don't know what you're talking about," I finally whisper back. I eye Mrs. Carter's printer. But it's still firmly jammed. Jessica jumps out of her seat and pretends she needs to get a ruler. She stops by the supplies cabinet and then scampers over to my desk.

"Just tell me what they said, because I know you did it," she says.

"*Nothing,*" I insist. "I didn't do anything!"

"Then why were you in there?!" Jessica asks.

I can tell this is killing her, not knowing. But I can't tell her! Even if I hadn't promised Carla, I would *never* tell her someone else's confidential police investigation. Unfortunately, Jessica mistakes my silence for an admission of guilt. The next thing I know, she points her ruler at me.

"You'll be sorry," she warns.

I throw a desperate glance at Mrs. Carter, but she's still on the floor, pushing buttons on the loud printer and yanking on paper.

"I'll give you one more chance," Jessica offers. "What did the sheriff want with you?"

"I can't tell you," I answer honestly.

Jessica shakes her head at me, her disappointment coming through every pore and molecule in her being as she walks back to her seat. I look over at Finn. But he's as pale as a ghost. Does *he* think I told, too? Preston and Nate are on their phones. Eleanor, Nora, and Tonya are huddled together, talking and looking over at me.

Finally, Mrs. Carter gets the printer working again.

As she claps her hands, Jessica gives me one final glare before turning and typing on her computer. I wipe my sweaty palms on my pants, telling myself to relax. Jessica's just being dramatic, as usual. She's not going to do anything. Besides, what can she really do?

At lunch, I dash toward Finn in the cafeteria, with my tray.

"Hey!" I say, sliding down next to him.

"Lina, Jessica is seriously stressing." He puts his sandwich down and leans over. "Did you tell?"

"No!"

"Really? Because it's okay if you did," Finn says. "I'd understand."

"Well, I didn't."

"Then why were you talking to the sheriff?" Finn asks.

"It's . . . private," I tell him. "But it has nothing to do with the Discord thread."

Finn looks relieved. "You don't know how terrified I was. I just saw a police car, and my mind immediately went to that *Worst Years of My Life* book. The one I was reading? And I thought, *Oh my God, this is how it starts!*"

As Finn dramatically grabs his hair, I chuckle. I could see how he'd be all worked up about that. His worst nightmare!

"Well, don't worry," I tell him, taking a bite of my burger.

He leans in, whispering, "Because I can't have that! I have to start middle school strong. I don't want to be like that kid in the book! I know I said some things on the thread, to Nate and Preston, but I didn't mean them—"

"I know." I nod. "It wasn't about that. I promise. The thread's safe."

Finn smiles. "Thanks, Lina," His whole face brightens. He reaches into his lunch bag. "You wanna share my Jell-O? It's chocolate!"

I hesitate, thinking of Carla's words. *You've got to tell him!*

"Finn . . . ," I say softly. "There's something I have to tell you."

But before I can get the words out, I hear my name on the loudspeaker.

"Lina Gao, will you please report to the office?" Ms. Egan, the office secretary calls.

AGAIN? The entire cafeteria stops eating and turns to me. I lower my head almost to the same level as my tray.

"What do they want now?" I mutter to Finn.

"I don't know, but you better go . . . ," Finn says.

Slowly, I start making my way over to the office. I tell myself it's probably an update from the police. Or a message from Carla. Or my mom. Maybe she's coming to get me early from school, because Carla's mom told her what happened, and we're going to do a movie marathon together.

But as I pass by Jessica, I get an eerie feeling . . . like I'm about to nose-dive in an airplane.

And she knows it.

Chapter 65

"Hi again, Principal Bennett," I say, walking into his office.

"Lina, take a seat," he says, pointing to the chair I sat on just this morning. I hug my arms to my chest as I sit, even though I'm hot. I'm sweltering. I can barely breathe in his office. I can't believe I've been in here twice in one day. At least the cops are gone.

"Is this about Carla and that guy?" I ask hopefully. "Have they found him?"

"No. This isn't about that."

I fight the nose-dive feeling in my tummy as he hands me a piece of paper.

"I received this in my inbox about ten minutes ago. Do you recognize it?" he asks.

It's a screenshot of my insult-a-thon on Saturday. Except everything that everyone else wrote is blacked out. The only thing you can see are my mean responses . . . and Jessica's announcement that it's me.

285

[REDACTED]

🅖 Ur the gross, cowardly, pathetic half hot dog bun!

[REDACTED]

[REDACTED]

🅖 Ur so mean, when u look into the mirror, it breaks

[REDACTED]

🅖 You have hairy eyeballs!

[REDACTED]

[REDACTED]

[REDACTED]

[REDACTED]

🅖 Ur as toxic as the gas that comes shooting out of a toad when he swallows a bombardier beetle! Because he can't handle it! He was just going about his day when all of a sudden, he sees a beetle out of nowhere. And it's so small and tiny, and it seems totally harmless. But it really really hurts! Now he has to flip his stomach inside out from his mouth, before the toxic beetle kills him! YOU'RE THE BEETLE!

[REDACTED]

[REDACTED]

[REDACTED]

🅖 Lina! I knew it! You're SO going down for this!

"Is this you?" Principal Bennett asks me, point-blank.

Alarm bells are ringing. The room is spinning. I feel like I'm going to throw up my lunch.

"Yes, but it's not like that! There were a lot of people!"

"Yes, I'm aware! At least seven of your classmates were very hurt by this, from the email I received this morning. *Very* hurt," Principal Bennett says. "We'll be discussing your actions in a group Justice Session on Thursday, which you and everyone in this thread will attend."

I gulp at the term—Justice Session. Sounds ten times scarier than recess detention, which is already the scariest thing I can think of.

"I want to make it clear, this kind of cyberbullying is *not* tolerated at Winfield. Frankly, I'm shocked, Lina."

"I know." My voice quivers.

He points to the blacked-out portions. "Can you tell me what else was said in the chat?"

"The whole chat?" I ask.

He nods. I stare at his Lego tie. If Principal Bennett knew the full extent of it all, about the memes and the making fun of our teachers and cafeteria workers, and *him*, he's not going to want just a Justice Session. He's going to want a Jail Session. I think of my promise to Finn. "I don't really know."

"C'mon, Lina," he says, frowning at me.

"I was just in there for a minute," I tell him truthfully. "It was an accident. I snuck in!"

"You *hacked* into a private chat room?" he asks.

Uh-oh. Is that even worse?

"No! I just started typing. I didn't even know what it was!"

"You expect me to believe you went into a chat without knowing a bunch of your classmates were on there and just started writing horrendously mean things?"

"No . . . but it's just more complicated than that," I squeak.

"How so?" he asks.

I fall quiet. Principal Bennett waits for a while, clicking and unclicking his pen.

"Lina, the things you wrote, they hurt people. Real people.

Your classmates. What would possess you to want to hurt your classmates like that?"

I cry out, "I don't want to!"

"Then why?"

"Because . . ." I start saying, then shake my head and swallow back my words. I can't.

He leans closer. "Lina, if there's something you're not telling me . . ."

I hold my breath, hoping he won't push me to say it.

After a long pause, he puts his pen down. "I'll give you two days to tell me the whole truth. Screenshots. Printouts. If there's another side to this, I *need* to see it. Otherwise, I'll have no choice but to discipline you for cyberbullying. Which, as you know, has serious ramifications. I've already told your parents."

My parents? My sweatshirt becomes an oven.

"What'd my mom say?" I ask.

"She was shocked."

I hang my head in shame as I walk out. I can't imagine how confused and deeply embarrassed Mom must have been. A new fear pops up. What if *she* doesn't believe me? I race for the library to print out the *real* truth, not the blacked-out version, so she can see!

But when I get there, I get a message on my computer.

Chapter 66

RROR. *The private group, Balloon Powered Car Challenge, does not exist.*

I click again on the library computer.

"Come on, come on," I pound on the keys. But every time I try, I get the same error message. Could they have deleted it? Is that even possible on Discord? I jump up to find Mrs. Hollins.

"What's the matter?" Mrs. Hollins asks.

"I need to print something urgently! But I can't get in!" I tell her. "Do you know anything about Discord?"

Mrs. Hollins puts her reading glasses on and follows me over to my computer. "That's odd. It says the chat room's been deleted."

It can't be! I need to show my mom! She has to see what was actually on there, not just my responses!

"Mrs. Hollins," I beg. "Is there any way we can get it back?"

Mrs. Hollins considers this. "Do you know who started the chat group?" she asks. "You could try asking them to reinstate it."

I thank Mrs. Hollins and race out of the library. I can't find Preston, but I see Finn walking out of the cafeteria.

"Finn!" I run up to him.

"Hey! What happened?" Finn asks.

I point to his phone. There's no time to explain.

"Can you ask Preston to let you back into Balloon?" I ask him.

"No. We deleted it this morning," he says.

"What?" I ask.

"When you were in the office. Remember when Jessica got all paranoid? She told Preston we gotta get rid of it. I'm actually sort of relieved. That thing was bound to blow up—"

"So it's *gone?*" I ask.

Finn nods. "Why? What's wrong?"

My ears are ringing. I crumple to the ground. That means all the evidence is deleted. Everything they said about me and Carla. All that stuff about me being a cartoon. Even if I wanted to tell Principal Bennett the truth, now I can't. How am I going to convince *anyone* to believe me?

"Lina, what's the matter?" Finn asks.

I shake my head. It's useless. There's nothing he can do to help. There's nothing anyone can do. On Thursday, I'm going to go down for cyberbullying. All because of Jessica. I'm probably going to get expelled.

Through the blur of my tears, I see Jessica. I scramble up.

"Why did you do that?" I confront her.

Jessica hollers back, equally angry, "Why did *you?*"

Finn runs up to us. Nate, Preston, and Eleanor all make their way over from the cafeteria.

"I didn't do anything! I never said a word about the Discord thread. I told you, that wasn't why I was in the office. But you refused to believe me!"

"You didn't tell?" Jessica asks, genuinely surprised.

"No! But now I'm in trouble, because of you!" I shout.

Preston and Nate look at Jessica. "What's she talking about?"

"I sent Principal Bennett a screenshot of what she said on Saturday," Jessica says, somewhat sheepishly.

Everyone turns to Jessica, mad.

"Why'd you do that??!" Preston asks.

"You took a screenshot of the thread?" Nate asks, making a horrified face. "I thought we agreed to delete it!"

"I blacked out all the stuff we said. I only sent it to Principal Bennett because I thought she turned us in first!"

I point to my chest. "Well, I didn't! You have to tell Principal Bennett the truth!" I beg them. "You have to tell him *why* I was so mad! What else was said on the thread!"

Jessica immediately starts shaking her head. "Oh no, no, no! We can't do that! If we tell him that, we'll get in trouble! ALL OF US," she reminds Finn, Preston, Nate, and Eleanor. "You guys know the punishment for cyberbullying! You heard the sheriff!"

"Exactly!" I cry.

"Don't worry," Jessica says to me. "He only has one page on you. It's going to be like a slap on the wrist. But if we tell him the whole thread . . . ?"

"My dad's going to kill me," Preston says. "He's already mad at me for not wearing a helmet at the skateboard park and threatening to take my skateboard away!"

"My mom's probably going to send me to some horrific summer camp for cyber delinquents over this," Nate says. "I can't risk that!"

I throw my hands up. "Summer camp and skateboards? That's what you guys are worried about?" I can't believe I'm hearing this.

"Don't worry, Lina, I'll tell him," Finn says.

I shoot him a grateful look. But then Jessica points a finger in Finn's face.

"If you dare say a single word about any of us, Finn Wright," Jessica warns, "I'll personally go down to the police station and tell the sheriff what you said about Preston and Nate. And he won't be happy."

Finn's glasses fog up as he stands stock-still. Jessica turns to the group, reminding them sternly, "There's nothing they can do to us. The chat's been deleted. There's NO evidence. NO screenshots. All *we* have to do is agree to say NOTHING on Thursday. And we'll be okay."

Yeah. Everyone except me.

I turn and run.

Chapter 67

Mom doesn't move.

I peer at her, waiting, studying her face. *Say something!*

But she just sits on the couch, absorbing everything I told her. I came clean to her as soon as I got home. About Discord. Using filters. Seeing all my classmates' posts and feeling like I was on the outside of a snow globe. Watching videos on makeup and skin care. Which led to more scary videos that had me twisting in hunger at night. My attempt to *become* the filter. I told her all the things I've been keeping inside, not the rosy highlights version but the *real* version.

The apartment is so quiet, I can hear my sister outside wheeling Alfie around on the small wagon Rosa got him after his surgery.

"Why didn't you tell me you were going through all this?" she asks finally.

"I wanted to be strong, just like you," I say, my voice catching.

Mom takes my hand. "Being strong doesn't mean you suffer silently. It doesn't mean you sweep things under the rug. It doesn't mean you put up with abuse online. And it *really* doesn't mean you keep your mother out!"

I nod, feeling awful. She has every right to be mad. I blew it.

"You're always saying, growing up means having a thick skin," I mutter.

"Let me show you something," she says, scooting from me on the couch and taking out her own phone. She shows me a secret hidden folder in Notes. In it, she has all the unkind comments people have made on her posts. And all the responses she wishes she could have said. She might have deleted them from her account, but she clearly didn't delete them from her mind. "The truth is . . . it doesn't matter how thick our skin is. We're all human."

She pulls me in for a hug. I look up at my beautiful, strong mama. *Why couldn't she have said that to me earlier?*

"I'm so sorry. I should have done a better job protecting you," she says.

I summon the courage to be brave, too, and tell her what *I* should have said earlier. What I've been keeping inside for months. "But I'm growing up, Mama. You can't protect me. I'm getting hair all over the place. And I might need deodorant soon." I gulp, bracing for her response. "And maybe even a bra."

Mom smiles through her tears. "Why do you think I've been working so hard? I *know*, sweetie."

I blink rapidly. "Since when?" I ask.

"Since you first put on that sweatshirt. I just wanted to wait until I made enough to finally buy you all the things," Mom says. "Because you're going to need them soon, sweetie. Things my mama couldn't always buy me. And I want so desperately to give them to you! But we had all those bills to pay!" Mom says. "And I got so focused on making content—"

"It's okay, Mom."

"No, it's not okay. I became obsessed with going viral, and I wasn't there for you," Mom says, looking into my eyes. "And I'm sorry. I wasn't there for you during your most beautiful, important time. You becoming a young woman . . ."

I wriggle under her gaze. "Doesn't feel so beautiful sometimes," I whisper. "Feels awkward and clumsy, like my body's a train station, and I'm not sure what part of me is staying or going."

"I felt the exact same way when I was your age," Mom says.

I look up. "Really?"

Mom nods. "I once stuffed tissue paper into my shirt, just so I can feel like I was with all the other girls at the train station," she tells me. "And why do you think I felt that way? Because of something a girl in my class said to me." Gently, Mom urges me, "You need to tell Principal Bennett the truth on Thursday."

The door unlocks. Dad walks in.

"Dad!" I yell, running over to hug him.

"I came home as soon as I could," he says, kissing my hair. "I talked to some other folks at my lab. Lina, do you have any screenshots of what the other kids said?"

I shake my head.

"Then you're going to have to throw yourself at the mercy of the court on Thursday. Tell 'em everything that happened!"

I gaze at my shoes.

"What's the matter?" Dad asks.

Mom turns to him and tells him, "She's worried about her friend. He's in the group, too."

Dad sighs. "I know you want to protect your friend, sweetheart. But you have to think about your future. This is America! These schools, they have records. I talked to all the people in my lab, and they said cyberbullying is very serious. Lina, you *must* try to clear your name."

I take Dad's words in as Mom reaches out a hand. At first I think she's just trying to hold my hand. But then I realize she wants something.

Reluctantly, I hand over my phone.

I'd be lying if I said I didn't feel like I was losing a limb. The most cherished, celebrated part of my identity these last few weeks.

But I'd also be lying if I said I wasn't curious. Curious to have a piece of me back. The piece that doesn't want to be in trouble in the principal's office. That still likes to dream instead of scroll. Play, instead of watch. The piece that tells my parents the whole truth and feels relieved afterward because there's real dopamine in my veins.

I hope Principal Bennett gives *that* piece of me another chance on Thursday.

Later that night, Millie and I try to find a way out of my Discord saga via the stuffed animal game. Millie pretends to be Principal Bennett, going around the circle, interviewing each stuffed animal.

But each time, the verdict is the same—either Finn goes down or I go down or we both go down. All three sound terrible, but I know I'd feel substantially worse if I dragged my friend down with me.

After the fifth game, I tell Millie, "Sorry, Mils, but I don't think this is something that we can solve tonight."

"Just one more game!" Millie urges. "You gotta *believe* in the power of the stuffies!"

"I do believe . . . ," I assure her. "But . . ."

Millie's eyes suddenly fill.

"What's the matter?" I ask.

She shakes her head, refusing to say. I think of Mom's words: *Being strong doesn't mean suffering silently.*

"Come on, out with it," I urge. "This is the stuffed animal game! All your concerns are valid!"

Finally, my sister tells me. "I don't want you to go to jail. . . ."

"No! I'm not going to jail," I say, hugging her.

"I heard what the policeman said," Millie says. "Who's going to play the stuffed animal game with me if you go to jail?"

Tears brimming in my eyes, I promise my sister, "There will be many many MANY more stuffed animal games."

I climb into bed, hugging Snowy and praying for a miracle.

Chapter 68

I n the car the next morning, Mom announces she's deleting her Instagram account.

"Why?" I ask. I realize she's been crying. "Is it the comments?" I put a hand over my mouth. Has it gotten out? Are people going after my mom now? "Let me see! What are people saying?"

"It's not important," she says, putting away her phone.

"I want to see."

"No." She throws her purse on the floor of the passenger side. "From now on, you two are not looking at the comments."

"Okay, but whatever they're saying, don't listen to them—"

"This time they're right. I messed up! I couldn't sleep all night, thinking of all the things you've been through. I should have done *everything I could* to shield you from this," Mom says. "Instead, I was totally out to lunch, irresponsible, and ignorant. Exactly what all the haters have called me."

I shake my head. "You weren't out to lunch. You've never even had time to go out to lunch!" I lean forward, putting a hand on Mom's arm. "You were busy being brave and inspiring. And I was too."

Millie glances at the two of us. "Maybe . . . you two don't have to be so brave . . . to each other?" she suggests.

We both stare at Millie.

For such a small person, she can be incredibly wise sometimes.

"We *definitely* don't have to be so brave to each other," Mom agrees.

Mom holds my gaze in the rearview mirror as she drives. And I stare back, encouraged that it's getting easier seeing my real reflection in the mirror.

"Please don't delete your account," I urge.

She's worked too hard. I know how much love and compassion and creativity she put into all those videos. And how empowered they made her feel. I'd be sad if she lost all that. At the same time, I hope she knows how great it felt to talk to her about my problems and to receive that love and compassion . . . just for me sometimes.

Walking onto campus, I run up to Finn. He's doing something with my posters.

"Hey, what's going on?" I ask.

"Nothing!" he says, hiding one of my posters behind his back.

I try to reach for my poster, accidentally bumping into a trio of third graders walking by. They scream like I'm going to take their lunch. That's when I realize . . . word *definitely* got out.

That must be what this is about.

I gesture for the poster. "Let me see."

With a sigh, he opens it. On it, someone had written the word *BULLY* across where it said *Be Kind*.

"But don't worry," Finn quickly says, putting the poster down for a second. "It's going to be okay. I told my mom and dad what happened, and they're going to help you. They're going to get you a lawyer. They told me to tell you don't say ANYTHING tomorrow. And that I shouldn't either."

"A lawyer?" I take a step back. "No, that's too expensive."

"They're going to pay for it." He smiles.

I shake my head. I don't understand. "Why would they do that?"

"Just say yes!" Shyly, he reaches for my hand. "They both know how much I like you. They think you're a great influence. It's the one thing they agree on!"

I realize I can't let this go on for a second longer. "Well, *I* don't agree," I say, letting go of his hand.

"What?" Finn asks.

"Finn, I tried to find a way to tell you this. I don't *like you* like you!"

Finn turns tomato red.

"I was just texting! I didn't know there were so many hidden meanings in emojis! My octopus was just an octopus!"

"What are you talking about?"

"You said you saw an octopus on the beach, so I put an octopus emoji. It didn't mean I wanted to cuddle! And the smiley face emoji that looked like it was drinking boba?"

"You mean the one that looks like it's whistling?" Finn asks.

"It's not whistling. It's kissing! And I didn't mean to use

it!" I wriggle at the thought. "I'm not ready for a crush! But it's just been so hard to tell you. That's why I went into that Discord thing to begin with!"

Finn is stunned. "You went into Discord to tell me you don't like me?"

Before I can say another word, he turns and dashes off, leaving a trail of posters.

"Finn, wait—" I cry.

As my friend takes off running, I think of Mom's words. *Be gentle and respectful, with your heart and theirs.* In the end, I was neither. I broke my friend's heart, like a grumpy, clumsy grizzly bear.

All day, I wish I could text Finn, *I'm sorry. Are you okay? Do you hate me?*

He went to the nurse's office right before lunch. Something about a stomachache and never came back to class.

I pace our apartment, willing the home phone to ring. Mom's at the UPS store with Millie.

Suddenly, it rings. I jump.

"Finn?" I answer.

"No, it's me!" Carla says. "Are you okay? I heard about what happened. How are you holding up?"

"Not well," I confess.

I tell her about the bully posters and the third graders. How Jessica's threatening everyone to keep quiet. Worst of all, how I have this sinking, churning fear in my stomach that Finn's not even going to be there at the Justice Session tomorrow. I wouldn't blame him if he skipped it, after what happened.

"And if he's not? Will you . . . ?" Carla asks gently.

"No."

"Lina . . . ," Carla starts to say.

"No," I repeat. My decision's been made. I am not going to throw Finn under the bus.

"Well . . ." Carla swallows hard. "If you want, I can tell Jessica the real reason you were in the office that day, with the cops, if you think it'll help."

I'm stunned by her offer. I know it can't be easy for Carla. But I also know, there's no way I can accept it.

"I'll be fine." I try to sound as strong and brave as I can on the phone. "How are you doing?"

"Better," Carla says. "Still terrified every time I check my email."

"Did the police say anything?"

"They're still working on it. They said it could take some time." Carla's voice lingers. "But it's been nice hanging out with my mom."

I smile. "Me too."

Today, when I came home from school, Mom actually put her phone in a drawer. And we looked over a catalog from a store called Happy Tweens together. It's a store for bras. I was relieved to see they didn't all look like power cords. She also gave me a crash course on what else to expect during puberty.

"That's amazing," Carla says when I tell her. "My mom and I had the exact opposite crash course. What to expect when nothing happens."

"And?"

"It was actually pretty cool! Lots of movie marathons,

ice cream nights, and hikes," Carla says. "And my favorite—making a journal of all our favorite Dad memories."

I beam. "That's amazing!" I say to Carla, thrilled for her.

"You sure you don't want me to talk to Jessica?" Carla asks.

I shake my head into the phone. As much as I appreciate the offer, the last thing she needs right now is to tell her most tender story to Jessica.

"I'm good," I assure Carla, trying to project the voice of total confidence.

Later, when it's just me and Lao Lao, talking by moonlight, I crumple.

"Lao Lao, I'm terrified," I say.

"I know, sweetheart," she says. "I'm so sorry this is happening to you. Do you know who's going to be there at the session tomorrow?"

"Principal Bennett and maybe a few teachers," I say, swallowing hard. "And Jessica and the others."

"Don't let them scare you," Lao Lao says.

"But I am scared. I don't want to get myself in trouble. But I don't want to get my friend in trouble either." I blink back the tears. "I know I'm supposed to care about my future over my friend. That's the grown-up thing to do. But Finn's important to me. He was the first person in my school to be nice to me. He showed me how to check out books in the library. To read. He believed in me when no one else would. . . ."

"It's very grown-up to care about a friend," Lao Lao says. "And you should never be ashamed of that."

I clutch the phone, tucking her words into my heart.

"Maybe there's a third way."

I sit up.

"One thing I've learned, from my seventy years of being alive, is there's always a third way," Lao Lao says. "Like this dance party. People thought we either had to have it the way it was or we had to cancel it. But there's *always* a third way. And it takes real courage, sometimes, to find it."

I wipe my tears. "I have courage."

"I know you do," Lao Lao says. "Tomorrow, when you get in there, you gotta look deep down inside you. And not be afraid to be your vulnerable, true self."

I think of Jessica and start shaking my head. *Vulnerable* in front of Jessica? No way!

"That's how I got all these retirees to fill out the survey. I went to every person and told them my most vulnerable truth. How I don't know when my daughter and my grandchildren will come back to see me. And I need to stop waiting for that and start making my own plans and giving myself something to look forward to."

Tears gush down my cheeks, listening to Lao Lao.

"And you know something? It inspired them to open up too," Lao Lao says.

"But it's Jessica! I can't be vulnerable in front of her! She doesn't deserve to see it!"

Lao Lao repeats a line she once said to me. "Sometimes those who don't deserve our kindness need it the most."

I gaze out at the full glowing moon, at my wise grand-mother on the other side. I wish I could tell the moon that Jessica's not like her friends in her nursing home. It's never going to work. But I also know, if there's anyone in the world who has earned my trust ten times over, it's my grandmother.

I close my eyes, and I picture the tiger in my head. This time I don't run. I still my beating heart and wait to face it in the morning light.

Chapter 69

Stepping inside the big, empty auditorium, I walk quietly up to the circle of chairs. I'm the first student to arrive. Principal Bennett, Mrs. Carter, and Mrs. Sanchez are already there. I take a seat next to Mrs. Carter.

One by one, my classmates start coming in. Jessica sits down next to Principal Bennett. I dodge her gaze. Eleanor and Nora take a seat next to her. Preston and Nate sit next to Nora. Tonya sits next to them. I stare at the empty chair next to me. *Where's Finn?*

After about five minutes, my heart slumps. Finn's not coming.

"Thank you, everyone, for coming," Principal Bennett begins. "Unfortunately, Finn couldn't make it today because he's still not feeling well—"

The auditorium doors open.

"I'm here," Finn says, walking in.

Finn! I whip my head around, and I give him the biggest smile.

"You came!" I say.

He shuffles over, taking a seat next to me. "'Course," he whispers back.

"All right, well, I'm glad everyone's here," Principal Bennett says. "As you all know, we're here to discuss the contents of the Discord thread that all of you were on. The goal of this meeting is for the faculty to understand the full extent of what happened, so we can make the most informed decision. And for all of you students to have the chance to address each other, to hopefully repair and heal as a community of peers."

Repair and heal. I repeat the words in my head.

"Who would like to start?" he asks.

I glance around the room, hoping for someone else to take the lead. But my fellow Discordees all stare at their shoe-laces. I think of Lao Lao's words and take a deep breath. I raise my hand.

"I'll start," I say. "I am sorry for all the mean things I said to all of you in Discord."

Jessica looks up, surprised.

"Looking back, I'm really ashamed."

Finn shakes his head at me, like, *You don't have to do this.* But I do.

"I shouldn't have written those things, because we never know what the person on the other side is going through. Even if they don't always show it."

Eleanor lifts her eyes.

"And I know that because . . ."

I glance over at Jessica. I know I can still stop. But I push forward, taking a leap of courage. Courage that I know lives in me, passed down from my grandmother to my mother, blooming inside me, along with all my other changes.

"Because I've been going through a lot."

In a tiny whisper, I tell my classmates all the things that happened to me that sent me spiraling.

"I know it sounds ridiculous to not eat rectangular foods

and put glue on my face, because of things I've read and watched," I say timidly. "But that's how much it affected me. To see everyone living such perfect lives online, day after day, night after night, while I'm scrolling under my blanket, wondering if I'm good enough, pretty enough, liked enough. Whether I'll ever have a chance to be somebody in the world when I grow up . . . Does anyone else ever feel that way?"

I look around at the stunned faces in the room. Finn raises his hand.

"Me. All the time," Finn says. "That's why I read so much. Because my life doesn't make a lot of sense to me right now. But I know that it will. And that's why I'm trying so hard." He looks over to Nate. "And I want to just say, I'm sorry, Nate, if I ever made you feel bad for skateboarding. You're an awesome skateboarder."

Nate turns red. He sticks his hands under his armpits.

"I'm sorry for making fun of you reading," Nate finally mumbles. "But sometimes it feels like you want to avoid me."

"I don't," Finn promises. "But I'm scared when you break rules, like no skating off the benches. That gives me a lot of anxiety."

Principal Bennett nods. "Me too. Can we save the skate-boarding for off campus?"

"Maybe at the skate park together?" Finn offers.

Nate quickly nods, exchanging a glance with Preston.

"Only if you put us in your script." Preston grins.

Finn fist-bumps with him. "Sure."

Next, Eleanor raises her hand. "And maybe, Lina, you and I can go to the trampoline park together sometime."

"What?" I ask, surprised.

"I'm sorry I didn't invite you to my birthday party," she says. "I wanted to! But the trampoline park people said I could only have fifteen guests and, because of what happened on Nextdoor, my mom made me invite some neighbors—"

"You don't have to explain. It's your birthday party," I tell her. "It was just hard seeing it online, that's all. . . ."

Tonya chimes in. "It was hard for me to see your Palm Springs pictures, too."

Now it's Eleanor's turn to be surprised.

"We were supposed to go, too, but my dad got stuck on a project," Tonya says. "I'm sorry I said your hotel wasn't cool."

"It's okay," Eleanor says. Then she turns to Principal Bennett. "You should know, I saw you at our hotel, and I told them all about your tattoo."

"You mean Owlbert Einstein?" Principal Bennett says.

"That is a very . . . cool name," Preston says. "And we're sorry we made fun of Owlbert."

Nate quickly adds a sorry to Mrs. Carter, too. Preston says he'll apologize to Mrs. Corso later, at lunch.

Principal Bennett claps his hands. "Well, I think this has been a *very* powerful Justice Session."

Mrs. Sanchez and Mrs. Carter both nod.

"Absolutely," Mrs. Carter agrees. "I'm so proud of all you kids. It takes guts to own up to your individual actions. It's a sign that you are really growing up—"

"Wait," Jessica interrupts.

We look over at her. So far, she's the only one of us who hasn't spoken.

"I'm sorry, too, Lina," she finally says. "For the things I said. And the videos."

As Jessica apologizes, I feel the air in my lungs expand. It's all I've ever wanted from her—to see me, to hear me. To know how her words and actions impact me.

"Why'd you do it?" I ask gently.

"Because! You made it look so easy!" Jessica bursts into tears. "Getting the views online! Getting small businesses to pay you! Meanwhile, I was struggling to come up with what to say. I even started copying people's reviews on Goodreads." She sobs. "I felt like such a fraud."

"You're not . . . a fraud," I tell her. "And it wasn't so easy for me either."

"I just wanted my mom to notice and be proud," Jessica says.

I nod. I never thought I'd relate to Jessica, but in that moment I feel everything she's saying.

"Clearly, we don't know what everyone's going through online," Mrs. Sanchez says. "Until we have a *real* conversation with them."

Mrs. Carter looks to Principal Bennett and Mrs. Sanchez.

"You know what I just thought of? Maybe we should start a social media club," Mrs. Carter says.

"Yeah!" We nod excitedly.

"That's a wonderful idea!" Principal Bennett says.

"I'll talk to Mrs. Hollins. Maybe we can have it at the library during lunch. Anyone can come. We can keep talking about the science of social media, and kids can have a chance to discuss face-to-face. Offline. So they can support each other."

"I would totally join that!" Eleanor says.

I grin. "Me too."

As we start making plans for our new club, I suddenly

remember the reason we got called in to begin with. I turn to Principal Bennett, "So what about the cyberbullying . . . ? Am I still . . . ?"

He puts a hand to his chin. "In light of everything that's happened here today, I feel sufficiently satisfied that the harm to the community has been healed."

"Not entirely . . . ," Eleanor says. "There's still one more person I need to apologize to. But we have to wait until she comes back to school."

"Me too," Jessica offers.

I smile. Lao Lao was right. When you show your real, vulnerable self, sometimes it really is powerful enough to inspire everyone.

Chapter 70

Walking out of the auditorium, Finn turns to me.

"Hey. Can we talk for a minute before going back to class?"

I nod. We walk over to a shady tree and wait until everyone's out of earshot. "I'm so sorry for making you uncomfortable."

"No, *I'm* sorry."

"Next time, if either of us uses an emoji the other person's unsure about, we should just . . ."

"We'll ask each other!" I volunteer. "Like, 'Hey, does this chair mean I'm tired or I need a haircut?'"

Finn grins.

"Does this unicorn mean cute hat or you owe me Halloween candy?" he jokes.

"Does this skull mean I'm dead or I love cheese?" I add.

"Does the pizza mean I'm hungry or there's a hole in your argument?"

It feels so great to be able to joke around with Finn again. I exhale in relief.

"So we're really okay?" I ask.

He nods. "For the record, I thought it was whistling," he says.

"And I was sure it was boba!"

He gazes down shyly at his hands. "Who knows, maybe one day . . . it can mean more?" he asks, blushing.

"Maybe," I reply. "When I'm ready."

He smiles.

"So, I talked to Brooke yesterday, about the whole emoji thing. And she showed me something."

I raise an eyebrow, surprised. He pulls out his phone to show me the yellow heart emoji.

"She says it means showing care to friends and family. I think I like it better than the red."

"I like it better than red, too."

We start walking back to class.

"So, things are going better with you and Brooke?" I ask.

"She's all right," Finn says. "She's kind of like having another doctor. Growing up is so complicated. . . . Now if I have a question and my parents can't answer it, I can get a second opinion."

When Mom picks me up, I tell her the wonderful news about the Justice Session.

"It was amazing, Mom! I was finally heard!" I tell her. "By everyone!"

"I'm so proud of you," she says, kissing my forehead. "This calls for a celebration!"

"Can we go to the mall for ice cream?" Millie asks.

"Great idea!" Mom says, stepping on the gas.

"You have time?" I ask, surprised and glancing curiously at her phone. There must be some emails she has to reply to or comments or packages to ship. . . . Something.

"Oh, I almost forgot," Mom says, handing me her phone.

It's her latest video. Unlike the others, this one's filmed in our apartment, with Mom sitting on our hole-in-the-cushion couch. I press play.

"Hi, guys. I just want come on here and say, I recently find out I was wrong about something. I thought social media making my daughters more confident and happier," Mom says. "But few days ago, one of my girls told me some things she's been dealing with—disordered eating, self-esteem problems, body-image issues, misinformation, anxiety."

Mom takes a deep breath.

"I blamed myself so hard. I regretted give her a phone. The truth is, it not the phone's fault. It was mine. I gave her a phone, but I didn't put in the work. I just left her to it and expect her to know how to control herself and control *it*. When what I'm giving her more powerful than any car."

Mom shakes her head.

"I know you all come to me for answers. The truth is, I'm not Modern Mama. I'm just a mama. Trying to do right by my daughters. Some days I get it right. Other days I mess up. And these last few weeks . . . I really blew it. I was on here, when I should have been with them more. And kids, they notice. They smart. They see what we're doing on these things. From now on, I want her to see balance. I want her to see me natural. Not worrying about the background or my hair. Just real talk, about real issues. I want her to see me make this work *on my terms.*"

Mom smiles into the camera.

"So if you want stick around and watch that journey, great. But if you're looking for perfect all time, I'm sorry I can't give that to you. I'm just a messy, tired, not-always-right mom, try-ing to raise two wonderful girls in this terrifying world."

My hands fly to my mouth.

"MOM!" I exclaim. "That's the *best* video you've ever made!"

She beams, taking back her phone. "Thanks. I'm very proud of it!"

I'm so relieved she didn't delete her account. I can't help but ask, "How many views are on it? Have you seen the com-ments yet?"

"Dunno." She shrugs. "Turned off comments this morn-ing. *And* I've changed the settings, so now I don't see the view count."

Now I'm truly speechless.

As she pulls out of the school parking lot, I marvel at Mom and how far she's come.

"I talked with Rosa, and she wants to start a class with me down at the Y," Mom informs me. "Teaching other small busi-nesses how to use social media in a creative, sustainable, and most importantly, balanced way."

I sit back, relieved. "That's so great!" I admit that these last few days, I've felt guilty about not being able to continue helping out all the aunties and uncles I've so enjoyed working for. I'm glad the small businesses around us can keep telling their stories!

As Mom tells us the things she wants to cover in her course, I realize she's driving the wrong way.

"Wait, Mom, the mall's this way," I remind her, when she turns left instead of right.

"I know," she says. "Just making a pit stop to pick up Carla!"

I grin, excited to see my best friend. "She knows we're coming to get her to go get ice cream?"

"Ice cream . . . and maybe something else."

As she winks at me in the rearview mirror, I gaze at Mom. *Where is she taking me?*

Chapter 71

Carla slides into the car in a tank top, jean shorts, and her unicorn backpack, giving me a huge congratulatory hug. I'd called her at home during lunch. Mrs. Hollins was so happy for me, she let me use the staff phone. I'm thrilled to see there are now two Pop-Its on her unicorn backpack. Next to the Popsicle, there's one of a butterfly, which her mom got her.

"Thanks for keeping my secret," she whispers as she hugs me.

"No problem." I smile back.

Mom glances in the rearview mirror, exchanging a look with Carla.

"You girls ready?" Mom asks.

Carla has a huge grin on her face, like she knows exactly where we're going. Mom turns up the radio. The song "I'm Every Woman" by Whitney Houston is playing. Millie giggles. Carla puts her fingers up and starts snapping to the bouncy beat. We dance the whole way to the mall.

At the ice cream store, Millie gets strawberry, while Carla gets chocolate. I stare curiously at the mango sorbet. I've never gotten sorbet before. It always seemed too grown-up. But today, the rich inviting yellow reminds me of Finn and our sweet yellow heart emoji.

"I'll try the mango sorbet!" I say.

The ice cream shop staff scoops it into a cone and hands it to me. As I'm licking the delicious cone and following Mom, she suddenly stops in front of a store.

I look up.

It's the shop for Happy Tweens, the catalog we were browsing. So *that's* the something else she was talking about. I gulp at the five half-naked mannequins in the display, wearing bold, colorful bras.

"Come on!" Mom says. "Let's go in and check it out!"

My sister immediately runs in and starts touching every single bra. She grabs two giant ones and wears the cups over her head like a hat, cackling. I'm glad this is hysterical to her.

"I don't know . . . ," I say to Mom. Mango drips down my hand. "I don't think I can do this." I lean in and whisper, "There are too many bras here. . . ."

"What are you talking about? It's not a bra!" Carla says. She polishes off the last of her ice cream cone. With a mischievous look, she grabs one. "Look! It's an entire store of slingshots!"

My best friend pretends to sling an imaginary gumball across the room. Millie immediately joins in, picking up bras and slinging. Luckily, the saleslady does not seem annoyed with us.

"Feel free to try on anything you want," she says. She's this smiling, older lady with short brown curls and a long tape measure around her neck that she wears like a scarf.

"Mom, what's that tape measure for?" I ask.

"Just try," she replies. Which makes no sense. That tape measure's got to be to measure something. But what? Then my eyes widen. No way is she measuring my chest with it. *No way.*

I pull on Carla's arm to get out of the store, but my best friend isn't quite done. She grabs a lacy bra, but instead of putting it over her chest, she holds it up and pretends to eat spaghetti out of it.

"What do you think? Pasta strainer?" Carla asks.

I giggle. My sister grabs a long one and starts trying to wrap it around a box.

"Bungie cord. Definitely," Carla says.

That's it. I can't resist the fun. I hand the rest of my cone to Mom, wipe my hands, and pick up an extra-padded bra.

"Travel pillows on long-haul flights?" I suggest.

"Or a headband!" My sister giggles.

"How about this? I'm thinking a purse!" Carla declares, wearing a strappy bra over her shoulders.

I laugh. Excitedly, I reach out for a baby-blue, cotton one. The minute I touch it, though, I stop. Whoa. The fabric is *so* soft. Like touching the neck of a baby chick.

"Like that one?" Tape Measure Lady walks over with a smile. "That's our Evie, our most popular starter."

Evie, I repeat under my tongue. It feels so feathery light in my hand. And there's no scary wire, unlike Mom's bras! Just a faint, gentle tissue hugging me. Like a sweatshirt. But not as hot.

"Does it . . . stay in place?" I ask.

"Absolutely!" the saleswoman says. "You won't even know it's on. You can run! You can jump! It's super breathable. Plus, it closes in the front. *Very* easy to put on, see?" the saleswoman says, showing me how it works.

I practice snapping and unsnapping.

Millie runs over and grabs the bra, eager to keep playing our charades game. "Cotton candy!" she calls out.

"Wait, no . . . ," I urge, taking the bra back from my sister.

Carla reaches out a hand, touching the fabric curiously.

"Ooooh, that's so soft!" Carla says.

"Right?"

"Maybe you should try it on," Carla suggests.

Mom nods eagerly. "Yes! Good idea!"

"What size are you, sweetie?" the saleswoman asks.

"It's her first time," Mom explains.

"Oh!" Tape Measure Lady grabs the tape measure from around her neck. "May I measure you?" she asks.

I immediately shake my head. Maybe this was a mistake. "No, that's okay. I'm good." I put the bra back. "I don't need this."

"You wanna just try it?" Tape Measure Lady encourages. "You don't have to buy it if you don't like it. But I think you might like it. . . ."

Mom nods encouragingly.

"I'm guessing you're a 32A," Tape Measure Lady says, handing me one in that size.

And just like that I have a number.

I feel a cascading gush of relief. 32A. It wasn't all in my head.

I really am growing up.

Chapter 72

"ow's it feel?" Mom asks from outside my dressing room.

I stand in front of the mirror, turning this way and that. It's been so long since I've actually looked at myself. Like *really* looked. With both eyes. These last few months, I've been fumbling in the dark. Getting changed in seconds, hoping the neck hole actually goes over my head. But with Evie on, I feel different.

For the first time ever, I gaze at my curves proudly. Bends that capture the light. Corners that radiate strength. Arches that deserve love. I really *see* myself.

Smiling, I lift my arms high. To my surprise, Evie doesn't move. It stays right where it is. I start hopping in place. Jumping. Reaching for the stars. She's still there. She's got me!

I gush to Mom, "It's weird. But I kind of think I like it!"

"Good!" she exclaims.

"What about you, Carla?" I ask.

Carla's trying on an Evie, too, in the next room. Tape Measure Lady gave her a 28AA, which Carla immediately nicknamed Astonishingly Awesome and marched proudly into the dressing room with. I know she's doing it for me, so I don't have to feel so alone. And I appreciate it.

"Yeah, really good!" Carla says. "It feels like it's just floating on me." A pause. "Maybe because it's actually floating. I don't really have anything for it to hold."

I throw on a T-shirt and walk out just as Carla's coming out of her dressing room. She hands her bra back to the Tape Measure Lady, sheepishly.

"There's a lot for it to hang on to," I remind Carla. "Like your heart and your kindness . . ."

Carla blushes. "Thanks."

"And your humor! Your brilliant charades skills," I add.

I hear a *humph* in the corner. I look over at my sister, sitting on the carpet all by herself. I walk over and take a seat next to her.

"Hey. I'm sorry I stopped playing. We can keep playing if you want."

"No," Millie says. "It's not fun anymore now that you're actually wearing it."

She hugs herself with her arms. She's terrified. I get it. I've been there. It's why I layered myself up with thick sweatshirts. But now I know there's nothing to be scared of.

"It's just a thin piece of cloth."

Millie sulks, staring at the carpeted floor, clearly unconvinced.

"No, it's not. You're gonna start acting all different and making me listen to slow love songs."

I laugh. Then I make a serious-newscaster face. "Today's top news—Girl walks into a store to get a bra and walks out singing Whitney Houston. Out of tune."

Millie chuckles in spite of herself.

"Let's interview her sister. Millie Gao, did you have any

idea when you walked into the bra store that this was going to happen?"

"No! *I* thought it was a place for pasta strainers!" Millie cries dramatically.

"And now that your sister's been pasta-napped, what is your greatest fear for her?"

Millie thinks for a long time.

I expect her to say something like, *She's going to hog up all the hot water! She's going to use up all the good shampoo!*

Instead, Millie says, "That she's going to think I'm not cool anymore."

Oh, Millie. My heart's a puddle. I pull my sister in for a hug.

"I promise you, I will always think you're cool," I tell her. "And if I don't, you and all your stuffies have my permission to bungee cord me back to my senses."

Millie's face softens into a smile. "I'm writing that in your Stuffed Animal Card!"

"You should!"

"You girls are going to make me cry!" Tape Measure Lady exclaims, reaching for a tissue from her pocket.

"Me too," Mom says, dabbing at her own eyes. "Now, where's that bra?"

The bra! I totally forgot about it! We all dash back to my dressing room to look for it. But it's not there! We look everywhere—the rack, the bench, the floor. I glance down at my shirt and suddenly realize . . . I'm wearing it. I've been wearing it this whole time. I couldn't even feel it on me! That's when I know . . . I'm ready.

"So we're getting it??" Mom asks.

"We're getting it!" I declare.

"WE'RE GETTING IT!" Tape Measure Lady screams, dancing with her tape measure.

I grab my sister's hand and my best friend's. We spin around in front of the giant mirror. With each spin, I smile bigger, beaming at my reflection, my imagination soaring as the feather-light cloud hugs me tight.

Mom pays for the Evie, and I wear it out.

"I have one final surprise for you," Mom says as we stroll out of the store.

We turn the corner and I look up. It's the trampoline park!

On the count of three, Millie, Carla, and I race toward it. With every step, I soar higher and higher. Skipping to the beat that I am a fearless young woman. I may not have everything figured out yet. Or know what the world's going to throw at me next. There may be lots of times when I mess up on this rocky, scary ride called growing up. But I am confident that I can get through it just being me. For I am enough just the way I am.

AUTHOR'S NOTE

My dear readers,

I have a secret to tell you. Much of Lina's journey was inspired by real issues my kids have gone through. This last year has been one of the hardest years for me as a parent, as my kids have cried over cruel things their friends wrote about them on Discord. Things that horrified me.

I've also been called in to the principal's office over things my kids wrote in response. Things I could never imagine any of them saying in real life.

But that's where we're at today. Two worlds. A real-life world. And an online world, where it's increasingly hard to tell even what's happening, let alone what to do.

As a parent, there's no more terrifying feeling than lying there awake, wondering what is going on with your kid. Not knowing whether your child is suffering silently. Whether what they're seeing online is taking another invisible stab at their self-esteem. Not knowing how to help.

I responded by doing all the things: I set screen times, took away laptops and iPads at night (only my oldest, in high school, has a phone), downloaded monitoring apps, and programmed every device in our household into the app, only to find out my kids were using the neighbor's Wi-Fi, and I had to beg her to change *her* Wi-Fi.

Some of it worked. Most of it didn't. All of it was exhausting.

In the end, the thing that's been working the most has been talking.

It started in the car. One day, I started talking about dopamine.

A funny thing happens when kids aren't just told that something's bad, but they're part of the conversation on why.

They become fascinated. They listen. They put on their scientific hats, and they start seeing their own behaviors and habits in a whole other light.

I started telling them about my own experiences with mean comments. What it's like to be judged by strangers. What it's like to be ghosted by friends. I shared with them my falling for various Tiktoks and Reels, only to feel like a real dope when I realized I'd spent one hundred dollars on an exfoliating sock.

Together we started brainstorming how to break the dopamine loop. How to not be played by the algorithm.

For the first time in a long time, we were really connecting. We were partners in this!

I started feeling hopeful. . . . Maybe I don't have to know every second of what my kids are doing in their adolescent lives. Instead, I can equip them with *tools*.

Tools to see beyond the likes and the views.

Tools to make them understand how it's impacting their brains.

Tools that can save lives.

We started talking about it, not just in the car but at the dinner table. For once my kids didn't just vacuum up the food so they could flee back to their computers. They actually stayed. They also pointed out when my husband and I were on *our* phones and told us to put them away. They suggested we go on hikes, so we could exercise and talk at the same time. Get double the *real* dopamine!

The more we talked, the more encouraged I became that we can *win*. We *can* set our kids up for success when it comes to the digital world!

And so I wrote this book. I hope Lina's story serves as a jumping point to start talking to kids about digital health before they get a phone. I hope it inspires, enrages . . . and ultimately leaves us with hope. I'm not going to lie. I still lie awake sometimes. But I'm hopeful that by having these important conversations, all our kids will be better prepared for the digital world.

With all my love,

Kelly

ESSENTIAL RESEARCH
ON SOCIAL MEDIA AND KIDS

I first joined social media in 2004 as a young student at Harvard University. There was a fellow student on campus who was asking everyone to join some little project he created. He said it would be huge, that it would change the world. We all didn't believe him. But we figured why not?

That kid was Mark Zuckerberg, and the thing he created was called Facebook.

Fast-forward to 2024. By now I have personally joined almost every single platform on the planet. I also have three kids—a high schooler, a middle schooler, and an elementary schooler. And every day, for the last five years, I've been asked this question by one of them, "Why can't I have a phone, Mom? Why can't I join social media?"

I wanted to give my kids a fair, objective, scientific answer to their difficult questions, so I started doing some research. The more I found out, the more shocked, fascinated, terrified, and wildly curious I became. Social media was not only changing the world, but it was also changing *us.*

Just How Many Kids Are on It?

A staggering 95 percent of teenagers ages thirteen to seventeen report using social media, and 35 percent report using social media "almost constantly," according to Pew Research Center.[1] Despite most social media platforms having a minimum age

---

1. Vogels, Gelles-Watnick, and Massarat. "Teens, Social Media and Technology."

of thirteen to sign up, nearly 40 percent of kids ages eight to twelve say they have used social media.[2] By eighth grade, kids spend an average of three and a half hours per day on social media.[3]

But *how?* you may ask. Well, in my house, neither my elementary schooler nor my middle schooler has their own phone. Yet every day, they are able to figure out some way to watch TikTok through YouTube or convince me that there is a group project that calls for Discord. Where there is a will, there is a way.

The Dopamine "Quick Fix"

At the heart of what makes social media so addictive is a tiny chemical that our brain produces called dopamine. Dopamine is our brain's way of rewarding and motivating us for beneficial behaviors, for instance, eating great food, accomplishing something, exercising, and having great social interactions. Dopamine feels so good that whenever we get it, we want more of it. With social media, we have a virtually unlimited supply of dopamine at our fingertips, giving us a "quick fix" with the tap of a button. Couple that with most tweens' and teens' still developing prefrontal cortexes (that's the part of the brain that regulates impulsivity), and it's no wonder kids are so interested in social media.

So interested.

With total screen time at eight hours per day among teens, and five hours among tweens,[4] the tech companies have our children hooked . . . but how?

2. Rideout et al., *Common Sense Census,* 5.
3. Miech et al., "Monitoring the Future."
4. Rideout et al., *Common Sense Census,* 3.

Welcome to Las Vegas . . . on Your Phone!

To understand just how powerfully addictive these platforms are, we have to look at how these social media apps are designed. Social media apps are free. So in order for the companies to make money, they have to keep you on the app for as long as possible, to sell your time to advertisers. This battle for your time has enormous ramifications.

Sean Parker, co-founder of Facebook, once said that when Facebook was being developed, the objective was "How do we consume as much of your time and conscious attention as possible?"[5] The answer?

Human psychology.

It turns out, if you want someone to be addicted to something, you can't reward them all the time. You need to withhold and sprinkle the dopamine randomly, so that they never know when they're going to get it and they always keep coming back to check. A psychologist named B. F. Skinner discovered in the 1930s that mice become more addicted to a stimulus when it is administered at varying intervals, such that the mice cannot predict when they will be rewarded.[6] We humans are no different. If we *know* we're going to get a certain number of likes on every post every time, we're less interested. But if we never know what we're going to get each time—it might be five, or it might be a million!—*and* it's so easy to check, we become obsessed.

As Tristan Harris, a former product manager at Google, once said on *60 Minutes* while holding up his phone, "This thing is a slot machine."[7]

---

5. Solon, "Ex-Facebook President Sean Parker."
6. Haynes, "Dopamine, Smartphones & You."
7. Cooper, "What Is 'Brain Hacking'?"

Brain Hacking

According to Harris, who designed products and studied their impact at Google for over four years, "Every time I check my phone, I'm playing the slot machine to see, 'What did I get?' This is one way to hijack people's minds and create a habit. It turns out that this design technique can be embedded inside of all these products."[8] The result? A never-alone, always-on, digital drug that hacks our brains or, in Facebook co-founder Sean Parker's own words, exploits "a vulnerability in human psychology."[9]

Dopamine Deficit and the Dopamine Loop

In her book *Dopamine Nation*, Anna Lembke, a psychiatry professor and chief of the Addiction Medicine Dual Diagnosis Clinic at Stanford University, explains how the constant hits of dopamine from social media actually create a dopamine deficit when we're off it, and we become unhappy. More unhappy, in fact, than before we even started.

As Professor Lembke explains, "The problem with things that release a lot of dopamine all at once is that our brains have to compensate. Our brains don't just then bring our dopamine firing back to baseline level. It actually pushes dopamine levels below baseline. We go into a dopamine-deficit state. That's the way the brain restores homeostasis: If there's a huge deviation upward, then there's going to be a deviation downward. That's essentially the comedown. . . ."[10]

Many of us have experienced this comedown. We're lying in bed. We're tired. We're no longer getting anything out

---

8. Cooper, "What Is 'Brain Hacking'?"
9. Solon, "Ex-Facebook President Sean Parker."
10. McNamara, "Science behind Social Media."

of watching the videos or posts, and we know it, yet we can't seem to put it down. This is called the dopamine loop: Our brain is in a dopamine deficit, and it's frantically fighting for a way to get back up. But the more we scroll, the harder we fall. According to Professor Lembke, this can feel similar to depression and anxiety. She believes that dopamine deficit is one of the main reasons social media has such a huge impact on mental health.

What Exactly *Is* the Impact of All This?

It's gargantuan. On a personal level, I've noticed that I sometimes have anxiety looking at the seemingly endless highlights from my friends, asking myself why do *they* get to go to such nice places for vacation? Why do *their* kitchens look so much bigger than mine? Why are *they* always doing fun things, and how can they afford all of it? I know I'm not alone in comparing and despairing. It's one of the biggest side effects of social media, and it capitalizes on another very human trait: our need to compare.

Compare and Despair

In 1954, American social psychologist Leon Festinger introduced the Social Comparison Theory. According to Festinger, we have an innate desire to evaluate ourselves in order to establish our identity and self-worth, and one of the key ways we do this is to compare ourselves to others.[11] Festinger categorized this into two types of comparisons: upward comparison is when we compare ourselves to someone who, say, we think is better off than us, and downward comparison is when

---

11. Festinger, "Theory of Social Comparison Processes."

we compare ourselves to someone who we think is worse off. It turns out, constant upward comparisons can lead to declines in self-esteem.[12]

The problem with social media is it's difficult to tell how people are *really* doing. Everyone is always putting up their *best* moments, their *biggest* wins, and their *hugest* brags, ignoring entire parts of their lives and experiences that aren't so rosy. From the outside, it looks like everyone else is doing so much better than us! So instead of balancing upward comparisons with downward comparisons, we are in an endless cycle of upward comparison. It's no wonder that depression is on the rise among young people, up an astounding 52 percent in adolescents ages twelve to seventeen between 2005 and 2017, and 63 percent in young adults ages eighteen to twenty-five.[13]

Effects on Body Image, Especially on Tween/Teen Girls

This is particularly troubling for teen girls—one out of every five teenage girls reports having experienced major depression.[14] In a separate study, researchers spoke with 881 female college students in the United States in 2016. They found that the more time young females spent on social media, the more they compared their bodies with those of their friends.[15] It's hard not to when so many images being thrown at us are filtered or edited yet seem perfect and totally real.

In September 2021, a Facebook whistleblower, Frances Haugen, testified before Congress that Instagram was harming

12. Warrender and Milne, "Use of Social Media and Social Comparison."
13. Twenge et al., "Age, Period, and Cohort Trends."
14. Neighmond, "Rise in Depression among Teens."
15. Eckler, Kalyango, and Paasch, "Facebook Use and Negative Body Image."

young women's mental health. She had inside knowledge of Facebook's own research into the matter. In an interview with *60 Minutes*, Haugen revealed Facebook's internal research which showed that 13.5 percent of teen girls said Instagram makes thoughts of suicide worse, and 17 percent of teen girls said Instagram makes eating disorders worse.[16] How did it do this? According to Haugen, the social media giant Facebook "exploited teens using powerful algorithms that amplify their insecurities."[17]

The Effects of the Algorithm

What exactly is an algorithm? An algorithm is a secret set of calculations and instructions that a tech company uses to automatically rank content to decide what to put in front of users, based on the user's history and likelihood of interacting with the post, in order to keep the user on the app. You may notice that if you look up "weather in LA," you'll get bombarded with a million videos on restaurants, hotels, shops, hikes, and beaches in LA. That's because the algorithm is constantly studying us. It's trying to figure us out, so it can give us more and more of what we want to see, so we'll stay in the app.

But what happens if we look up a worry, like Lina does? We all have insecurities. In the hands of an all-powerful algorithm, though, an insecurity is not just an insecurity. An insecurity is money. An insecurity is a bankable, exploitable commodity, which the algorithm could sell, sort, and feed back to us in a never-ending loop.

---

16. Pelley, "Whistleblower: Facebook Is Misleading the Public."
17. Bond and Allyn, "Whistleblower Tells Congress."

In doing so, the very technology that's supposed to just be analyzing us can actually *shape* us.

My personal fear is that the algorithm can change our society, by subtly dividing us, polarizing our opinions, potentially helping spread misinformation, and slowly eroding the fabric of democracy that our ancestors worked so hard to build . . . without us even realizing.

As Tristan Harris says, "Inadvertently, whether they want to or not, [these apps] are shaping the thoughts and feelings and actions of people. They are programming people."[18]

So What Do We Do about It?

I believe that young people are most empowered by knowledge. The earlier we have conversations with kids about social media, the better prepared they are going to be for when they accidentally or intentionally stumble upon it. I hope Lina's story and the information in this book serve as a jumping point for families and classrooms to talk openly about our digital health and the ramifications of social media.

The more we talk about it with kids and open up about our own struggles, the more we educate them on all the various ways in which this powerful technology has the potential to manipulate as well as captivate. The better we prepare them for what's coming ahead, the happier they'll be when the time comes to get their own devices.

I wish a book like this had existed when I first signed up for my classmate's app. I'm so grateful *Finally Heard* exists now, so I can give it to my own children. If I could go back to Harvard and say one thing to young Mark Zuckerberg, I would say this:

18. Cooper, "What Is 'Brain Hacking'?"

Yes, you made the thing that changed the world.

But you forgot the responsibility that comes with changing the world.

The next generation deserves better. They deserve the honest truth, so they have a chance to find out who they are before they're shaped by an invisible machine.

Bibliography

Bond, Shannon, and Bobby Allyn. "Whistleblower Tells Congress That Facebook Products Harm Kids and Democracy." NPR, October 5, 2021. https://www .npr.org/2021/10/05/1043207218/whistleblower-to -congress-facebook-products-harm-children-and-weaken -democracy.

Cooper, Anderson. "What Is 'Brain Hacking'? Tech Insiders on Why You Should Care." CBS News, April 9, 2017. https://www.cbsnews.com/news/brain-hacking-tech -insiders-60-minutes/.

Eckler, Petya, Yusuf Kalyango, and Ellen Paasch. "Facebook Use and Negative Body Image among U.S. College Women." *Women Health* 57, no. 2 (April 7, 2016): 249–67. https://doi.org/10.1080/03630242.2016.1159268.

Festinger, Leon. "A Theory of Social Comparison Processes." *Human Relations* 7, no. 2 (May 1954): 117–40. https:// doi.org/10.1177/001872675400700202.

Haynes, Trevor. "Dopamine, Smartphones & You: A Battle for Your Time." *Science in the News*, May 1, 2018. https://sitn .hms.harvard.edu/flash/2018/dopamine-smartphones -battle-time/.

McNamara, Brittney. "The Science behind Social Media's

Hold on Our Mental Health." *Teen Vogue*, November 10, 2021. https://www.teenvogue.com/story/the-science -behind-social-medias-hold-on-our-mental-health.

Miech, Richard A., Lloyd D. Johnston, Jerald G. Bachman, Patrick M. O'Malley, John E. Schulenberg, and Megan E. Patrick. "Monitoring the Future: A Continuing Study of American Youth (8th- and 10th-Grade Surveys), 2021." National Addiction & HIV Archive Program, October 31, 2022. https://www.icpsr.umich.edu/web/NAHDAP /studies/38502/versions/V1.

Neighmond, Patti. "A Rise in Depression among Teens and Young Adults Could Be Linked to Social Media Use." NPR, March 14, 2019. https://www.npr.org/sections/health -shots/2019/03/14/703170892/a-rise-in-depression -among-teens-and-young-adults-could-be-linked-to-social -medi.

Pelley, Scott. "Whistleblower: Facebook Is Misleading the Public on Progress against Hate Speech, Violence, Misinformation." CBS News, October 4, 2021. https://www .cbsnews.com/news/facebook-whistleblower-frances -haugen-misinformation-public-60-minutes-2021-10-03/.

Rideout, Victoria, Alanna Peebles, Supreet Mann, and Michael B. Robb. *The Common Sense Census: Media Use by Tweens and Teens, 2021.* San Francisco: Common Sense, 2022. https://www.commonsensemedia.org/sites/default /files/research/report/8-18-census-integrated-report -final-web_0.pdf.

Solon, Olivia. "Ex-Facebook President Sean Parker: Site Made to Exploit Human 'Vulnerability.'" *Guardian*, Novem-

ber 9, 2017. https://www.theguardian.com/technology
/2017/nov/09/facebook-sean-parker-vulnerability
-brain-psychology.

Twenge, J. M., A. B. Cooper, T. E. Joiner, M. E. Duffy, and S. G. Binau. "Age, Period, and Cohort Trends in Mood Disorder Indicators and Suicide-Related Outcomes in a Nationally Representative Dataset, 2005–2017." *Journal of Abnormal Psychology* 128, no. 3 (2019): 185–99. https:// doi.org/10.1037/abn0000410.

Vogels, Emily A, Risa Gelles-Watnick, and Navid Massarat. "Teens, Social Media and Technology 2022." Pew Research Center. August 10, 2022. https://www.pewresearch .org/internet/2022/08/10/teens-social-media-and -technology-2022/.

Warrender, D., and R. Milne. "How Use of Social Media and Social Comparison Affect Mental Health." *Nursing Times 116, no. 3* (February 24, 2020): 56-59. https:// www.nursingtimes.net/news/mental-health/how-use-of -social-media-and-social-comparison-affect-mental -health-24-02-2020/.

ACKNOWLEDGMENTS

I'm forever grateful to the following people, without whose unwavering support this book would not be possible: Krista Vitola, Faye Bender, Justin Chanda, Tara Shanahan, Lisa Moraleda, Antonella Colon, Beth Parker, Michelle Leo, Nicole Benevento, Caleigh Flegg, Alyza Liu, Kendra Levin, Erin Toller, Brendon MacDonald, Ashley Mitchell, and Nadia Almahdi. Huge thanks to Maike Plenzke for your masterful work on the cover!

All my love to Sylvie Rabineau, Paul Sennott, and all the wonderful folks at Curtis Brown, including Enrichetta Frezzato, Roxane Edouard, Isobel Gahan, Savanna Wicks, and Isobel Leach. My publishers all around the world. My friends in tech who provided much insight. My dear friends Lindsey Moore, Paul Cummins, Bill Isacoff, Christine Ni, Victoria Piontek, Mae Respicio, thank you for feeding me, supporting me, cheering me on, encouraging me even when it felt at times like this book was going to be impossible to finish.

A huge thank-you to Professor Jennifer Harriger of Pepperdine University for your important research on social media and the impact on body image and for reviewing *Finally Heard* and giving me your enthusiastic feedback!

To my readers, thank you for trusting me and coming with me on this journey. Thank you for putting your faith in me to write honestly about the important issues we're going through today. It is the honor of my lifetime, writing for you.

To my husband, Stephen, and my parents, thank you for

not blinking when I said, *I want to write a book that will change the world.* Even though it took me eight full complete drafts, you cheered me on every step of the way.

Finally, to my kids, Eliot, Tilden, and Nina—thank you for always being real with Mommy. For letting me in. For asking questions. For your incredible generosity, sharing me with the world. And for keeping me all to yourself when it matters. I love you. ♥